Templar Prize

'There is no need to be afraid,' he said in a deep voice that sounded as smooth as silk. For a second she had not realised that he had spoken to her in fluent French tinged with just the faintest of accents. Part of her was curious to see this man – after all she was expected to couple with him – yet a voice was nothing to judge someone by and she feared she might find him repulsive. 'Will you not look at me?' he asked as a firm hand took hold of her chin and turned her face towards him.

Very reluctantly, she opened her eyes and found herself staring at a young, surprisingly attractive man, probably about the same age as Stephen. Of course he looked like a Saracen, with dark olive skin, black hair and dark eyes, and like all Moslem men he wore a beard, but it was small and neatly trimmed. Edwina had not expected him to be this good-looking and, although his face was square jawed and his features inherently masculine, there was a gentleness in his expression that made her feel just a little less terrified. Nevertheless she knew that, like voices, looks could be deceiving.

By the same author:

Savage Surrender
Wild Kingdom
Doctor's Orders
Barbarian Prize

Templar Prize
Deanna Ashford

BLACK LACE

Black Lace books contain sexual fantasies.
In real life, always practise safe sex.

First published in 2007 by
Black Lace
Thames Wharf Studios
Rainville Rd
London W6 9HA

A catalogue record for this book is available from the British Library.

www.black-lace-books.com

Typeset by SetSystems Ltd, Saffron Walden, Essex

Printed in the UK by CPI Bookmarque, Croydon, CR0 4TD

The paper used in this book is a natural, recyclable product made
from wood grown in sustainable forests. The manufacturing process
conforms to the regulations of the country of origin.

ISBN 978 0 352 34137 2

Distributed in the USA by Holtzbrinck Publishers, LLC, 175 Fifth Avenue,
New York, NY 10010, USA

1

1191 – Sicily

The candles lighting the small chamber flickered and spluttered as if they might expire at any moment. Edwina shuddered, not wanting to be trapped here in virtual darkness. With the heavy shutters tightly closed not even a small amount of light could creep in through the narrow window and the room was becoming steadily hotter. The stifling air was now tainted by a sweet sickly odour and the terrible smell drifted into her nostrils and slid insidiously down her throat, making her stomach churn. She swallowed anxiously, praying that she would not retch as she tried not to look at the corpulent form of Hugh de Moreville lying on the narrow bed covered by a white linen sheet.

Yet she could not ignore the corpse of the man she had been married to for almost three and a half years; somehow it managed to draw her eyes towards it time and time again. Determinedly she tried to pray for his eternal soul and ask that he rest in peace but however hard she struggled she could not find anything appropriate to say. If she were honest with herself, at present she felt nothing: not pain, regret, joy or even relief. It was as if her mind were totally numb and devoid of any emotions. Yet, as her thoughts became more and more clouded, she became acutely conscious of every part of her body. She was used to kneeling in prayer as her husband had not been a particularly religious man and, during their marriage, the chapel in their castle had become a refuge for her on numerous occasions. She had often spent extended periods of time on her knees praying to God to help her endure her loveless union to a man she loathed.

Despite those previous endless hours of devotion, kneeling here on this hard floor was now becoming acutely uncomfortable. Edwina could feel every nuance of the rough paving stones of the floor beneath her pain-wracked knees, while her back and shoulders ached with the strain of being in one position for a prolonged time. Even her arms felt amazingly heavy from being held in front of her as she kept her hands clasped together in an attitude of prayer, unable to relax her pose for even a moment. She had to remain where she was and retain the posture of a pious grieving widow.

Edwina tensed as the candles flickered again and a number of them died, leaving dark menacing shadows in every corner of the small room. She thought she detected a movement out of the corner of her eye and she feared, quite foolishly, that her husband would rise from his bed like some evil spectre and lurch frighteningly towards her. It appeared that she was not bereft of all emotion, she considered, as she told herself not to be so weak-minded. Tiredness had overtaken her senses and was making her imagine things that were not there. She could not even remember when she had last slept as she had spent the last few days nursing Hugh through his unexpected illness.

Once again, she forced herself to look at the corpse. His hard-featured face looked kinder in repose and she felt a sudden elation as she realised that he could no longer hurt her any more; her tribulations had at last come to an end.

There was a sudden scraping sound, followed by the creak of an unoiled hinge as the door of the chamber was pushed open. Remaining on her knees, she peeked through her lowered lashes and saw four Knights Templar enter the chamber. Edwina had always found something rather unsettling about the sight of these devout knights with their white surcoats, emblazoned on the front with large blood-red crosses. They had not come for her, of course, they had come to pay their respects to her husband. Hugh had often told her that he wanted to die in battle so it was ironic that he had instead died quite ignominiously from quartan fever, most probably contracted, so the Hospitaller who had first attended him claimed, by drinking water drawn from a contaminated well.

Totally ignoring her presence, the knights stood at the four corners of the bed. Edwina heard a rasping sound as they drew their swords, then a clatter as they positioned their weapons, holding them with the blades pointing downwards so that the tips rested on the stone floor. Bending their heads they stood in silent contemplation as they paid their respects to Hugh de Moreville.

Edwina wondered what she should do now, unsure whether she was expected to remain where she was or slip silently from the room. I am free now, but for how long, she wondered, very aware that her fate now lay in the hands of her sovereign lord King Richard the Lionheart.

Still all too concerned with her own physical discomfort, she wasn't even aware that someone was standing beside her until she felt a gentle hand touch her shoulder.

'My lady,' William de Preaux, one of the king's loyal retainers, said softly. 'It is time for you to leave now.'

'Leave?'

'Yes. You look exhausted,' he continued in a low voice. 'Come. I'll escort you to your chamber.'

'I am obliged to you, my lord,' she said wearily, as he took hold of her arm and helped her to her feet.

Edwina winced as the blood flowed freely into her cramped limbs and she was forced to lean heavily on William as he escorted her from the room. The narrow corridor was empty and she was relieved because she knew that she must look a terrible mess in her crumpled gown, her long hair untidily escaping its plait, with not even a veil to cover her head at present.

They had only walked a short distance when they came upon an open window that overlooked the garden. She glanced pleadingly at her escort. 'A moment, if you would allow it, my lord.'

'Of course.' William de Preaux stopped and smiled understandingly at her. 'Judging by the atmosphere in that damnable chamber, I can now understand why the Sicilians insist on such swift burials,' he muttered, almost as if he were talking to himself rather than her.

Appreciating his kindness, she took a deep breath of fresh air, trying to ignore the sudden rush of emotions that unexpectedly filled her mind. It was as if a door had been opened to all the memories and feelings she had tried to ignore for so long. The experience left her feeling weak and helpless, while unbidden tears suddenly filled her eyes. 'I am sorry,' she murmured, keeping her face averted from her escort.

'I quite understand,' he said in a gentle voice. 'It is a terrible time for you, is it not? You look pale and drawn. I fear you have made yourself sick, my lady. You should not have nursed your husband for so long without any help.'

'He ordered it,' she said flatly, so wanting to tell William de Preaux that even during his illness Hugh had continued to make her life a misery. She knew full well that it was a wife's duty to care for her husband. Did not the marriage vows say both in sickness and in health? Even so, he could have allowed her to bring in some help and not bear the burden of his care alone. King Richard had offered Hugh the services of his own personal physicians but he had refused even that and, perhaps because of that very stubbornness, he had died of what was sometimes a recoverable illness.

'I am aware, my lady, that you have no servants of your own to care for you now.'

She blinked back the tears, which she knew were prompted by the sudden turbulence of her emotions and had nothing really to do with the loss of her husband. 'Hugh claimed that we could not afford such luxuries. Holy quests are expensive undertakings are they not, my lord?'

'Indeed they are.' He tenderly touched her hand and the brief gesture made her tremble. It was so long since a man had touched her with gentleness in his heart.

'Forgive me for delaying you, my lord,' she said, struggling to compose herself. 'I do appreciate your kindness.'

'Come,' he urged her. 'I have not much time. I have to meet with His Majesty as soon as I've conducted you to your chamber. Plans are already underway to at last set sail for the Holy Land.'

As he escorted her further up the corridor, Edwina wondered what would happen to her now: would she be expected to travel onwards with the king or would he provide her with an escort to return to her family home in France, or Hugh's gloomy castle in northern England?

They entered the large hall which presently served as the royal audience chamber where the king held court. It was fuller than usual and she could sense a strange mood of anticipation in the air as she glanced briefly at the eager faces of the courtiers.

'Is something amiss?' she asked curiously.

'You have not heard, then? The Dowager Queen Eleanor has arrived and she has brought the king's betrothed, Princess Berengaria, with her.'

'I was not aware of that. I have heard tell that the daughter of the King of Navarre is comely and sweet-natured.'

They had almost reached the far side of the hall, to her relief, as she was embarrassed at being seen in such a state of disarray.

'She is indeed. I am sure that Princess Berengaria will be eager to get to know you and the other ladies as soon as possible,' William said with a warm smile. 'She has been resting since she arrived but it is expected that the king will present her to the senior members of his court today. Hence the crowd.'

'I see.' Edwina suddenly stiffened and she felt the blood drain from her face as for a brief second she thought she saw a tall dark-haired man who looked uncannily like Stephen. Then he disappeared behind a crowd of courtiers. Her heartbeat quickened and she feared for a moment that she might fall to the floor in a swoon.

'My lady?' William said as she clung even more tightly onto his arm.

'It is nothing,' she insisted, shaking her head. 'I thought for a moment that I saw someone I knew. Someone I did not expect to see here of all places.' She made a determined effort to recover her shaky composure. 'No doubt I was mistaken. He couldn't possibly be here.'

'You are exhausted,' he pointed out. 'The mind easily plays tricks,' he added, guiding her out of the crowded hall and up the wide staircase to the second floor of the palace.

Edwina's limbs felt leaden and she was all but exhausted by the time they reached the door to the room she had so recently shared with her husband. 'I'm obliged to you for your kindness, my lord.'

'Just promise me that you will rest for as long as you need to. His Majesty does not expect you to attend the interment. As the climate necessitates, it will be carried out swiftly with little ceremony. I'm certain that your husband would have wished that.'

Edwina doubted that were true. Hugh had a high opinion of himself and would have expected a ceremony befitting his status as one of the premier knights of the realm. 'I will do so willingly,' she assured him with a weary smile.

He lifted her hand to his lips and then took a step back. 'If there is anything you need, Lady Edwina, you have but to ask.'

'Thank you, my lord,' she acknowledged, and she watched him walk away.

Pleased to be alone with her confused thoughts, she stepped into her chamber, shut the door behind her and sat down shakily on the bed as her shattered emotions threatened to overwhelm her again.

It was only relief, she told herself; relief that she no longer had to bear the burden of a husband who had not cared one jot for her and had been uncommonly cruel and brutal to her at times. It was that emotion that had somehow made her believe for a second that she had caught sight of the one and only man she had ever truly cared for. She had thought that she'd seen Stephen because she had secretly wanted him to be here. Nevertheless, she knew full well that he'd not accompanied his king to Sicily and she had never dared to ask Hugh why. So she must have been mistaken. After all she had only caught a fleeting glimpse of the man and he had been some distance away from her. She knew from past experience that sometimes one saw precisely what one wanted to see. When she had been forced into marrying Hugh she had been convinced that she had caught sight of Stephen's strained features among the crowd of people waiting outside the chapel where the wedding had taken place.

Edwina sniffed and wrinkled her nose; she stank of the sickroom. Once again she was reminded of the strange, sweet and yet noxious odour that had filled the small chamber. Not wanting to dwell on such morbid thoughts, she unfastened her girdle and removed her crumpled linen gown, which was stiff with perspiration and soiled with all manner of unpleasant effluents. She did not have many clothes; her husband had never been generous with her. After their hasty marriage, he had even taken away many of the fine garments her brother had provided for her trousseau and she suspected, but had never been able to prove, that he had given them to one of his many mistresses. Nevertheless, this was one garment she would never wear again, she thought, as she threw it in a corner. There had been no time to wash, let alone bother about her own appearance while caring for her demanding, ill-tempered patient and she was too weary to do so now. She just wanted to rest.

It was odd, she thought. Now that she looked back on all that had happened in the last few days it had never crossed her mind that Hugh would actually perish from his fever and she would be left a widow.

She slipped off her soft leather shoes and undid the loose plait, letting her blonde hair spill around her shoulders. Then she lay down on the bed clad only in her sleeveless shift. Wearily, Edwina closed her eyes but she could not sleep; her mind was suddenly filled with memories of far happier times in her life, memories she had suppressed for so long.

The canopy of green in the forest protected them from the searing heat of summer as she and Stephen rode side by side along a little-used path. Edwina couldn't resist glancing at the handsome features of the tall dark-haired man she adored. Her family was influential and as she was an heiress many young men had courted her, but she had only ever had eyes for Stephen.

'I fear that I shall never be *this* happy again,' she shyly confessed.

When she had first come to the Duke of Aquitaine's court in Poitiers in the spring of the year of our Lord 1187 she had never expected to fall in love; such emotions rarely figured in unions between noble men and women. She had believed that her marriage would be one of convenience, arranged by her older brother, Fulk. Now, just five months later, she had been given this most precious of gifts and sometimes she felt her heart would explode with the strength of her happiness.

'Of course you will.' Stephen smiled lovingly at her and Edwina felt a tingle of pleasure fill her stomach and slide delightfully down to the tips of her toes.

'I shall miss you desperately,' she said with a sad smile. Stephen had to depart in a couple of days. Richard, the Duke of Aquitaine, had charged him with a special task that was so secret that he could not even tell her where he was going.

'I'll return as soon as I am able. Even so I trust that on our wedding day you will be even happier than you are right now,' he teased as he smiled lovingly at her.

'Of course I will.' She gave a soft laugh. 'I still cannot believe that life has been so good to me.'

'When we are wed you will have to become accustomed to such partings. Richard is my liege lord and he expects me to be at his side in all his campaigns,' he said as they rode through the entrance gates of what appeared to be a small estate. 'When he becomes king no doubt he will have many other knights to also carry out his bidding and we can perhaps spend more time together. In the meantime you will have my sister Blanche to keep you company and, if God wills it, strong sons and daughters as well in the future.'

'For the time being then our reunions will have to be all the more precious.' She wrinkled her nose. 'I do hope that when he becomes king, he does not expect you to reside in England. I hear that it is cold and it rains there most of the time.'

Stephen gave a soft laugh. 'Do not believe all that others tell you, my love. In many ways England is just as beautiful as Aquitaine.'

'Why are we here?' she asked, as they approached a small, quite exquisite, manor house.

'Why indeed.' Stephen smiled wickedly and then dismounted. Stepping forwards, he helped her down from her palfrey. 'Just be patient, Edwina,' he said, his green eyes twinkling as he handed the reins to a groom. 'This is one of the homes of my friend Gilbert de Fevre. He thought I might be able to make use of it while he is away in England.' Stephen led her through the arched doorway into a small entrance hall. 'We are never alone at court, whilst here . . .'

Edwina knew full well that they were breaking all acceptable conventions by being alone like this when they were not yet wed. Yet she made no protest as Stephen led her into an elegantly furnished chamber. When she saw that it contained a large four-poster bed, her heart began to beat faster and the blood pounded excitedly through her veins. This was so wrong, she knew that, but she could deny Stephen nothing. At court they had occasionally been able to steal a few moments alone together and the brief but passionate kisses they had shared had left her breathless and wanting far more. More of what she wasn't entirely sure, but the touch of his lips had made her entire body grow weak and her stomach churn with a strange wild excitement.

'Stephen . . .' she said questioningly.

'Don't look so fearful, Edwina.' He removed her light cloak and flung it onto a nearby carved chest. 'I'll not hurt you, my love, you know that,' he said softly as he pulled her into his arms.

'We should not,' she protested, all too briefly, before his lips covered hers. Stephen kissed her far more passionately than he had ever done before and she thought she would swoon from the sheer bliss as his tongue unexpectedly eased its way into her mouth. She clung onto him like a drowning woman as the pleasure overwhelmed her, making a soft entreating sound as he pulled her even closer, crushing her breasts against his muscular chest.

One of his hands moved to the back lacing of her gown and she felt his fingers plucking at the knot. 'Edwina, my love, you know full well that fortunes change in the wind these days. Especially because of the constant conflict between the King Henry and his sons. Women are used as pawns and I would not have you used so. I may well be away for some months and in the meantime I fear for your safety. We are betrothed but promises such as that can easily be broken. Your brother agreed to our union but he displays more loyalty to King Henry than he does to his liege lord Richard. So if I take your virginity, then our betrothal is sealed by our conjoined flesh. I could not bear it if you were forced to wed another because your brother suddenly thought it more advantageous.'

'You do not trust Fulk's intentions?' She felt him pull the lacing apart, then start to ease her gown slowly from her shoulders.

'Do you?'

'No,' she admitted. She loved her brother but like most men he would always choose what was right for him and would never take account of her feelings on the matter. She shivered with anticipation as she felt Stephen slide the dress down to her waist, then he eased it lower until it was heaped around her feet. Edwina felt rather embarrassed as beneath it she was wearing only a thin chemise which concealed little. She glanced nervously down, fearing that Stephen could see her nipples distorting the fine fabric.

She was here in front of Stephen clad in just this thin undergarment; only her maid and her friend Blanche had seen her so unclothed. Was it right to feel exposed yet also so liberated as she stood scantily dressed in front of the man she loved? She looked up at him, seeing his desire for her reflected on his handsome face, and at this moment in time she knew it was right to give him the thing most precious to her, her own virginity. Holding her protectively in his arms, Stephen brushed his mouth tenderly against hers. His lips sensuously caressed the pale skin of her cheeks, the side of her neck and the exposed column of her throat.

The sudden overwhelming desire she felt excised any lingering doubts that this might somehow be wrong as he removed the silver filet encircling her brow and the short veil that covered her hair. Since she had become a woman, no man apart from her late father and her brother had ever seen her with her hair uncovered like this.

'Your hair is so beautiful,' he said softly as he removed the pins that held it coiled around her head, pulling them out one by one until her long, heavy, wheat-coloured locks cascaded down her back. 'You must wear it unbound at our wedding ceremony,' he added, then kissed her again with passionate longing.

She tasted the sweetness of his mouth and felt his tongue touching hers as he held her close to his muscular chest. She was desperate now to see him unclothed and feel his warm skin pressed close to hers; to lose herself in the pleasures of his flesh and to let him take anything he wanted from her. If this was absolute submission, the strange need for a woman to be conquered by a man, then this was what she wanted. It felt as if she had waited all her life for this one precious moment.

There was an unfamiliar warmth in her belly and tingling tremors of pleasure slid across her skin as Stephen held her close and kissed her, until all sense and reason deserted her. Before she knew what was happening, he'd lifted her into his arms and carried her to the bed. He lay her down on the soft mattress and then bent to slip off her shoes. Then he rolled the thin woollen hose down her legs and eased them from her feet. Edwina tensed in surprise as he kissed her toes one by one, sucking on them gently until she gave a gasp of delight, never having realised that something so simple could be so unbelievably titillating.

'Will you not remove your clothes also?' she asked shyly. 'I want to see all of you.'

'Aye, my love.' Stephen gave a soft chuckle as he immediately straightened and began to remove his garments, one by one.

Soon he had cast them aside and he stood before Edwina in all his naked glory. He showed no embarrassment as a maiden might, but appeared proud of his strong body. But then he was a man and had most likely been with many other women before her. However, like most young noblewomen, she had been kept blissfully ignorant about matters of the flesh. Her priest had told her on numerous occasions that it was a sin for a woman to enjoy coupling with any man, even her husband. Surely God would not have designed it so that only men enjoyed the pleasures of sex?

She stared curiously at Stephen; he was beautiful, more beautiful than the wickedly decadent statues of naked Greek and Roman gods that the duke kept in his private quarters. Blanche had heard tell of them and when the duke was out hunting they had bribed a servant to let them into Richard's chambers, merely to satisfy their girlish curiosity, of course. They had giggled over the marble statues of naked muscular men and stared in awe at the carved renditions of male anatomy, wondering what it would be like to see a living breathing man unclothed. Now she could do so and Stephen was even more perfect than every one of them.

The muscles of his chest and arms were firm and well developed, his waist was narrow, his belly flat and his legs made hard and strong by riding and swordplay. She looked at little nervously at his manly parts and her heart beat a rapid tattoo in her chest. They looked much like those on the statues but considerably larger and that was troubling. Her mother had died when she was only seven, so she knew little of what happened between a man and a woman in bed.

'I'll not hurt you,' Stephen promised as he lay down beside her and pulled her close.

Gently, he eased the loose neck of her chemise downwards until her breasts were exposed. Lovingly he caressed the soft globes and she felt her nipples harden. Did all women feel like this? she wondered, as a jolt of pleasure travelled down to her loins, almost as if her breasts and her womanly parts were conjoined.

He stroked her breasts, cupping them in his large sword-roughened hands, and she found his caresses intensely pleasurable. Edwina shivered, almost overcome with the wild delight he aroused in her, as his fingers focused on her nipples, pulling at them gently as he rolled the hard nubs between finger and thumb. There was an accompanying ache between her thighs and to her consternation her sex became hotter and somehow surprisingly moist all at the same time.

'I want you,' she said haltingly, still unsure what the act of copulation ultimately entailed. 'But I do not know ...'

'Hush, my sweet,' Stephen said as he tried to ease the chemise further down her body, but the soft folds caught beneath her hips. With a muttered oath of frustration, he pulled on it hard, and when that did not free the fabric he ripped the garment from neck to hem. As the material fell away, her entire nakedness was exposed to his gaze. She shuddered, filled with a strange heady mixture of excitement and embarrassment. The hungry way his green eyes were raking her body sent a surge of fire through her veins.

Edwina's lids closed and her dark lashes fanned against her pale cheeks, where two small spots of red were starting to form. She was half afraid of his powerful need for her, certain now that his gaze had slid down over her belly and was directed towards the small triangle of hair covering her womanly parts. Now that she was unable to see, all her senses were focused on the feel of his fingertips as they brushed the soft skin of her stomach, than trailed tantalisingly down to her mons. She shivered as they slipped between her thighs, parting her full lips to explore the complex folds of her sex. Her pleasure began to increase exponentially as they brushed against a small soft nub of flesh that sent a dart of exquisite fire through every inch of her body. Then they reached the entrance to the ultimate essence of her femaleness and she stiffened nervously.

Stephen kissed her passionately as his fingers continued on their magical journey, sliding into her moist sheath. Edwina's eyes fluttered open in surprise as she felt the sweet indescribably wonderful sensations – a pleasure the like of which she had never experienced before.

His fingers edged slowly deeper, into the very core of

her body. She held her breath, entirely overcome by the intoxicating sensations that invaded every part of her being.

Unconsciously, her hands reached for him. She caressed the hard curve of his hip and his firm belly, while his fingers continued to work their enchantment inside her. Cautiously, she brushed her fingers against his sex, feeling the organ leap at her touch, and she was filled with a sudden trepidation. It was no longer soft and malleable, as it had appeared when he'd been standing in front of her; now it was hard and impossibly huge, massive in comparison to the male organs of the statues that she and Blanche had examined so curiously not long ago.

'Do you know what happens between a man and a woman?' Stephen asked her as he continued to slide his fingers seductively in and out of her vagina. It felt so good and yet it also made her feel as if she were striving for something which was just tantalisingly out of reach.

'How they come together to make children?' she said shyly, then she bit her lips trying not to reveal just how much pleasure the gentle thrusting movements of his fingers were giving her. She was so very tempted to beg him to move harder and faster and venture deeper, but she was too shy to voice such thoughts aloud. 'I've seen animals . . .'

'We are all part of nature, my love. Yet this is so much more perfect. Do not believe what the priests say, this is a God-given pleasure to be shared between a man and a woman,' he said with feeling. 'Now let me show you how blissful this union can be.'

Stephen withdrew his fingers and gently edged her legs apart. Moving onto his knees, he crouched between her open thighs, staring down at her. His green eyes were dark with desire as he gently eased the tip of his hard cock between her swollen sex lips and pressed it gently and very cautiously against the mouth of her vagina.

Very carefully and evidently all too conscious of the fact that she was still a virgin, he slowly eased his engorged shaft inside her. To her amazement, her body easily expanded to accommodate him. Yet, when he had only penetrated her partway, he paused.

'What's wrong?' she asked in a trembling voice. 'Does my body displease you in some way?'

'It pleases me exceedingly, but you are a maiden, there is one last barrier before we can complete our union. Be warned, my love, when your maidenhead breaks it will hurt a little.'

He drew back slightly and she tried not to tense, yet she still clenched her fists nervously, not knowing what measure of discomfort to expect. With a firm jerk of his hips, he thrust his cock deep inside her. Edwina felt something give way and, for a brief second, she experienced a sharp tearing pain, but to her relief it was gone in an instant and was replaced by a multitude of wonderful sensations which she had never experienced before.

He had paused and was looking down at her with concern, his green eyes still reflecting the love he felt for her. 'It only hurt a little,' she gasped as she experienced the absolute intimacy of being conjoined with the man she loved and savoured the perfectly exquisite feeling of his body buried deep inside hers.

She wanted to clasp him close and hold him tight, just enjoy this strange bliss. However, female instinct told her that there was more to this act of union and even more incredible pleasures to come. Very cautiously, Stephen began to move his hips, sliding his engorged shaft partially out and then back inside her again. Surprisingly, the moisture inside her seemed to increase. The movements were fluid, while the friction and the feeling of fullness were amazingly pleasurable and she unconsciously lifted her hips. 'Please,' she gasped. He responded, quickening his pace and the sensations she was experiencing increased exponentially.

Her hands reached for his muscular arms and she clung onto them as he thrust harder, his hips pounding against hers. The feelings were so powerful that they astounded her, making the muscles of her legs tighten and her toes curl as he thrust harder and deeper. Suddenly, there was a strange overwhelming bliss growing deep inside her, blossoming and expanding. It was followed by a violent explosion of intense pleasure as Edwina experienced an orgasm for the very first time in her life.

As her body shuddered beneath his, the desire Stephen had been holding onto by little more than a thread exploded. He gave one last powerful thrust, followed by a deep groan of gratification as he lost all sense and reason in the depth and power of his own climax. Gently he rolled her onto her side, his shaft still buried inside her body, then he held Edwina close and murmured tender words of love in her ear.

2

Stephen strode along the wide corridor passing only a couple of courtiers, neither of whom he recognised. Apart from them this part of the building seemed empty and he couldn't help wondering why Richard had gone to the trouble of constructing this large wooden edifice, which he had dubbed Mategriffon, when there was, so he had been told, a perfectly adequate royal residence only a short distance away in Messina.

Philip of France had thought the palace good enough for him but perhaps that was the very reason Richard had declined to live in it, Stephen considered with a wry grin. The two men had once been friends but their relationship had changed over the years and now they were just reluctant allies on the same quest to recapture the Holy Land from Salah ad-Din.

All of a sudden, Stephen heard a deep booming voice, from somewhere behind him, call out, 'Stephen, by God. I've been looking for you.'

Stephen swung round. 'Your Majesty.' He bowed as Richard strode towards him.

'Come now, my friend, let us not stand on ceremony.' Richard flung a companionable arm around Stephen's shoulders and grinned at him. 'It is good to see you again.'

The king looked far more relaxed and rested than usual. This long sojourn in Sicily seemed to have done wonders for him. Stephen stared into his friend's blue eyes. He was a tall well-muscled man but now he looked even fitter. His pale complexion had become ruddier and the Sicilian sunshine had bleached his reddish-gold hair, turning it a pale strawberry blond.

'The pleasure is all mine, sire. I am relieved to be here at last,' Stephen replied as Richard waved away the group of men surrounding him.

'Come.' Richard led Stephen into a luxuriously furnished anteroom. 'Sit.' He pointed to a couple of chairs.

'I was just admiring Mategriffon.'

'Philip hates it.' Richard chuckled. 'He thought that he bested me by being first to occupy the palace in Messina so I snubbed my nose at him and built this. He also resents the fact that my forces are far larger than his,' he added as he flung himself down on one of the chairs.

'He has a multitude of reasons to be jealous of you,' Stephen replied, only sitting, as convention demanded, after his monarch had done so. 'You outshine him at everything, do you not?'

'And you allow me no modesty, my friend.' Richard picked up a pitcher from a nearby table and poured wine into two silver goblets. He handed one to Stephen.

'Thank you, sire.'

'It is a good wine, one Philip gifted me, surprisingly.' Richard paused, and then added, 'How fares my mother?'

'She is as beautiful and sprightly as ever.' Stephen had not been happy when Richard had charged him with escorting Eleanor of Aquitaine to Navarre to begin negotiations for Richard's marriage to the Princess Berengaria. He would have far preferred to accompany his king to the Holy Land but, because of the bad weather, Richard had been forced to hold his forces here until spring so he had only missed a long boring winter in Messina.

'And did you find Mother's company pleasing?' Richard had a teasing twinkle in his blue eyes.

'She is a most delightful companion,' Stephen lied.

Truthfully, Eleanor was an overpowering strong-willed woman, who had proved very difficult to please, but even so Stephen couldn't help admiring her. 'The journey from Navarre was not easy but both your mother and your betrothed bore the discomforts without complaint.'

'Yes, Berengaria,' Richard murmured as he thoughtfully sipped his wine. 'My mother insists that she will be the perfect bride for me, even though she knows that I have no interest in marrying.'

'That is one of the burdens of being a king, sire. You cannot always do what you want, you also have to consider the needs of your kingdom,' Stephen replied. 'She is pretty and sweet natured. No doubt she will make a fine queen.'

Truthfully, Stephen doubted that his friend would have much in common with the plump and pious princess, who appeared to have little interest in any serious matters. Richard had always been drawn to strong intelligent females like his mother, Eleanor of Aquitaine.

'Unfortunately, as you say we monarchs rarely have a choice in such matters.' Richard pursed his lips thoughtfully. 'I do not find her particularly attractive but she does not repulse me, so she will have to suffice.' He gave a bitter laugh. 'After all, how long can it take to beget a child?'

'No time at all,' Stephen said, then paused in surprise as a man he did not recognise strode into the room unannounced.

When the young man caught sight of the king, he blanched and looked very concerned. 'Forgive me, Your Majesty,' he stuttered awkwardly.

To Stephen's amazement, Richard didn't appear angry at being disturbed, which was unusual for him. He just smiled rather indulgently at the young stranger and Stephen's curiosity was aroused. The man didn't look much like a Frank as he was dark haired and swarthy skinned, his features reminding Stephen of the Saracens he had seen when he had lived in the Holy Land, which at the time had still been under Christian rule.

'Stephen, this is Armand de Mirabel,' Richard said as the young man bowed elegantly, bending so low that it appeared too much of a fawning gesture for Stephen's peace of mind. He had never taken an instant dislike to a man before but he did now and he had no idea why. 'Armand, my good friend the Comte de Chalais.'

'I have heard much of you, my lord.' Armand smiled warmly at Stephen. 'His Majesty speaks of you often.'

'Armand arrived here a few weeks ago from the Holy Land. He has been at the siege of Acre with the forces of the King of Jerusalem, Guy de Lusignan.'

As Stephen nodded, Armand said, 'Forgive my intrusion, Highness. I did not realise you were in here. Queen Joanna asked me to fetch her psalter which she left somewhere in this room.'

'My sister constantly leaves her belongings all over the place,' Richard said with a smile as he spotted the Book of Psalms on a low chest. 'There it is. Please take it to her, Armand.'

'Yes, sire.'

The young man retrieved the psalter and then bowed for the second time, once again far too obsequiously in Stephen's considered opinion. After he had left the room, Richard said, 'Perhaps you recall meeting Armand's father at King Baldwin's court in Jerusalem?'

'I do not recall doing so,' Stephen said. 'But I was young and far more interested in training to be a knight than becoming acquainted with all the noblemen of the royal court,' he added, thinking of the time in his early teens when he had gone to live with his godfather, Raymond of Tripoli. As was the custom, his father had sent him to Raymond to serve as a squire in his household, prior to beginning training as a knight. His godfather was dead now sadly but Stephen's memories of him were as strong as ever as he had been a most remarkable man. Not only had he been a great warrior and highly intelligent, he had also been interested in many diverse matters. Stephen was grateful for that because as well as training him in all the skills of warfare, Raymond had also taught him to speak Arabic and encouraged him to study various Saracen texts.

'Armand's mother was a Syrian Christian and his father a Frankish knight, so he has a unique understanding of the Saracen mind. I thought that he could also be useful as an interpreter when we reach Acre. I know that I cannot rely on your abilities all the time and I prefer men I can trust to act as my translators.'

'Yes, indeed.' Stephen found it unusual for Richard to so easily place his trust in someone he barely knew. It wasn't like him. He normally relied just on the council of his most loyal advisors and Stephen was proud to be included as one of them.

'In the meantime –' Richard spoke carefully as if he was about to say something of great importance '– I have another task for you, my friend.'

Stephen's heart sank as he imagined a multitude of unwanted tasks, including having to escort Richard's mother back to England. She had told him that she planned to return home soon to keep a close eye on Richard's younger, rather disreputable brother, John, who the king had, rather unwisely, left in charge of his kingdom. 'What task?' he asked charily.

'Hugh de Moreville, who was, as you know, one of my father's most loyal knights, has just died.' He paused as he saw Stephen tense. 'His wife accompanied him here,' he added in a gentler tone.

'Edwina here?' Stephen stuttered, dumbfounded.

'She is indeed and, as I recall, you and the lady were once betrothed?'

Stephen's heart thudded out of control as he tried to keep a check on his sudden rush of emotions. Even the sound of her name was opening up old wounds which he had begun to believe were more or less healed. Richard of all people knew how devastated he had been when he'd returned to Aquitaine and discovered that King Henry had arranged for Edwina to break off their betrothal and marry one of the king's most loyal knights: a man who had already sent two previous wives to their graves.

'Will you say nothing?' Richard prompted.

'You know the truth of it, sire. For my sake you tried to prevent Fulk taking her to England, did you not?'

'I did, but as you recall my father and I were at open warfare at the time and Fulk was always my father's man.' He smiled at Stephen. 'Now you have the opportunity to make some amends with the noble lady. I doubt very much that she is overly devastated at the loss of her husband. Hugh was a brutal man and my sister tells me that they did not fare well together. In the circumstances I thought perhaps that you might take it upon yourself to care for her. Perchance bring a little cheer back in her life.'

Stephen walked slowly along the corridor on his way to see Edwina, his thoughts in total turmoil. He was sweating so much beneath his elaborate tunic that his linen shirt clung to his chest and back while his palms felt damp and clammy. Even when readying himself for battle he always felt quite calm and controlled as if death held no fear for him any more. Yet thinking of this one woman, who had wed another almost three and a half years ago, made him feel nervous, confused and excited as if he were a callow youth once again. Time healed wounds, so he had been told, but none had told him that they could be ripped open again so easily.

How had she had fared with that brute of a husband? he wondered. Part of him dreaded finding out as he'd met Hugh once and found him an unpleasant individual. Even thinking of her with him and being forced to share his bed made Stephen feel sick to his stomach.

At Richard's suggestion, he had spoken to William de Preaux and he'd told Stephen that Edwina had been close to exhaustion a few hours ago after having spent days nursing her dying husband. Despite that warning, Stephen was determined to see her now even though his conscience told him that he should let her rest a while longer. He had always been a patient man but today that virtue had deserted him completely.

Following Stephen was a small troop of royal servants. One carried food and wine, two others a large wooden tub and the rest large jugs of hot water. He was certain that she would want to bathe after spending many hours in a sickroom tending to her husband. She apparently had no personal servants to care for her needs at this unhappy time and he'd learnt that Hugh had cruelly denied her many comforts, even the services of a lady's maid.

By the time he arrived at her door, his heart was beating at what felt like a thousand times a minute and he had to swallow hard and pause for a second before he could recover a measure of composure. Stephen knocked softly on the wooden door but there was not even the slightest sound from within so he cautiously lifted the latch. It was not locked so he opened the door and stepped inside her chamber, feeling somewhat apprehensive.

He saw her, lying fast asleep on the bed clad only in her shift. 'One moment,' he instructed the servants. He stepped towards her, took the damask coverlet from the end of the bed and draped it over her. 'Come,' he said softly.

The king's servants set about their tasks swiftly and in virtual silence. Soon the bath was ready and the food and drink laid out on a low table. During all that time Edwina had remained in the deep sleep of total exhaustion.

After the servants had departed, Stephen barred the door and picked up a three-legged stool which he placed beside the bed and sat upon. He had been unsure what to say when he first saw her again and now he didn't have to cope with that problem, he could just sit and stare at her lovely face. Stephen felt a shiver slide down his spine and an even stronger surge of troubling emotions that made his entire body feel unaccountably weak as he looked at the woman he had once loved more than life itself.

The softness of youth had left her exquisitely delicate features and she was now stunningly beautiful; lovelier in his considered opinion than she had ever been. She had the face of an angel, with skin as pale as ivory, while her glorious hair was still the same pure brilliant gold he remembered it to be. Her long, surprisingly dark lashes lay thick against her pale cheeks as she slept, yet there were now dark shadows of exhaustion, like bruises, under her eyes.

Stephen's thoughts were in turmoil and he was unsure how he actually felt about her after all this time. The desire was still there, there was no doubt about that, but he was no longer the relatively innocent young man who had been her betrothed. Life had honed and hardened him, until he had come to believe that he could never love any woman ever again.

Now that he had at last opened his mind to his painful memories, he recalled how desperate he had felt when he had returned from that mission for the Duke of Aquitaine to find her gone. Against all warnings, he had followed her to England, knowing full well that it was foolhardy when Richard and his father were still at war and that he risked being arrested and thrown into prison.

Unfortunately, he had arrived just in time to see Edwina and the tall grizzled man, who was now her husband, leaving the chapel. As he stared at her pale distraught face, his tortured mind had been filled with the words of the marriage ceremony – *'whom God has joined together, let no man put asunder'*.

Not so long after that King Henry had died and Richard had become king. When he had accompanied Richard to England, Stephen had hoped to see Edwina again but Hugh had never brought her to court, keeping her sequestered instead in his castle in the depths of Northumberland.

Stephen looked thoughtfully at Edwina. All the time he had been thinking of the past she had been sleeping soundly. He was not sure if he wanted to wake her just yet as she still looked exhausted. But her bath would cool too much if she didn't make use of it soon. Of course, after she had bathed and eaten, she could always sleep again, he told himself.

Suddenly she sighed and to his consternation began to thrash about on the bed as if she was having a terrible nightmare. 'No,' she murmured. 'Please no, Hugh,' she cried out in a terrified voice.

'Hush, Edwina,' he said softly as he stroked her cheek, longing to take her into his arms and comfort her but knowing that in the depth of her dream that might frighten her even more. Yet the sound of his voice appeared to calm her a little. 'I am here,' he added reassuringly.

Her frantic movements gradually ceased and she

opened her eyes. Blinking sleepily, she stared at Stephen as if he were some kind of strange apparition. 'Am I dreaming?' she asked in a weary, hesitant voice.

'No, it is I.' He gently brushed the stray fronds of golden hair away from her face.

'Stephen?' Her blue eyes widened in surprised disbelief. 'Is it really you?'

'I am as real as you are.' He smiled tenderly at her.

'I thought I saw you earlier...' she stuttered. 'I convinced myself that I was mistaken.'

'No mistake. I am here, Edwina,' he said, as she shakily tried to lift herself. 'Let me help you.' Sliding a strong arm around her, he helped Edwina into a sitting position and tenderly placed an extra pillow behind her back.

'How? Why?' she asked in confusion.

'I arrived here with Queen Eleanor and Princess Berengaria,' he explained.

'And why are you here in *our* bedchamber?' She suddenly looked terrified. 'Hugh!' she gasped, glancing around apprehensively.

'Edwina,' he said as gently as he could, 'he's dead, don't you remember?'

'Remember?' she replied, her body still as tense as a bowstring. 'Dead – yes.' She hunched back against her pillows like an old woman.

Her terror reignited his hatred of Hugh. He cursed her late husband and hoped that he was where he belonged, in the depths of hell. When he had first met Edwina she had been well rounded with a perfect bosom, slim waist and curvy hips, but at present she was rail thin. Now that her face was no longer in repose, he saw that her pale skin was drawn way too tightly across her high cheekbones. Then he spotted a large number of fading bruises on her thin arms and his stomach churned angrily. It was clear that she had been misused.

Gently, he took hold of one of her hands, which had been moving restlessly against the coverlet. Clasping it tenderly, he stared into her troubled blue eyes. 'Hugh died, Edwina. You nursed him to the end, did you not? You are clearly exhausted, that is why you are confused.'

'Yes.' Tears welled up in her eyes. 'I remember now. I was so scared, Stephen.' She clenched his hand so hard that her nails dug into his palm but he didn't even feel the discomfort. 'I prayed to God that he would die and now he has. Do you think that means that I will go to hell?'

'No.' He shook his head. 'From what I know of Hugh de Moreville, he deserved all that came to him. He committed many sins in his lifetime and I just wish he had died long before he wed you.'

'If only fate had not treated us so badly.' She shyly lowered her eyes as two spots of colour formed on her pale cheeks.

Stephen could only guess at the travails she had been forced to endure at the hands of that loathsome man. No doubt she had suffered even more, he thought with a sudden surge of guilt, when Hugh had discovered his supposedly innocent bride was no longer a virgin. 'Did you confess to Fulk and tell him what happened between us when he told you that you were to break our betrothal and marry Hugh?'

'That I was no longer...' She choked on the words. 'My brother didn't believe me. He said I was just lying in a desperate attempt to stop my marriage. I had hoped that when my husband discovered the truth he would set me aside, but he did not.'

'So he punished you instead?' he said as he brushed his fingers over the fading bruises on her arms.

Edwina did not reply to his question; she seemed lost in her thoughts for a moment. Eventually she gave an unhappy sigh and glanced towards the table containing the food and drink. 'I'm uncommonly thirsty. Could you get me something to drink?'

'Of course.' Stephen rose to his feet and stepped over to the table. He poured out a goblet of light Rhenish wine. 'Here.' He sat back down on the stool and handed her the goblet, conscious that his hand was shaking a little. How could this woman move him so much and so easily, when he could stand cool and unafraid in front of a whole troop of Saracen soldiers?

'You have not changed at all, Stephen.' She sipped the wine and then smiled tremulously at him.

'I have a few more battle scars,' he admitted with a wry smile.

'As have we all...' Her words trailed off and she stared into her cup of wine, appearing not to want to meet his gaze for a moment.

'You are as beautiful as you ever were, Edwina.' Perhaps, even if he could not be anything else to her, he could be her friend, he thought as, taking hold of her free hand, he lifted it to his lips. As he kissed it, she stiffened slightly almost as if she were afraid of his touch. 'What's wrong?'

'Hugh said that I had become loathsome and that no man would ever desire me again.'

'He lied.' Desire for her coiled like an insidious snake deep in his belly, even though he knew that it was wrong to feel like this at this moment in time.

'I fear that he did not.' She glanced down at her thin arms. 'I am ugly and sullied both without and within.'

Tears filled her eyes and she looked so unhappy that he could bear it no longer. Wanting to reassure her, and unable to resist the temptation her beauty afforded him, Stephen leant forwards and tenderly brushed his lips across her pale cheek. All sense and reason told him that he shouldn't be doing this, but regardless of all that had happened his body still ached to touch her again.

Ignoring the sudden tensing of her limbs, he meshed his hand in her hair and drew her towards him. Stephen captured her lips with his, kissing her tenderly and with restraint, his touch by necessity caressingly delicate. At first she kept her lips tightly closed but slowly, as he continued to kiss her, his mouth moving gently against hers, they eased open a little.

He was overcome by powerful emotions he did not even care to examine let alone explain. Eventually he ventured to dip the tip of his tongue into her mouth slowly and sensuously, holding back on the fierce desire that suddenly consumed his body, fearing that he might frighten her with the strength of his passion. Sex was most probably not the answer but now that he was here with her, his only excuse was that he couldn't help himself.

With a soft sigh, the tension left her body and her mouth softened as her tongue tentatively brushed his. Their kiss deepened, becoming more passionate, and he felt sexual desire well up even stronger inside him as his stomach tensed and his cock began to harden. He was desperate to pull her close and caress her breasts, then possess her again completely, no longer just in his fevered imagination but in reality once more. Instead he was forced to hold back on his desires as he kissed her with affection and reassurance.

The empty goblet slipped from her hand and made a clattering noise as it fell on the floor. Edwina jumped in surprise but Stephen held her close and whispered softly, 'You are still beautiful, Edwina. As beautiful and desirable now as the day we first met.'

'Stephen,' she murmured, relaxing in his embrace for a moment. Suddenly, she drew away from him a little. 'We should not be alone like this. I'm newly widowed. It is not seemly.'

'Not even when the king himself commands it?' he

said, smiling reassuringly at her. 'We are under royal protection. He thought it might help if he sent me to care for you at this unhappy time.'

'The king commands it?'

'He knows how much we once cared for each other, does he not?'

'Stephen, I don't know anything any more.' She didn't appear at ease in his company; and why should she be, he asked himself. The present situation was very different now from what it had been in the past.

'I arranged for a bath, I thought it might please you.'

'I stink of the sickroom and the water looks so tempting.' She glanced longingly at the tub of water where a thin trickle of steam was still rising lazily in the air. 'It is a luxury that has been denied me for such a very long time.'

'Then bathe you shall, at once.' He drew back the coverlet and watched her shakily slide her legs from the bed.

Edwina winced a little as she planted her feet on the wood floor. 'I'm more exhausted than I thought, it seems,' she said tremulously as she smiled awkwardly at him.

As she stood up, her shift slipped from her shoulder, revealing the upper curves of one small, firm, creamy breast. Her full bosom had shrunk with her loss of weight but she was as desirable as ever to him. Lust filled his loins and he felt his cock stiffen even more beneath his clothing. He wanted to bed her right now and the licentious side of his nature told him it wouldn't be inappropriate because she was a widow and now had a measure of freedom for the first time in her life. Hugh had no living heirs and, with the money and land she had brought to her marriage, combined with his riches, she was now an extraordinarily wealthy woman.

Many men would clamour for her hand. Yet she was exhausted and he knew that it would be wrong to take advantage of her weakness and even think of bedding her at a time such as this.

'Come.' He rose to his feet. 'Let me help you.' He went to take her arm.

'No, Stephen.' She tensed nervously.

'I'll expect nothing you are not prepared to give,' he assured her. 'I wish to help you bathe, nothing more.'

'The water does look inviting.' She took a cautious step towards the tub. 'A bath would be wonderful.' She gnawed anxiously at her lip.

'Do not be so modest, Edwina. It is not as if I've never seen you unclothed before.' He stepped closer but did not touch her. 'You are so weak I doubt you can manage alone, but I will keep my eyes averted as much as possible.'

'My body is not as it was then,' she said tremulously as she glanced down at the soft fabric of her shift, which had moulded to her diminished breasts.

'You are as beautiful to me as you always were. I can assure you that you'll soon grow fit and well again, especially after I feed you some of the rich sweetmeats that Princess Berengaria loves so much.'

'They say that the Saracens like their women well fleshed,' she said awkwardly. 'So they would not like me either.'

'You placed your trust in me once. Can you not do so now?' he pleaded.

She might be embarrassed about her looks and her situation but surely she knew she could trust his words above all else. However, what troubled him most was that he sensed that her concern at present was prompted by more than just mere modesty.

Edwina took another couple of hesitant steps towards

the tub. Stephen frowned. She was wearing something quite bulky beneath her shift and he couldn't understand what it could possibly be.

Pausing, she looked nervously at him and, when she realised what he was staring at, fear and concern clouded her eyes again. 'No, Stephen . . .' she faltered. 'It was Hugh, he made me wear it.'

'Wear what?' he asked in confusion as he saw tears start to roll down her pale cheeks.

'He has the key.' She looked wildly around the room. 'I know not where it is or how to find it now that he's gone. I have looked before and it is not in this room.'

'The key to what?' Her words were not making any sense to him.

'I'm ashamed,' she said uneasily. Biting her lip, she nervously pressed the fabric of her shift to her body and he could see that she appeared to be wearing what looked like some kind of heavy belt around her slim hips. 'And I cannot get it off.'

'You've no reason to be ashamed,' he said gently, feeling very confused. 'If you need my help then there can be no false modesty. You must show me what concerns you so much.'

She stood there, looking forlornly at him. 'I cannot,' she said with a sob, shaking her head.

This was certainly not the time for maidenly indecision. 'Yes, you can,' he said determinedly, as he stepped forwards and gently took hold of the hem of her shift. Stephen lifted the fabric slowly, first revealing her slim legs, which were trembling visibly. As he reached her hips and lower torso she gave a murmur of embarrassment but he ignored it as he saw the strange contraption fastened securely around the lower half of her body. 'By St George!' he gasped. 'What is it?'

'I know not what you would call it,' she said shyly, her face flushed with humiliation. 'Hugh obtained it from a master craftsman who came from Florence. He told me that in some lands men force their women to wear these things to ensure their chastity.'

As far as he could ascertain it was a wide metal belt with elaborate hinges set at intervals to give it a measure of flexibility. It girded her body just below her waist and another, wider piece of metal, ran down the front, over her belly to disappear between her legs. Stephen was appalled and the thought of her being forced to wear such a contraption made him feel sick with disgust.

'How long has he made you wear this thing?' he asked with concern as he examined it more closely. It was terrible to be sure, but it was also exquisitely crafted with metalwork finer than anything he'd ever seen before.

'When the mood took him. Or when I displeased him in some way,' she explained awkwardly, clearly mortified by his discovery. 'Of late, far more often, perhaps because practically everything I did seemed to anger him. Here, he could not keep me hidden away like he did back in England. This time it was because some young nobleman smiled at me. Hugh was insane with jealousy even though he claimed not to desire me one jot. He made me put it on some days ago, just before his unexpected illness.'

'Yet surely it is not designed to wear for such long periods,' Stephen said. He wondered if it might have been fashioned to be used on a fleeting basis, just as titillation between lovers, nothing more. Nevertheless, Hugh had cruelly strapped her into this contraption as a punishment because she had displeased him in some minor way. He presumed it must have some provision to allow normal bodily functions, but he could see wide red weals on her skin where the metal had chafed her delicate flesh.

'It is uncomfortable most of the time,' she confessed, tensing as he reached out to touch it. 'Now I fear that I will never get it off.'

'Have no fear of that, Edwina.' Stephen swept her into his arms and carried her back to the bed. As he lay her down on the mattress, he made sure her shift was rucked around her waist so that he could see all of the belt clearly.

'What will you do?' Her face was scarlet with embarrassment but she made no attempt to cover her modesty.

'I never told you of my friend Robert,' he said with a warm smile. 'His father was the local blacksmith but in his youth had been a thief. I hasten to add that he had paid dearly for his crimes and obtained the necessary absolution from the village priest, so my father agreed to employ him in our castle. Merely to amuse us both as young boys, Robert's father taught us how to open just about any lock. Believe me, the skill has proved very useful on a number of occasions when I have been carrying out missions for the king.'

He glanced around the room and eventually his gaze rested upon an ornate tray filled with hairpins. Striding over to them, he selected one. 'This looks suitable.' He stepped back to the bed.

Edwina watched as he bent the pin into the shape he required. 'You can open it with that?'

'I know I can,' he said sounding far more confident than he actually felt. A door lock was huge in comparison to this exquisite piece of ironwork, a tiny padlock barely bigger than a walnut which held the belt together at her waist. 'Stay still,' he warned her as he eased the tip of the pin into the tiny keyhole and moved it gently until he connected with the lock mechanism inside. He wriggled the pin carefully until he heard just the faintest of clicks. 'As I said – it was simple.' He smiled, happy that he'd managed it so easily as he eased the hasp of the lock open.

Edwina gave a sigh of relief as he pulled the waistband of the belt apart. Her skin looked red and inflamed but was not damaged as much as he had expected it to be because the inside of the waistband was padded with soft leather. 'Stephen!' she gasped in horror as he leant down and gently prised open her legs.

'I cannot get it off otherwise,' he said lifting her bottom to ease the two hinged metal straps, which rested either side of her buttock cheeks, down towards her thighs. Just as he'd suspected there were lines of small perforations in the piece of polished metal that cupped her sexual parts, but he could see that the sides had dug into the tender flesh of her groin, rubbing it raw in places. 'Hugh was a monster,' he muttered angrily as he eased the cruel contraption away from her body. It made a noisy clattering sound as he threw it on the floor with disgust.

'Thank you.' She went to pull down her shift but he gently stayed her hand.

'One moment.' After rising to his feet he strode over to the tub and wrung a washing cloth out in the water. He walked back to Edwina, knelt before her and lovingly cleansed her sexual parts, trying to ignore his sudden surge of lust at the sight of her secret pink flesh. Swallowing hard, Stephen suppressed his shameful desires as he felt her shudder every time the damp cloth brushed her abused skin.

'You will soon recover,' he reassured her as he tossed the cloth aside. 'I have a wonderful salve in my baggage, which I obtained from an Arab doctor. It will heal your skin in a couple of days or so.' He tried to concentrate on her face and stop himself from looking down at her tempting sex again. 'I'd kill Hugh if I could. You know that?'

'It appears that fate has already accomplished that task.' She smiled nervously. 'I do not know what I would have done if you'd not been here, Stephen. I could never have asked anyone else to free me from that thing.'

'I give thanks that I was here then.' As he moved his hand away from her, his fingertips briefly brushed her mons and he couldn't be entirely sure if it was an accident or whether unconsciously he wanted it to happen. 'Forgive me,' he muttered awkwardly as he saw her shudder in response. He was mortified that he could still feel desire just by looking at her sexual parts, when all he should feel was anger for the suffering she had been forced to endure.

'There is nothing to forgive ... it felt ... it felt good,' she said shyly. 'You will never know how much I have missed the loving touch of a man I desire. Sex with Hugh was cold and brutal; all I felt was loathing and disgust. When I couldn't bear it any longer I used to close my eyes and try to pretend it was you.'

'Edwina,' he groaned, unable to resist the temptations of her flesh a moment longer. Wanting to replace all the pain she had suffered with pleasure, he leant forwards and brushed his lips against her mound. Her soft sparse pubic hair tickled his lips and he longed to slide them downwards towards her cleft.

'Please,' she murmured as she allowed her thighs to roll open.

The unspoken invitation was clear. Gently he slid his fingers into the slit of her sex and caressed the soft pink velvety flesh. To his surprise it was already becoming moist.

'I thought that you would not welcome such intimacies so soon,' he murmured, looking back at her to see if her expression displayed any revulsion, but she had a half smile on her lips and her eyes were closed. Tenderly, he explored her soft folds until he found what he sought, the small bud of her clitoris. At least the casual liaisons he'd indulged in since their parting had taught him more about pleasuring women, he thought wryly. Yet he still found it amazing that touching something so small and insignificant could arouse a female so much. As he gently stroked the bud, he heard Edwina give a low keening moan of bliss. Then he could have sworn that he felt the tiny nub of flesh stiffen as her sex grew even moister.

'I'd forgotten how good this felt,' she gasped, then tensed in surprise as Stephen dipped his head between her slim thighs and ran the tip of his tongue along the folds of her sex. 'What are you doing?'

'I've learnt that there are many different facets to lovemaking, my sweet girl,' he murmured as his tongue delved deeper, lapping and teasing her sensitive flesh.

Edwina stiffened as his lips found her clitoris and fastened around it. His tongue flicked against the small nub as he sucked on it gently. Stephen heard her gasp with pleasure, and she thrashed her head against the pillow as he began to suck harder, pulling the nub deeper into his mouth while his fingers continued to delicately explore every part of her sex.

Stephen ignored his own needs, the aching rigidity of his cock and the tenseness in his balls as he continued to use his mouth and lips until she was moaning and twisting beneath him like a woman possessed. He slipped two fingers into her soft sheath, and the smooth interior seemed to swallow them up willingly. He moved his fingers gently, finger-fucking her until she was beyond anything but her own imminent release.

3

Edwina lay on the bed and watched Stephen strip off his clothes, feeling almost euphoric and hardly able to believe that her life had changed so much in an instant. Stephen looked so gloriously masculine, fitter and more muscular than ever, although there were a number of unfamiliar scars on his body which reminded her of how much time had passed since they had been forcibly parted.

She shivered with anticipation as he turned towards her, his delicious-looking cock swinging free between his muscular thighs, and she felt faint at the thought of that thrusting inside her again. How could she suddenly feel so wanton, she wondered, as he eased her shift from her body and swung her into his arms.

'Your bath awaits, my lady,' Stephen said as he strode over to the tub and gently deposited her in the water. It felt warm and deliciously smooth, lapping around her soiled skin like a soft caress.

'That is wonderful.' She felt that she could just close her eyes and drift dreamily in the comforting warmth but clearly Stephen had no intention of letting her slip into an indulgent lethargy. He picked up a washing cloth, wrung it out in the water and then rubbed it over her shoulders and down her back.

'My soap,' she said, pointing to the small jar which Fulk had sent her from France. It was a sweetly scented concoction which was far kinder on the skin than the acrid-smelling potion they used in Hugh's castle in England.

Stephen poured some of the soap into his palm and began to rub it gently onto her skin. First he massaged her arms, then her back and shoulders, but it was clear that his thoughts were not just connected with cleanliness. Her breasts were not covered by the water and her skin prickled sensually as his gaze roved over the upper half of her body. Edwina sighed softly as his hands brushed her breasts. Cupping the small globes in his palms, he squeezed them gently and shivers of pleasure darted down to her groin. Soon, his soapy fingers focused on her nipples, squeezing and pulling at them until they hardened into firm peaks.

'Your body is so tempting, my sweet,' he groaned as he leant forwards and kissed her lips. He carefully rinsed the oily soap from her body with the soft cloth.

'As is yours,' she murmured, conscious of how impossibly firm his body was as she felt his muscular chest pressed close to her shoulder. Edwina resisted the sudden temptation to look down at his cock, knowing that by now it must have already started to grow hard. Dear Lord, how she wanted this man and needed to feel his swollen shaft thrusting inside her.

She had clung onto her wonderful memories of Stephen for such a long time, until they had gradually been swallowed up by Hugh's constant brutality. Even on her wedding night he had been cold and vicious, unconcerned with her feelings and intent only on his own release. Her memories of Stephen's sensual lovemaking helped keep her sane in the early months; even though Hugh had been furious beyond belief when he had discovered that she wasn't a virgin. Yet, he had refused to set her aside and annul the marriage as he had no wish to relinquish her generous dowry. Even so, he had never for one moment let her forget that she had not been a maiden when they wed, castigating her about it constantly, using it as another reason, among many others, to treat her cruelly most of the time.

Yet none of this mattered now, the past was long gone and Stephen's hand had crept under the water to stroke her flat stomach. She shivered with pleasure as he cupped her sex, then gently eased his fingers inside her. The wonderful sensations, combined with the feel of the warm water caressing her flesh, made her body melt with bliss. Grabbing hold of his shoulders, she boldly pulled him close, her mouth seeking his. The kiss they shared was long and passionate and his tongue pushed its way into her mouth and played tantalising games with hers, while his fingers worked their magic inside her.

'Join me,' she said a little breathlessly. 'The tub is big enough for two.'

'Barely,' he responded as he pulled away from her.

'We will manage no doubt.' Teasingly she splashed water onto his bare chest and the sparkling droplets rolled temptingly downwards. 'I've made you wet.' She peeked over the rim of the tub and saw the thin trickle of water running down over his flat stomach to disappear in the dark hair clustered around his already erect manhood. 'Hurry,' she begged, so wanting to feel the entire glorious length of it inside her.

'As my lady wishes.' He sprung to his feet and strode towards the bed.

'What are you doing?' she asked as he picked up the coverlet and carried it back to the tub.

His cock bobbed enticingly as he moved, while the heavy sac of his balls brushed against his muscular thighs. The mere sight of his sexual parts made her weak with need for him again. Unconsciously, she opened her legs, feeling the smooth sensuality of the warm water lap against her open sex.

'I know not what lies beneath this room,' he explained as he draped the coverlet round the base of the tub. 'For all I know it could be the king's bedchamber. When I join you the water is bound to spill over the sides.'

Edwina giggled at the thought of King Richard awakening from a deep sleep to find water dripping from the ceiling onto his bed. 'A wise move,' she agreed with a warm smile.

'Richard may be my friend but he has a foul temper at times and such thoughtlessness would not be excused,' Stephen said as he planted one foot in the tub.

Edwina eased herself back and pulled her knees up to her chest to give him enough room to sit down. Stephen sank down, now happily able to ignore the thin trickle of water that began to spill over the sides of the tub. He sat facing her, knees also drawn up to his chest. 'This will not do,' he said, grinning wickedly. 'Lift your legs and open them a little.'

As she did as he asked, Stephen leant forwards, grabbed hold of her waist and pulled her towards him. He angled his back against the sides of the tub, which gave her just enough room to squat rather awkwardly astride his hips. She smiled: Stephen was way too tall for this tub and had to bend his long legs as he braced his feet against the wooden sides. Suddenly, he pulled her down hard onto his groin and she felt the wonderful pressure as the side of his engorged shaft rubbed sensuously against the entire length of her open sex. He leant forwards and fastened his lips around one of her nipples and, as he pulled the teat deeper into his mouth, she gave a soft sigh of bliss.

He sucked on her nipple, pausing to graze it teasingly with his teeth now and then, while at the same time he slid an arm around her and cupped her buttocks in the palm of his hand. Gently he kneaded the firm cheeks, while he continued to suck on her aching teat. She became more and more aroused as all the time his engorged shaft continued to press tantalisingly against the open valley of her sex.

Desire made Edwina become bolder. She reached down into the water and curved her fingers around his cock. 'Careful,' he gasped. 'My endurance wanes. I want you so much.'

'Then you must endure a while longer,' she purred softly as she lifted herself so that she could more easily guide his penis inside her. Sighing with pleasure, Edwina pushed her body downwards and felt the entire length of his shaft slide smoothly into her vagina. For one precious moment she remained motionless, just enjoying the glorious sensation of her body being speared completely by his.

'Edwina,' he groaned, his fingers digging into her buttock cheeks, while she fought the slight buoyancy of the water as she ground herself against his firm groin. 'How I've longed for this moment,' he said, his voice husky with need.

'As have I.' She kissed him with passionate intensity, pressing her breasts against his powerful chest. Then, bracing her feet against the floor of the tub, she began to move her hips. The gentle swirling of the water lapping around her body and against her open pussy, coupled with the feel of his hard flesh buried deep inside her, was intoxicating. Grabbing onto his shoulders, she began to move faster, pumping her body up and down on his cock, the intense friction and fullness driving her wild beyond belief.

Her vigorous movements made water slop even faster over the side of the tub but they no longer cared as they were captivated by the sensual delights of the moment. Edwina worked her hips harder, savouring every erotic sensation as the pleasure overwhelmed her completely. Meanwhile, Stephen was digging his fingers deeper into her buttock cheeks, urging her to move even more vigorously, while his other hand dipped into the water and slid between their smoothly pounding flesh.

His searching fingers found her clitoris and he rubbed it briskly, adding to the erotic sensations rising up inside her. As she bounced up and down on his cock, her breath coming in small urgent gasps, she felt the pleasure envelop her in a tidal wave of amazing proportions. It rose to a swelling crescendo, which swept her up to the heights and beyond. As her extended orgasm reached its climax, she vaguely heard Stephen's accompanying grunt of pleasure as he too came, spilling his seed inside her.

'Are you sure this is the right place?' Edwina turned to look questioningly at the page, who had sought her out a short time ago and asked her to come to the stables as one of her horses was unwell. However, to her consternation, the boy had disappeared completely. She really didn't have time for this. Edwina looked around the large royal stableblock, not even certain if her late husband's horses had been housed in this place.

'Hello?' she called, but there was no reply. The building seemed to be empty apart from the horses.

She heard a noise but it was only a stallion snorting, while a couple of other mounts stamped their feet restlessly. The rest of the horses were contentedly chewing their feed. It was a mistake, the message couldn't have been for her, she decided, thinking that she should leave and return to the princess as soon as possible.

Yet she so wanted to linger a while as just the smell of this place brought back so many happy memories. The pleasant earthy odours of horses and fresh straw reminded her of her home in Angoulême. It was early and still a little chilly outside but the stables had been warmed by the heat of the animals' bodies and she was tempted to just sit down on a bale of straw and relax for a moment. She felt a little weary as today she had been obliged to rise at dawn in order to accompany Princess Berengaria to the chapel to pray for the king. Now that she was one of the princess's ladies-in-waiting she found her life almost as restrictive as it had been with Hugh. Berengaria was a sweet but overly pious lady and Edwina often spent just as much time on her knees now as she had during the years she was married.

Edwina heard a faint noise. 'What?' she gasped as a strong arm coiled around her waist and she was pulled into an empty stall. 'Stephen!'

Stephen's lips covered hers as he kissed her passionately, and Edwina melted into his embrace, twining her arms around his neck. Since they had been reunited, she could think of nothing else but her desire for him and the more she was with him, the more she wanted to be with him every time of the day or night, even though that was far from possible at present.

As he at last drew his lips from hers, she drew in a ragged breath. 'What are you doing here?' she asked.

'I sent word, did you not receive my message?' he said softly, as he plucked off her veil, tossed it aside and kissed her ear lobe.

The feel of his lips on that sensitive spot made her shudder with pleasure. 'I received a message that one of my horses was unwell,' she said as he pulled the pins from her hair. Within seconds her carefully arranged hairstyle was destroyed and her golden locks fell around her shoulders and tumbled in disarray down her back.

'Quite so.' He grinned cheekily at her. 'You were with the princess and such a message seemed more circumspect. After all,' he said as his lips caressed her neck. 'I could not say that I have to fuck you because my cock is so swollen it feels as if it might explode.'

'Stephen.' She giggled. 'You are so wicked.'

'Is it wicked to tell the truth?' His green eyes were dark with desire as he pulled her further into the stall.

'It is a conundrum, is it not, my lord?' she teased as he began to pull up the sides of her skirt so that he could slide his hand between her trembling, eager thighs.

'Wool is way too heavy to wear in this climate,' he said frustratedly, letting go of her skirt and reaching for the back lacing of her gown. 'I'll buy you silk, it is so much cooler and lighter to wear when in the Holy Land.'

'Now that I am in control of my own purse, I can buy it myself,' she murmured, her heart beating faster as, in his haste to unfasten the gown, he snapped the laces.

'I shall choose them all because you need to have a number of Eastern-style garments such as the Saracen ladies wear. The noblewomen at the court of Jerusalem often wore such clothing and it is far more attractive and comfortable in this warmth.'

'The princess is very modest and strait-laced. No doubt she would not approve.' She paused. 'Yet I should like to enjoy the sensual feel of silk next to my skin,' she added as she ran her hands over the hard lines of his back, enjoying the feel of his strong muscles tensing slightly beneath her fingertips.

Edwina was fascinated by the stories Stephen had told her about the Latin Kingdom of Jerusalem. It was a world so different from her own: elaborate palaces, opulently furnished houses with their own bathing facilities, the strange and varied customs of the inhabitants of different creeds and races. However, what fascinated her most of all were his stories of the Saracen harems where women lived in secluded luxury, existing only to please their Arab masters.

'Then the princess would consider such comfortable garments sinful?'

'No doubt. She is a very religious lady who confers often with her priests.'

'Even so, they were not thought sinful in the Holy City,' he said as he eased her dress down her body until it fell in a heavy pool at her feet. 'So why should they be sinful here? I agree with Richard, priests speak foolish nonsense at times.'

'Hush.' She lifted a finger to his lips. 'The king may be able to speak such heresy but you should beware.'

'And you concern yourself too much.' He lifted her off her feet and placed her gently on a soft brightly coloured blanket that had been laid over a pile of straw. 'And before you worry about anything else, I should tell you that my squire is on guard outside. We shall not be disturbed.'

'Even so you should hurry.' She felt excited, longing to couple with him again as she lay there, just clad in her shift, watching him disrobe. 'Princess Berengaria worries even more than I do. If I am too long she will send one of the maidservants to look for me.'

'My squire can easily cope with one curious maidservant,' he said as he threw his plain tunic on the ground and kicked off his loose leather slippers. 'Anyway, Berengaria expects far too much of you.'

She smiled as he undid the cord at his waist and let his loose breeches drop to display a very delicious-looking cock that was already partially aroused. 'Just as King Richard expects too much from you, Stephen. In the last couple of days I've barely seen you at all.'

Grinning, he flung himself down beside her and pulled her into his arms. 'But we still have the nights.'

'You creep into my bed when I am half asleep and leave before I'm awake.'

'Only because convention demands it. I have no wish to sully your reputation, my lady.'

'I care not for my reputation.' She sighed as he pulled

off her shift, not appearing to care whether he ripped it a little in the process. 'If I could, I would make you stay in my bed morning, noon and night. I've never truly known how intoxicating sex can be. But you, no doubt, have had many other women in the past.'

'Too numerous to mention,' he said teasingly. He pulled her closer to him so that their bodies were pressed sensuously together, flesh to flesh. He kissed her passionately until she was gasping for breath, while all the time his hands gently caressed her back and buttocks.

Edwina felt the familiar need for him grow even stronger inside her until it became a tearing pain of desire. Her body felt weak and her sex grew moist and ready for him. She could feel the swelling length of his shaft digging into her upper thighs and she was now desperate to feel it inside her. Yet she was also tempted by the thought of something that Hugh had forced her to do often in the past. Would Stephen like it as well, she wondered, unsure whether she should be so forward in this early stage of their newly burgeoning relationship. Or should she even consider it at all? She knew that Stephen was no prude, however. He had lived in the East where, according to the tales he had told her, women did all they could to pleasure a man and never even thought to consider if what they did was even remotely sinful.

'Wait.' She wriggled from his embrace and slid down the blanket.

She had become quite expert at pleasuring Hugh with her hands and mouth, and she had made every effort to improve these skills, because then she could bring him to fulfilment as soon as possible. Thankfully, most times after he had climaxed he would leave her alone. That was not what she wanted this time, however, as she knew the experience with Stephen would be very different. After all his engorged penis looked deliciously tempting and she was eager to experience the feel of its pulsing strength in her mouth.

She moved until she was crouching astride her lover's legs. Then she leant forward until the tips of her nipples all but touched his upper thighs, and gently took hold of his shaft. Tenderly she curved her fingers around its meaty bulk, sensuously caressing the taut organ just as she had learnt to do with Hugh in the past.

'Edwina, please desist,' he groaned. 'I want to come inside you.'

'After I have pleasured you as much as you have pleasured me,' she murmured and she guided the tip into her mouth. Stephen swore softly, his entire body tensing as her lips closed around the bulging helmet. Then she ran the tip of her tongue teasingly over the tightly stretched skin on its domed peak.

He did not protest again as he lifted his hips, forcing more of his shaft into her mouth. She accepted it eagerly, swallowing as much of his rigid flesh as she could while her hand reached between his legs to tenderly stroke his balls.

She began to gently suck on the organ, sliding her lips tantalisingly up and down its length, and she was delighted when she heard Stephen give a throaty gasp of pleasure. He meshed his hands in her long blonde hair as she pulled his cock deeper into her mouth. She caressed the rigid shaft with her tongue, while her fingers continued to play sensually with the soft sac of his scrotum.

Remembering all she had learnt, Edwina moved her mouth, sliding it up and down his burgeoning shaft, amazed to find how much she was enjoying an act that she had always found so distasteful before. There was something sexually invigorating about feeling the power and strength of his manhood quivering between her lips. Unconsciously, she sucked harder, teasing the sensitive flesh with her tongue, milking him rhythmically with her lips.

'Dear Lord,' he gasped as her fingertips moved to the extra-sensitive strip of skin between his cock and balls. All the while the warm wetness of aching desire kept growing deep inside her. 'Edwina!'

Before she could act to stop him, Stephen jerked his cock from her mouth, grabbed hold of her waist and pulled her body upwards until she was poised above his engorged penis. She caught a brief sight of its glistening strength, the surface still covered with the moisture of her mouth before, with one smooth movement, he pulled her downwards. She felt his hard cock slide inside her only partway, then he held her there with his strong arms, letting her open sex swallow him up a mere finger's breadth at a time. He was teasing her, moving far too slowly and, filled with a desperate need, she struggled to force her body downwards. Determinedly, she thrust her hips down hard and, with one smooth movement, he was inside her, filling her completely, almost driving the very breath of life from her lungs.

Then he rolled over until he was atop her, his knees between her open thighs. Edwina grabbed hold of his muscular shoulders, pressing her fingers into the hard unresilient flesh as he began to thrust, pounding his cock in and out of her sex until she thought she might faint just from the exquisite intensity of the sensations he was arousing inside her.

Stephen was not feeling at all happy this evening. They were due to depart for the Holy Land tomorrow and he would be travelling with the king on the royal war galley, while Edwina was obliged to accompany Princess Berengaria in one of the slower, sturdier and much larger vessels. No doubt they would not see each other again for two or three weeks, so instead of being in this brothel in Messina, he would have far preferred to be in Edwina's bed.

Idly, he looked around the large high-ceilinged room with its marble floor and walls decorated with brightly coloured silk hangings; it had an opulence and luxury that Stephen had only seen before in the homes of the richest Frankish knights in the Holy Land. A group of blind musicians, sitting in the far corner, were playing haunting Eastern music, while very scantily clad young women served Stephen and his two companions food and drink.

Stephen glanced at Richard, who lay on a damask-covered couch dressed only in his linen braes. He looked happy and relaxed enough, far more at ease than Stephen felt, but then the king had consumed a fair few goblets of wine. Armand had arranged this visit tonight and he lay on a couch next to Richard's. The spotless white linen of Armand's braes contrasted spectacularly with his smooth olive skin, flashing dark eyes and shoulder-length black wavy hair. Armand was very good-looking and could be immensely charming but first impressions counted and Stephen still didn't like him overmuch. He felt there was something a little sinister and untrustworthy about the young man, but unfortunately Richard didn't appear to see it and enjoyed his company.

The brothel owner, a plump overdressed little man, appeared, bowed obsequiously at Richard and then clapped his hands. The pace of the music changed as two lean but muscular young men ran into the room. They wore only tiny blue loincloths and their skin was heavily oiled, making it gleam attractively in the lamplight. They began to perform an acrobatic routine, which included the most amazing somersaults, all in time to the strange, rather jarring music. Stephen was entranced by the display as he watched the two beautifully supple bodies moving lithely and in near-perfect unison. They were far more skilful than any tumblers he'd ever seen before, twisting and turning, their feats growing even more improbable by the moment, almost as if they had invisible cords pulling them smoothly in the air. With two final spectacular backward flips they finished their performance and bowed low before the three men. Richard nodded his appreciation as they stood there motionless and breathing heavily.

Stephen expected them to leave but they remained where they were as the music became slower and more seductive. A young woman glided into the room, sensually swaying her slim hips. She was quite tall but delicately built with long slender limbs and jet-black hair, which hung in a dark cloud down her back, and all she wore was a tiny bolero covering her small breasts and filmy, sky-blue silk trousers. They were gathered at her ankles and cut so low that you could just see the top of the crack of her buttocks at the back and a thin line of inky-black pubic hair peeking over the jewelled belt girding her hips.

As she danced closer to them, moving seductively in time to the music, Stephen saw that her dark eyes were outlined with kohl and her full moist lips were stained a shining scarlet. She danced, moving so expertly and in such a tantalising manner that, even though he'd so far remained immune to the eroticisms of this place, Stephen found himself becoming physically aroused. His cock started to stiffen of its own accord, and soon he was forced to lay a casual hand across his lap to cover the telltale growing bulge in his thin linen braes. He had never seen a dance so entrancing; the girl moved in a way that turned all his thoughts and feelings instinctively towards lustful sex.

He found himself leaning forwards intently as she

began to tempt the two young acrobats, circling them slowly, edging towards them to run her hands over their legs and chests, then brushing her fingers teasingly against their groins. Gracefully, she rubbed her body against theirs, twining her long limbs around one young man as she deftly jerked off his loincloth. His cock was already engorged and standing lewdly out from his groin. Immediately, the other man, who was a shade taller, pulled off his loincloth with a flourish and tossed it on the floor. Not surprisingly he too was aroused and the two men's semi-erect organs bobbed erotically in the soft lamplight as they stepped towards the girl.

Smiling enigmatically she glided teasingly away from them, moving her body sensually in time to the music, swinging her hips and undulating her belly as she led the two young men tantalisingly around the room. Every time they went to touch her, she smiled and darted just out of their reach, teasing and taunting them as she glided enticingly away time and time again.

Within minutes Stephen felt the atmosphere in the room begin to change as the two naked men relentlessly pursued the young dancer. It was clearly all part of a display for their benefit but the two men's apparent frustration at her ability to elude their reaching hands seemed amazingly real. A crackling tension filled the air as the play-acting suddenly changed from teasingly erotic to brutal and sexual.

In perfect unison, much like their display, the two men lunged for her at once, grabbing hold of the girl, their fingers digging into her flesh as they pulled her roughly towards them. Her useless struggles didn't look like play-acting to Stephen and appeared frighteningly real as one ripped her bodice, jerking it off to reveal her small breasts. Stephen tensed. Her nipples were large and erect, painted a glistening scarlet like her mouth.

The taller man's hands closed over her breasts as the

other tugged the jewelled girdle down her slim hips, and she was left naked, standing in a pool of blue silk, with just an inky-black triangle of pubic hair covering her sex. Giving a sharp, surprisingly convincing scream of terror, she struggled to get away but the taller man grabbed a handful of her long dark hair and forced her to her knees, pulling her face towards his tumescent shaft. Curving his fingers around his cock, the man pumped it to make it grow even harder and then thrust it between her moist scarlet lips.

By now Richard was breathing heavily and Stephen was also highly aroused by the inherent brutality of the moment. He told himself this was all just a display put on to entertain them, but the strange angry fire he usually only experienced in battle surged excitedly through his veins, making him forget everything but the overwhelming urge to ravish and conquer.

He watched, totally enthralled, as the girl was forced to suck her aggressor's cock, sliding her lips up and down the engorged organ. Stephen felt his own cock grow even harder. Before the man could climax, however, he pulled away from the girl, his shaft glistening enticingly in the lamplight, and his companion moved forwards to take his place. Grabbing her head, the shorter man eased her face towards his groin and obediently she placed her hands on his hips and began to caress his penis with her mouth and lips.

Stephen was so enthralled by this vision of brutal lust that he didn't even notice the other man walking to the side of the room to pick up a padded stool. Striding back to his companion, he grabbed hold of the girl and placed the stool under her stomach, then kicked it back so that the two small rounded globes of her buttocks were lifted provocatively into the air. Even so she somehow managed to keep the other man's cock in her mouth. Stephen tensed with expectation as the taller man grabbed hold of her buttocks and positioned himself. With a hard jerk he penetrated her, while her mouth still worked on the other man's shaft.

Stephen stiffened as he felt his cock grow even harder and his balls tighten. Vaguely he heard Richard give a soft groan of desire, as he too was turned on by the highly charged, erotic brutality of the moment. Stephen had to fight the sudden urge to curve his hand around his own cock and jerk off as he watched the young man pumping wildly into the girl, while she greedily sucked on the other man's organ, sliding her scarlet lips up and down the bulging shaft.

This was beyond belief. Paying for a whore was one thing, but a sensual display such as this was an entirely different matter. Stephen had never thought of voyeurism as a form of entertainment and as far as he knew no brothel in Christendom had ever put on a show like this. It appeared that his companions were just as entranced as he was. Stephen watched, becoming more and more aroused by what he was witnessing, even though he knew it was all utterly contrived and just put on to excite and inflame the brothel's clientele. Even so, he was totally immersed in the eroticism of the moment and the climax of the act came far too swiftly for him as, with an exultant gasp of pleasure, both of the men reached orgasm at the same time.

'Sweet Jesus,' he heard Richard say softly as the manner of the two suddenly changed. There was no violence in their movements now as they solicitously helped the girl to her feet and she stood there smiling provocatively at the king.

'You chose well, Armand,' Richard said gruffly. His face was flushed with excitement and there was a very visible bulge now under the thin fabric of his braes.

'Now you have to choose, Majesty,' Armand said with a sly, rather knowing smile.

Stephen frowned and looked with confusion at Armand; surely he couldn't believe that the cruel rumours that had circulated about Richard were remotely true. Everyone at court knew they were put about by his enemies, purely to soil his reputation.

Richard didn't respond angrily. Fortunately for Armand, he was most probably a little too drunk by now to realise exactly what was intended by the remark 'Come here, girl.' Richard smiled and beckoned to her.

The dancer's cheeks were pink with exertion and she was clearly excited at being presented to Richard as she walked towards him. Stephen wondered if they performed this act often or had it just been arranged for his monarch's benefit. Whatever, it appeared that the woman had enjoyed taking part in the display as much as the two young men.

'Your Majesty,' she said in a husky voice in heavily accented French as she went to sink to her knees. 'My name is Leila.'

Stephen was surprised; it was unusual for a Sicilian whore to speak their language, especially as she looked to have Saracen blood in her veins. 'No.' Richard patted the couch. 'Come sit beside me, Leila.'

'I'm honoured, great king.' She sank down beside Richard and he twined an arm around her slim waist and pulled her close to him.

Richard stared into the dancer's dark eyes. 'You are lovely,' he growled, his large hand sliding downwards to caress her buttock cheeks, while his other hand stroked her tiny breasts.

She smiled seductively as Richard slid his hand down to her groin and pressed his fingers against the dark curls guarding her sex. 'My lord, I am here to give you pleasure in any way you would wish,' the dancer purred, wriggling excitedly as Richard's fingers slid into the crack of her buttock cheeks. 'Any way at all,' she added huskily.

It appeared she was happy to offer even more unusual pleasures to Richard and Stephen knew that few whores in Christendom would even think of affording such strangely diverse delights. Tactfully, he tried to keep his gaze averted, but out of the corner of his eye he could see her boldly caressing Richard's bare chest. Then she leant forwards and kissed him full on the lips. Richard gave a muffled groan of pleasure and wrapped his strong arms around his new exotic plaything.

Stephen tried to keep from looking at Armand as well, but he was amazed when he at last glanced over at him because Armand appeared to be displaying far too much interest in one of the muscular young men. Was that the reason he had sensed such ambiguity in the young man? Stephen frowned as he saw the young acrobat move to squat beside Armand's couch. Armand had removed his braes and his erect cock was on display to all who cared to look at it, and that made Stephen tense uneasily.

Stephen glared rather disapprovingly at Armand, who did not seem overly concerned by his disapproval. But then Richard was now quite oblivious to their presence. The dancer had removed his braes and he lay on his back, his cock standing proudly out from his groin as she caressed it. She then bent forwards to take it reverently between her scarlet lips. Stephen found the sight of all this highly arousing but he still jumped nervously when he felt a firm hand touch his groin.

He tensed in concern as he realised that it was one of the male dancers. 'No,' he said sharply, pushing the man away as Armand watched, an insolent smile on his full lips.

Stephen wasn't entirely sure whether he should leave or stay but he needed the king's permission to depart and Richard would not be happy if his sexual enjoyment was intruded upon at such an inopportune moment. He glanced around the room, trying not to look at Richard and doing his best to ignore the tantalising sounds of sex coming from the couch next to his, although it wasn't proving easy.

He had vowed not to partake in any of the eroticisms on offer this evening, but even so he was highly aroused and hearing Richard groaning with pleasure only a couple of feet away was making his lust grow even stronger. His cock was so hard now it was almost painful and he shifted uneasily on his couch. Perhaps he should slip quietly away and hope that the king didn't realise that he had gone, let alone object to his leaving.

The decision made, he went to sit up but gentle female hands pushed him back against the pillows. He found himself surrounded by three naked, full-bosomed slave girls. Soft lips were pressed to his, hands started to stroke and caress his body and a gentle mouth began to slowly engulf his aching penis, drawing him deep down into a pit of erotic bliss.

4

The timbers of the massive vessel creaked and groaned as it ploughed through the stormy waters of the Mediterranean. It sounded as if the entire ship might break apart at any moment, Edwina thought anxiously. The floor of the cabin tilted perilously, forcing her to cling desperately onto a wooden table, which was fortunately bolted down. Everything that was not fixed in place slid across the floor and slammed against the flimsy wooden interior walls of the cabin.

Berengaria gave a scream of terror, which was almost drowned out by the crash of the waves and the noise of the wind, wailing like a banshee around the floundering vessel. As the floor briefly righted itself, Edwina staggered gracelessly towards Berengaria and grabbed hold of the edge of the bunk on which the princess was huddled.

'How do you feel, my lady?'

'Terrible,' Berengaria groaned.

The cabin was dimly lit by a number of lamps, which swung wildly at every movement of the vessel, casting sinister shadow on the walls, and the place stank of stale vomit and the sweat of fear. Edwina was the only one of the four women in the cabin who had not been violently ill. Berengaria's two other ladies-in-waiting, Agnes and Matilda, were crowded together on pallets in one corner laid low by the seasickness, which also plagued their royal mistress.

Still clinging onto the edge of the bunk, Edwina smiled reassuringly at the ashen-faced princess whose skin had taken on a peculiar greyish tinge. Berengaria prided herself on her neatness and piety but she looked more like a slattern at present than a princess. Her nightgown was crumpled and stained, while her light-brown hair lay in tangled disarray around her plump shoulders. At least, she was no longer vomiting, most probably because her battered stomach must be totally empty by now, but she still gave pitiful, wrenching coughs every now and then.

'You should at least drink some water, my lady.'

'No.' Berengaria weakly shook her head. 'I cannot. I fear that God is punishing us, Edwina,' she wailed in a distraught voice, her entire body trembling as she clutched with desperate fingers at the bejewelled rosary, which was one of Richard's betrothal gifts to her.

'We will survive,' Edwina said with all the confidence she could muster. She placed a damp cloth on Berengaria's warm clammy forehead. 'The storm will soon be over.'

'No, we will die. The sea will swallow us up,' Berengaria whimpered, hunching back against her pillows in terror as the sound of the wind grew louder and even more threatening. The vessel rocked wildly as it continued to be buffeted by the enraged waters.

Edwina sat down on the bunk next to the princess and placed a comforting arm around her shoulders. 'This craft is large and designed to sail in the worst of weathers,' she said, although to be honest she knew almost nothing about these ships except that they were of Byzantine design. 'Dromons have sailed these waters for centuries and are said to be far safer than any other vessel.'

'If they are the safest,' Berengaria said tearfully as she let the rosary fall into her lap and reached out to cling onto Edwina's other arm, 'then why does it feel as if this ship is about to sink at any moment? This storm is so terrible. No doubt by now Richard's galley has already foundered and I will have lost my future husband.'

Edwina sighed. 'Not so, Princess. The king will come through this unscathed and so will we. God will protect us, we are on a holy quest,' she said, certain that surrendering to fear was not the answer.

'Then why do we have to endure this at all?' Berengaria complained weakly.

'Perhaps God is testing our resolve?' Edwina paused and listened intently, certain that the noise of the storm was abating just a little. The ship was still battling through stormy seas but the movements of the vessel were becoming slightly less violent. 'See, it is improving, is it not?'

'You think so?'

'I do,' Edwina replied.

'Then it is possible that God, in his eternal wisdom, has spared us.' Berengaria picked up her rosary again and began to mumble a prayer of thanks.

'I think perhaps I should discover the whereabouts of your maids.' Edwina was desperate to get out of this foul-smelling cabin for a moment. Thankfully, she had not suffered from seasickness but the stuffy interior and the terrible smells were now making even her stomach feel a little queasy. Also she felt that she should try to locate the princess's maidservants and make sure they were safe. The two young women had never put in an appearance, despite that fact that she had sent for them to help care for Berengaria. She could only presume that they were huddled in terror somewhere in the bowels of the ship.

'Do not be long,' Berengaria said in a weak voice. 'I cannot cope without you, Edwina. You are my strength in this adversity.'

'I promise that I will return in a few moments.'

Removing her arm from Berengaria, Edwina stood up and, doing her best to keep her footing on the pitching floor, she staggered towards the door of the cabin. Opening it, she stepped into the cooler, salt-laden air of the dimly lit corridor.

Pulling the door shut behind her, Edwina took a deep unsteady breath to cleanse her lungs. Bracing herself against one of the walls to stop herself being flung about too much, she thought of Stephen, wishing that he was here with her, needing to feel the strength of his arms around her. She would not even allow herself to consider that he might not have survived this appalling storm.

When they had set out everything had been so wonderfully different. The sea had been a calm endless sheet of azure and the sky clear and cloudless. The three massive dromons had embarked first, the fleet of some two hundred-odd vessels following on behind, looking to her like a great flock of white-winged birds. The dromons carried most of the king's precious possessions: his betrothed, his sister and a fair portion of the royal treasury along with the king's vice chancellor. The other vessels carried the knights, men-at-arms, horses and all the necessary equipments of warfare including, so Stephen had told her, massive deconstructed catapults, which would be used, when they arrived, to batter the walls of Acre.

At first their voyage, which was expected to take between 14 and 21 days, had proceeded smoothly. Berengaria had been quite happy and had even insisted on arranging a special mass for all the occupants of the ship on Good Friday. While they were worshipping, the wind had dropped and the entire fleet had become becalmed, but it had been the prequel to something far worse.

The sky had turned black and threatening and the

sea had become a seething mass of ugly green waves, then the torrential rain and the blustering winds had started. Edwina could only guess at how terrible the conditions were on deck as the captain and crew battled to keep this vessel afloat.

Suddenly, she felt a blast of icy damp air and she realised that the hatch had opened and someone was climbing down the steps. At first she could see only the lower half of his body but, judging by the black clothing, it was one of the Hospitaller knights. She heard him slam the hatch shut and saw him jump lithely down the last few steps. Yet she couldn't quite make out his features in the dim light. Most of the lamps in the narrow corridor had been blown out in the ferocity of the storm and only a couple were left burning.

'My lady,' the Hospitaller said worriedly as he strode towards her, seeming untroubled by the uncontrolled movements of the ship, which did not make walking along the corridor at all easy. 'You should not be outside your cabin, it is not safe.'

'I just came out here for a breath of fresh air.'

He was young and quite good-looking, she couldn't help noticing, as he stopped and looked down at her. 'Martin of Edessa at your service, my lady,' he said, inclining his head politely. 'You are the Lady de Moreville, are you not?'

'I am, sir,' she said, feeling a little uncomfortable as he stepped even closer and placed his hands on the wall either side of her to protect her as the ship pitched violently again. Nevertheless, she couldn't stop herself falling forwards and found herself pressed rather inelegantly against his hard muscular chest. 'Forgive me,' she muttered awkwardly.

Edwina felt remarkably safe for a moment as the violent movements of the ship forced her to remain where she was, pressed close against his hard unyielding form. She inhaled the pleasant spicy aroma that perfumed his long black tunic, which had the white Hospitaller cross on its front.

'And forgive my bold behaviour,' Martin said softly against her blonde hair, which she realised uneasily was not even modestly covered by a veil at present.

'Protecting a lady from falling is not bold, it is kindness itself,' she said rather bashfully, as to her relief she was at last able to pull herself back against the cold damp wood of the corridor wall. 'I had hoped that the storm might be abating.'

'I fear not,' he said with a troubled frown. 'To be sure it appears a little less violent at present. The captain tells me it is because we have reached the centre of the storm. Sometimes the winds and stormy waters abate for a short while before they resume their ferocity again.'

'And will we survive?' She at last allowed the apprehension she felt to surface for a moment. Now that she was away from the princess, she didn't have to appear quite so brave and steadfast in this time of adversity.

'I am certain that we will, my lady. God will protect us,' he said confidently. 'I have endured storms as bad as this before. How fares Princess Berengaria?'

'She has been violently ill; she is not a good sailor.'

'I feared that might be the case,' he said softly, as the ship pitched violently once more and Edwina found herself pressed against his chest again. Martin's cloak was held away from her by his braced arms, but she could see that it was soaking wet.

'You should change your cloak, Martin of Edessa, or you will catch your death,' she said as she managed to force herself back against the wall.

'I am a soldier. I have endured far worse, my lady. My only concern is for your welfare.'

'And your concern is most heartening,' she said.

He removed one hand from its place beside her and reached into the leather bag at his waist. 'Here, I have brought this for you and the other ladies.' He handed her a small packet wrapped in oiled parchment.

As Edwina took it from him, the floor of corridor tilted wildly and Martin clamped his strong arm beside her again. 'What is it?' she asked as she was jerked forwards again and her face was pressed to his chest. She was so close she could feel the heat of his body and hear his regular, comforting heartbeat.

'One of the Hospitallers, who served for some time at our large hospice in Acre, suggested this remedy. He was aware that the princess and her attendants had little experience of weather such as this. He tells me that it helps with all kinds of sickness and he has added some ground poppy seeds to allow her to rest easy for a while. No doubt she is exhausted and needs to sleep.'

'As do we all,' Edwina agreed, craning her neck to look up at his rather strained features. 'How much do I give her?'

'The packet contains at least five strong doses so I am told. I am sure you can measure that out. Perhaps you could take some yourself?'

By now the embarrassment she had initially felt had all but ceased. Even though she did not know him at all, she was finding the experience of his strong arms around her at this perilous time strangely comforting. 'I will give it to the ladies-in-waiting as well. But I will not take any as fortunately I do not suffer from seasickness and at least one of us needs to remain on our feet.' She gave a soft embarrassed laugh as the ship tilted again and she was pressed even harder against his chest. 'If I can manage to do so, of course.'

'No doubt you will. From what I have heard you are an enterprising lady. The Comte de Chalais speaks very well of you and he requested that I do all I can to help you, if and when the need arises.'

'You are a friend of Stephen's?'

'I have that honour,' he replied.

'Then I am indebted to you, Martin.' She paused thoughtfully. 'I really should be returning to the princess, she will get concerned if I leave her alone for too long. Yet I had hoped first to ensure that her maidservants were safe.'

'They are,' he reassured her. 'I came to tell you that unfortunately one of them slipped and fell while trying to reach the princess's cabin. She is not badly hurt. Her companion and the Hospitaller who provided the remedy are looking after her. Yet I fear that it has left you with the responsibility of caring for the princess alone.'

'It keeps me occupied, and takes my mind off the storm,' she replied. 'I will survive. After all I have survived far worse,' she added, thinking of her life with Hugh. 'Now I must return to the cabin.'

'So you shall.' He stepped back a pace and took a firm hold on her arm. 'I will escort you there myself.'

Stephen looked around the deck of the royal galley. The crew were all busy repairing the minor damage done by the violent storm. They, like many of the other vessels, had survived virtually unscathed but the fleet had been scattered in all directions. However, such a likelihood had been accounted for and a meeting place had been arranged here, off the island of Rhodes. Now there were at least sixty vessels anchored close to the rocky shoreline of this small island.

Ships were arriving hourly and no doubt more vessels would soon be joining them. Nevertheless, what concerned Stephen most of all were the three missing dromons. None of the other captains had spotted the massive Byzantine vessels, so they could not be anywhere in this vicinity. Either they had been blown far off course or they had been wrecked in the storm and the last eventuality was one Stephen didn't even wish to contemplate.

Stephen sighed. A page had come to him a few moments ago, carrying orders from Richard to meet him in the king's cabin and give him a report on the current situation. He just wished that he had better news for his friend as he climbed down the steps that led to the lower deck where Richard's large stateroom was situated.

He didn't bother to knock as the king was expecting him; he just opened the door and stepped into the spacious well-appointed cabin. He saw Richard immediately, sitting behind a large table, which was piled high with documents and maps. However, he looked a little strange as his face was red, his eyes bulging and his skin was beaded in sweat.

'Are you unwell, Your Majesty,' he asked with concern.

Richard didn't reply, he just raised his hand to stop Stephen approaching as his eyes glazed over and he gave a loud groan followed by a grunt of what sounded to Stephen like pleasure.

Two spots of bright scarlet formed on Stephen's cheeks. Richard appeared to have just experienced an orgasm and he didn't quite know what to do. Should he leave or should he stay? In his indecision he just remained where he was, awkwardly rooted to the spot.

'Of course I am not unwell,' Richard said curtly. 'I am fully recovered from my seasickness now.'

'I can see that,' Stephen said awkwardly. 'Forgive me, sire. I came at an inopportune moment. I'll leave.' He began to back towards the door.

'Christ in heaven, Stephen,' Richard exclaimed. 'It is

too late for such prissy behaviour now.' He reached down to adjust his clothing. 'You have seen it all before at the brothel in Messina.'

At that moment, to Stephen's amazement, he saw the dancer from that very brothel move out from beneath the table and rise gracefully to her feet. What was *she* doing here? The dancer didn't appear troubled in the slightest by his presence at such an intimate moment between her and the king, which perhaps was not surprising: after all she was a whore.

Casting an insolent smile at Stephen, she turned and sauntered towards Richard's wide bed. She was dressed very indecorously in a long filmy garment, which was near translucent. Through the thin fabric he had caught sight of her erect, rouged nipples and her inky-black triangle of pubic hair, before she turned away from him.

'I was not aware.' He cleared his throat nervously as he watched the girl sit cross-legged on the feather mattress and stare thoughtfully at the king with her dark kohl-ringed eyes.

'Of course you were not. Armand arranged it.' Richard grinned. 'To keep me company on the voyage. Perhaps it might have been wiser to acquaint you of her presence as you are the only person who has unprecedented access to my private quarters.'

'It might well have been wiser. Then, if needs be, I could have helped you conceal this ... er ... lady's presence from everyone else onboard ship.'

Stephen thought that Richard had acted most foolishly, without any consideration for the consequences of such actions. There were both Templars and clergy on this vessel, including the grand master of the Templars, Robert de Sable, and the Bishop of Evreux. He knew that such religious men would disapprove highly of Richard bringing a whore onboard, even more so because he was now betrothed.

'Leila tired of Sicily and she has a mind to travel to Tyre. She has kin in the city.'

'No doubt she does, sire,' Stephen acknowledged as he stepped closer to Richard, who was relaxing back in his chair appearing quite unconcerned. 'In the circumstances might it not have been wiser to allow Leila passage on another vessel?'

'Indeed it would have.' Richard grinned wickedly. 'But then I would not have been able to avail myself of her exceptional talents.'

'Yet if the grand master or the bishop learnt of her presence . . . ?'

'You know full well that their piety irritates me at times,' Richard confessed with a shrug of his wide shoulders. 'They have both sworn a vow of chastity, so what do they know of such intimate matters? I have always thought it foolish to set aside the pleasures of life. They should not even think to criticise me, after all I was one of the first princes to take up the cross after Jerusalem was captured by Salah ad-Din.'

'I know that, sire.'

'Then do not lecture me on this matter.' Richard glanced back at Leila and smiled indulgently at her.

She returned his smile, lasciviously licking her scarlet lips, as she provocatively stroked her nipples and pressed her hand against her groin. 'I am waiting, lord,' she said in heavily accented French.

'I have no intention of presuming to lecture you, sire,' Stephen replied patiently. He found Richard's sometimes thoughtless behaviour incredibly frustrating. 'I can report later on the status of the fleet, if you so wish?'

'No. Tell me now. Did we lose any ships?'

'At least one galley is known to have been lost. One of the captains saw the vessel sinking off Crete. While the dromons . . .' Stephen paused and cleared his throat once again. 'There has been no sign of them as yet.'

Richard clasped his hands together. 'That gives you cause for concern? I was assured that they could endure the worst of weathers. That is why I chose to send Berengaria in one of those vessels.'

'No ship is unsinkable,' Stephen replied uneasily.

'I am certain that Berengaria and my sister Joanna are safe.' Richard looked knowingly at Stephen. 'As no doubt is Lady de Moreville. You have been discreet, my friend. But I am well aware that she is now your mistress. Would it not be wiser in the circumstances for you to refrain from judging my behaviour?'

'I have no wish to judge you,' Stephen replied. 'I am just asking you to be discreet also. Most noblemen on this vessel are not as open-minded as you and I.'

'Quite so.' Richard tapped his fingers on the table top. 'Have you sent out galleys to search for the dromons?'

'I have, sire.'

'Then, unfortunately, my friend, all we can do is wait.'

Edwina heard the bottom of the longboat grate against the sand, whereupon most of the occupants, including Martin, jumped out and dragged it closer to the shore.

'My lady.' Ankle deep in water, Martin held his hand out to Berengaria. 'Allow me.'

She stood up rather gracelessly and looked down at the water swirling around his boots. 'I have no wish to get my feet wet,' she said regally.

'In that case, you will have to forgive my presumption.' Reaching forwards, Martin swung her into his arms and carried her out of the water and up the beach. Gently, he deposited her on the golden sands.

Edwina had no desire to be carried as she knew that she was perfectly capable of wading through the water herself. Slipping off her soft leather shoes, she held them in her hand, and stepped cautiously down into the sea, keeping her skirts lifted so they didn't get too wet. It was quite pleasant to feel the water lapping at her ankles and she wished she had thought to pull off her hose as well as she waded forwards until she reached dry land.

They had arrived off the island of Cyprus yesterday and, as they were running a little low on water, Martin had decided to bring a longboat to shore. Against Martin's advice, Berengaria had stubbornly insisted that she and Edwina accompany him. According to Martin, the Byzantine emperor of the island, Isaac Comenius, was no friend of the Franks, and landing might not be altogether safe. However, this place looked deserted, Edwina thought, as she walked up the beach to join Berengaria who was perched on a large rock half buried in the sand.

'Your stockings are soaked,' Berengaria said reprovingly.

'So they are.' Edwina plonked herself down next to the princess and began to discreetly roll down her hose. Removing the wet woollen stockings, she rolled them into a ball and dug her damp toes into the surprisingly warm golden sand. 'Have you never taken off your shoes and walked barefoot outside, my lady?'

'Of course not.' Berengaria frowned rather disapprovingly at the sight of Edwina's bare ankles and feet. 'It is not seemly.'

Further down the beach, Martin was busy organising the men. Yesterday, the lookout had spotted wreckage close to the rocks of Aphrodite and Martin feared it might be one of the other dromons. Edwina saw one small group set off, walking south along the shoreline, so presumably they were going to try to locate the wreck and find out if there were any survivors. The rest of the men were lifting empty casks from the boat and carrying them up to the rear of the beach in the hope of finding a supply of fresh water close by.

Eventually, Martin walked over to them. 'Princess,' he acknowledged, his expression becoming a little more serious, 'I am leaving a couple of men to guard the boat and to ensure your safety. This area appears very quiet even though we are only a short distance from Limassol. With luck no one should discover we are here.'

'But I wish to go into town,' Berengaria said haughtily, 'and seek lodgings there. I need a short respite from that dreadfully cramped cabin and my seasickness.'

'That would not be wise, Majesty, as I told you before,' Martin said politely, but Edwina could sense he was frustrated as he'd discussed this with the princess already. 'However, if you insist I will have to find some form of transport, unless you wish to walk the few miles to Limassol, my lady.'

'Walk!' Berengaria exclaimed in horror. 'Princesses do not walk.'

'Of course they do not,' Martin agreed. 'Once we have located a supply of fresh water, I will endeavour to find something.' He paused and looked penetratingly at the princess. 'You are still determined to go ahead with this foolishness, my lady?'

'Of course.' She spoke curtly. 'I am not foolish, Martin. You will soon discover that I am right and you are wrong.'

'I truly hope that is the case.' He turned away from them and began to stride up the beach to join his men.

'That young man is most irritating,' Berengaria commented. 'And quite wrong in his presumptions.'

Edwina, however, feared that Martin might well be right and that it was the princess who was wrong in placing her trust in this so-called emperor. Nevertheless, she was only a lady-in-waiting and it was not her place to question Berengaria's judgements.

There was silence between them for some time and eventually Edwina looked up the beach, wondering when the men would return. Even though it was well past noon, it was still getting warmer and it might be prudent in the circumstances to find some kind of shade soon.

Edwina dug her toes further into the sand and wriggled them, enjoying the feel of the rough grains against her skin. 'When I was little I used to escape from my maids and run around barefoot,' she said, wanting to break the silence even though Berengaria seemed lost in thought. 'There was a pond nearby, hidden in a small copse, and when no one was around I used to strip down to my shift and swim in the icy cold water.'

'Was that not foolish?' Berengaria sounded horrified by such behaviour and Edwina found herself pitying the young woman. Most likely she had lived a protected regimented existence with none of the freedoms of childhood that most other people were allowed to experience.

'I was safe enough. There was no one around to harm me.' Edwina just happened to glance casually along the beach in the other direction and spotted a small troop of mounted men riding towards them. 'I wonder who they are?' she said, suddenly feeling very uneasy.

'Perhaps it is our escort.' Berengaria shaded her eyes with her hand and stared at them. 'No doubt the emperor has sent them.'

'It is way too soon for that.' Edwina rose to her feet, her concern increasing as she noticed that the men guarding the longboat looked agitated and appeared to be beckoning to her. 'I think they want us to return to the boat.'

'Return to the boat? Of course not,' Berengaria said. 'There's no need for that.'

'But we do not know who those men are.'

'They look like soldiers to me,' Berengaria said coolly. 'This is convenient, is it not? They will be able to escort us to the emperor.'

By now Edwina was becoming even more troubled. One of the crew, brandishing his sword, was running protectively towards them. However, he was easily overtaken by the leader of the soldiers, a dark-haired man in a gaudy uniform, who was galloping straight for her and Berengaria.

As a couple of mounted men stopped to restrain the armed crew member, the dark-haired soldier brought his horse to a halt directly in front of them in a wild flurry of sand. Brushing away the grains that had showered onto her skirt, Berengaria stood up and glared irritatedly at him. 'Who are you?'

'I think the question is, who are you, my lady? You are the trespasser on our land, not I,' he responded in excellent French as he dismounted.

Berengaria stiffened and for a moment the plump, rather unprepossessing young woman looked incredibly regal. 'I am Princess Berengaria of Navarre, the future Queen of England.'

'Princess.' He bowed, his manner becoming far more respectful. 'How fortunate to come upon you like this. We saw your ship at anchor in the bay. My emperor was planning to despatch an envoy to your vessel to invite you to enjoy the pleasures of his castle in Limassol.'

Riding pillion behind a Cypriot soldier was far from easy and very uncomfortable, Edwina thought as they at last entered the bailey of the castle in Limassol. She glanced over at the princess who was perched behind the captain, her skirts rucked up rather inelegantly to display her plump hose-covered calves. Berengaria seemed blithely unconcerned by the situation but Edwina had seen the soldiers take the two crew men captive and they had not treated them at all kindly. They had bound their hands and forced them to run behind the horses, tethered by long ropes to one of the riders' pommels. If one of them had fallen they would have been dragged over the rough ground and might well have been badly hurt. Fortunately, both had managed to remain on their feet until now. As she glanced back at them, Edwina saw that both had fallen to their knees and were breathing heavily, clearly exhausted by their ordeal.

What had happened to Martin and the others? she wondered worriedly as her escort dismounted and politely helped her down from the horse.

'Not an altogether pleasant journey, but at least now we will be housed in comfort,' Berengaria commented after she too had dismounted. She smiled at the captain who was handsome in a dark, rather swarthy fashion.

'I will have you escorted to your rooms,' he said, gesturing towards a skinny, hatchet-faced women who stood on the steps leading into the keep. Before they had left the beach Edwina had seen a soldier ride off so they were clearly expected. 'No doubt you will wish to bathe and have something to eat before resting.'

'First I need to speak to the emperor,' Berengaria announced.

'Regretfully, Majesty, he is not here but he returns on the morrow.'

'How inconvenient!' Berengaria exclaimed. 'Then it will have to be a meal and a comfortable bed.'

'Which you shall have.' The captain bowed and then strode off to supervise the prisoners. They were being led down some steps, which appeared to go underneath the side of the keep, perhaps to the dungeons, Edwina surmised uneasily.

'Noble ladies, this way.' The hard-faced woman gestured for her and Berengaria to follow her.

As they walked into the cool interior of the castle,

Edwina was surprised by the opulent luxury that confronted her. It was far more elaborately furnished than any of the castles she had ever been in, either in England or in France; everywhere she looked there were gilded ornaments and oriental-looking lamps.

'This is all rather exotic,' Berengaria said disapprovingly as she looked at the ornate fabrics covering the walls and the elaborately carved furniture and sumptuous, brilliantly coloured upholstery. 'I prefer simpler furnishings myself.'

They were escorted up a wide stone staircase into a large finely appointed room, which to Edwina's amazement had a thick carpet covering most of the floor and gold-threaded damask curtains at the wide windows instead of shutters. There was a massive bed in one corner of the room and a large bathtub, which had been lined with a white sheet, and was now being filled with water by a long line of servants. Judging by the pleasant odour, the water was scented and Edwina decided that she would take the opportunity to bathe even if Berengaria refused to.

'Your clothes need wash,' the woman said in hesitant French. 'You give me, I find more for you to wear.' She looked rather disapprovingly at their plain woollen gowns. 'Better clothes,' she added emphatically.

'First I want to eat and rest,' Berengaria informed her.

'No, bath,' the woman said stubbornly.

'We are guests, my lady. No doubt customs here are different and it would disrespect them in some way if we did not bathe,' Edwina said, desperate to avail herself of the pleasure of the steaming perfumed water.

'I suppose.' Berengaria sighed heavily. 'Then it appears I will bathe.' She stood there and watched the servants file from the room, then turned to look expectantly at the woman. 'You are dismissed.'

'I stay,' the woman insisted, crossing her arms. 'Want clothes to wash.'

Berengaria gave her a frosty look and walked over to the tub to dabble her fingers in the water. 'At home bathing was always so chilly and uncomfortable. Navarre is much colder than Cyprus and drying myself afterwards in a draughty chamber was far from pleasant.'

'It will not be so here,' Edwina pointed out, 'and you will discover, when we reach the Holy Land, that many houses there have separate rooms for bathing, with pipes that carry hot water so that few servants are needed to provide such comforts. The Comte de Chalais has told me all about it. '

'Even here, life and customs are so different from ours.' Berengaria glanced back at the woman who stubbornly stood her ground. 'I suppose I will have to avail myself of the bath but there is not even a screen to protect my modesty when I undress.'

'Here.' Edwina picked up a linen towel. 'I will unfasten your gown, and then hold this towel out in front of you.'

'So I undress myself?'

'Are you not able to do so?' Edwina asked.

'As you are well aware, my maidservants have always done it for me,' Berengaria replied rather curtly as Edwina began to unfasten the back lacings of the princess's gown. 'But I am quite able,' she added stiffly. 'Now be sure to hold the towel out as wide as possible. I have no wish for that woman to see me undressing.'

As Edwina did as ordered, Berengaria removed her veil and began, rather awkwardly, to struggle out of her dress. Edwina's widespread arms were beginning to get a little uncomfortable by the time Berengaria had rather clumsily divested herself of her shoes, hose and petticoats. At last she stood there dressed in a long, lace-edged linen shift, cut low at the neck, which displayed her plump arms and large breasts to full advantage. It made Edwina even more conscious of the skinniness of her body at present. Although the large amounts of food Stephen had insisted she consume recently were gradually helping to make some of her missing curves reappear.

Berengaria was just about to step into the tub when the maidservant brusquely pushed Edwina aside and bent to pick up the princess's discarded garments. 'That also,' she added, straightening and pointing to the shift Berengaria was wearing.

Berengaria looked at her in disbelief. 'But I always wear a shift when bathing.'

'Wash this too.' The woman grabbed hold of the skirt of the offending shift.

'Stop her, Edwina.' Berengaria tried to shy away from her.

'I find more servants,' the woman said in a decisive voice.

'I think she means that she will bring more servants in and force you to remove it,' Edwina explained.

'This is ridiculous. She wants me naked,' Berengaria said anxiously. 'Tell her that this is no way to treat a princess.'

'We are in a strange castle in a foreign land with no one to protect us. Do you not think in the circumstances it might be wiser to concede to her wishes? Bathing in the nude will not harm you, I do it all the time.'

The woman was still resolutely clinging onto Berengaria's shift. 'Very well,' the princess said. Jerking herself away from the woman, she glared at her. 'Close your eyes,' she ordered as she turned her back on her. 'And you close your eyes also, Edwina.'

Edwina had no idea if the woman had done as Berengaria asked but she closed her eyes, not opening them again until she heard a loud splash as Berengaria sat down in the water.

'Good.' The woman moved to put the discarded clothes in a woven basket by the bed. Then she walked back to Edwina. 'Now you.'

5

'Is this not ridiculous?' Berengaria gave a girlish giggle

'Indeed it is,' Edwina agreed. She had bathed after Berengaria and, as the servant had taken away their clothes for washing, they had both resorted to wrapping the linen towels around their bodies to provide them with temporary clothing. 'I do find it strange that they have not yet provided us with something suitable to wear,' Edwina added with a trace of concern.

'No doubt they will soon,' Berengaria replied airily. 'It is not as if they were expecting us. They may have had to send someone into the town to find garments appropriate for a princess.'

Berengaria shifted rather awkwardly on her small stool. The low seats were all they had to sit on but at least they were the right height for the table on which their meal had been served.

'I do not want any more,' Edwina said as the princess eyed the last portion of spiced lamb and rice. The food was delicious but they had been obliged to eat with their fingers as there had been no sign of any eating utensils.

Berengaria gobbled it up greedily. 'It is a pity they did not serve sweetmeats as well.'

'We can always ask the servants when they return.'

'If any of them understand us,' Berengaria complained. 'That horrible woman seemed to be the only servant in this castle that has even a smattering of French.'

'I know a few Arabic words, Stephen taught them to me, but I do not know any Greek at all.'

'Stephen, the Comte de Chalais?' Berengaria smiled knowingly. 'He is handsome, though not quite as good-looking as my betrothed. You have a fondness for him, do you, Edwina?'

'Stephen and I have known each other a long time,' she admitted. 'We were once betrothed but my brother decided that I should marry another.'

'I do not judge you, Edwina. We cannot always help where our heart lies.' She smiled understandingly. 'I am a fortunate woman. I fell in love with my betrothed the first moment I laid eyes on him. Princesses are not often that blessed in their choice of husbands.'

Berengaria cleansed her fingers in the bowl of lemon-scented water that had accompanied the meal. Then she picked up her goblet and finished off the delicious, rather powerful red wine. Edwina found that the wine was making her feel rather light-headed. Perhaps it was having a similar effect on Berengaria, who seemed far more relaxed and at ease than usual.

'I like this habit of putting carpets on the floor,' Berengaria commented as she dug her bare toes in the thick pile. 'It seems a waste just to put them on walls as ornaments, does it not? Walking barefoot on these is quite delightful. And I must admit that wearing so little is strangely invigorating, although my priest would tell me it was sinful to enjoy such simple sensual pleasures.'

'Surely it cannot be sinful to enjoy the freedom of our own bodies? After all it was God who fashioned them, was it not?'

'I have never really thought about it,' Berengaria admitted. 'In the past I was expected to accept what I was told by my religious advisors and never question anything.'

'When you are queen you can question whatever you want.'

Berengaria smiled. 'Apart from my husband. I doubt

that Richard would like that.' She looked rather anxiously at Edwina. 'You will not tell anyone about this, will you? Such indiscretions must be kept secret.'

'I would never think to tell anyone.' Edwina found that she really liked this side of Berengaria, a side she had not seen before. Relaxed like this, the usually rather repressed princess was so much easier to get along with. 'Even so, at present it strikes me that we should be more concerned about the fate of Martin of Edessa and his men.'

'No doubt they are safe,' Berengaria said with a serene smile.

'Did you not see them bind the men they captured on the beach?'

'Do not forget, Edwina, that they were foolishly brandishing their weapons when the emperor's soldiers approached,' Berengaria replied. 'Once the Cypriots learn that my men are no threat to them, they will all be released. I promise that I will raise the matter with the emperor when I see him in the morning.'

Edwina did not feel as positive as Berengaria sounded, especially when she recalled Martin's warnings about the emperor. However, she just had to be patient at present. She glanced over at the window and saw that it was very dark outside. 'It must be getting late, I suppose.'

Berengaria yawned, delicately covering her mouth with her hand. 'As there is nothing else to do, we might as well retire. You'll share the bed with me, of course.'

Edwina had already discovered that there was no maidservant's pallet, on which she could have slept, stored beneath the large bed. 'We have no nightgowns,' she said, not certain that Berengaria would consider sleeping in the nude, even though she rarely wore anything in bed with Stephen these days. There was no point, he would have it off in an instant.

'Then we will have to sleep in these towels,' Berengaria said. 'Although mine does not feel that secure.' She readjusted the top so it covered a little more of her ample breasts. 'I will get into bed first. You blow out the candles, Edwina. But leave at least one alight; I do not like total darkness.'

As Berengaria went to stand up, the corner of her towel snagged on the table and somehow the basin of lemon-scented water toppled over and its entire contents spilled into her lap. 'Oh!' she exclaimed. 'I am soaked.'

'You cannot sleep in that,' Edwina said. 'I'll turn my back and you remove the wet towel and get into bed. Once you are safely concealed under the covers I'll spread it out to dry.'

'But I'll be naked in bed,' Berengaria pointed out uneasily. A faint blush formed on her cheeks.

'You can wear my towel if you wish.'

'No, leave it be.' Berengaria coloured even more. 'I'll sleep unclothed.'

'The bed is large and wide enough for three at least. I will not even know that you are not wearing a nightgown,' Edwina reassured her. 'After all you may have to become accustomed to being unclothed when you are wed and share a bed with your husband,' she added as she stood up and turned around. 'I am not looking now, to preserve your modesty.'

Edwina heard the princess scuttle towards the bed. There was a rustle of sheets and then Berengaria said, 'I am safely in bed.' Edwina moved around the room, blowing out the last of the candles apart from the one on the nightstand. Still keeping her eyes averted from the princess, she picked up the damp towel and laid it out to dry. 'Did you mean what you said? Will I be expected to be naked in bed with my husband?' Berengaria asked in a small voice.

Edwina climbed into the other side of the bed, feeling the towel pull away from her a little as she slid between the cool sheets. 'The king does not strike me as a man who will appreciate too much feminine modesty.' Edwina glanced over at Berengaria who had the bed-clothes clutched to her bosom.

'But sleeping unclothed.' Berengaria drew in her breath. 'Would that not be sinful to share a bed with a man when naked?'

'Are marital relations considered sinful?'

'Of course not,' Berengaria said stiffly. 'As long as the wife is not enjoying them. My priest says that it is sinful for a woman to enjoy coupling, she is just there to give pleasure to her husband.' She looked thoughtfully at Edwina. 'Did you enjoy relations with your husband?'

Edwina shook her head. 'I did not. However, he was a cold and brutal man, unlike King Richard, who will no doubt treat you with gentleness and understanding.'

'You think he will?' Berengaria asked, appearing a mite uneasy. 'He seems kind and he is charming, he has even written poetry for me. But I spend little time in his company.'

'Only because he has been busy with his plans to recapture the Holy Land,' Edwina said reassuringly. As she turned towards Berengaria, she felt the towel pull away from her even more.

'You think that is the only reason? I fear that he does not like me and that he is unhappy with me in some way.'

'Not so.' Stephen had told Edwina that Richard was not altogether enamoured with his betrothed but surely when he got to know her better, he would come to see how sweet-natured and appealing she was beneath her pious exterior. 'You are wrong in your assumptions.'

'I hope so.' Berengaria frowned uneasily. 'I am begin-ning to fear that I was wrong to insist on coming here.

clothes Do you not find that troubling?'

'It may well be that it is the custom here to sleep unclothed,' Edwina pointed out. 'However, to be truthful I do not know if your decision was right or wrong. Perhaps we will discover that in the morning, when you speak to the emperor. If his intentions are in any way dishonourable then he is a fool, because King Richard is a powerful warrior, who could easily crush the emperor and his army underfoot.'

'Why else would they call him the Lionheart?' Berengaria said with pride. 'Yet I feel so confused.' She slid a little closer to Edwina. 'And a little wicked being naked beneath the bedclothes.'

'Why wicked?'

'Because the soft linen sheets against my bare flesh feel oddly sensual,' Berengaria admitted shyly. 'Especially when you are so close to me.'

'Sensual,' Edwina muttered, having no idea why her heart was suddenly beating faster. There was a strange kind of excitement about being in bed with Berengaria when she was near naked and the princess was unclothed. Yet what could be stimulating about that?

'Tell me.' Berengaria suddenly slid closer and cautiously touched Edwina's bare arm. 'What is it like to couple with a man? Your skin is so soft, yet I presume that a man's would be smooth but more resilient somehow.' Her spice-scented breath brushed Edwina's cheek and she could sense the heat emanating from Berengaria's body.

'A man's flesh is different,' Edwina admitted. The unaccountably strange emotions she was experiencing became stronger and she had no idea why. 'It is smooth and unyielding because of the strength and hardness of their muscles. Their bodies are far larger and more powerful than ours. It is very pleasant to be close to them and you feel so secure in their embrace.'

Berengaria gently trailed her fingers up Edwina's arm and she felt the hairs on the back of her neck and arms prickle as if her body was somehow becoming more and more alive. Gently, Berengaria brushed the tangled golden locks of hair away from Edwina's collarbone and breasts.

'Tell me more,' Berengaria said huskily. 'I know nothing of what men and women do when they come together. My confessor told me that I should not ask, that it was my husband's place to show me.'

'A woman should have knowledge of such matters.' Edwina recalled the gentle, loving way Stephen had seduced her the first time they had made love. The tender understanding he had displayed when she had gifted him her virginity. Richard did not strike her as a man who would bother to be that gentle and cautious with his new bride. 'Has no one ever told you anything?'

'Nothing at all. I like you, Edwina, and I feel comfortable in your presence. Although usually I do not find placing my trust in others at all easy.' Berengaria did not seem concerned by the intimacy of their contact now as she snuggled closer until the soft curves of her stomach pressed against the fabric that was untidily bunched around Edwina's slim hips. 'Being close to you is oddly comforting. You can be like the sister I never had, and you can tell me everything you think I need to know about matters of the flesh.' She smiled innocently at Edwina. 'First, does he kiss you? I came upon one of my ladies-in-waiting in Navarre when she was passionately embracing a young knight. He was kissing her and she seemed to be enjoying it.'

'Kissing can be delightful,' Edwina cautiously admitted, still confused by the strange emotions Berengaria's close proximity was arousing in her. The princess's body was warm and felt incredibly soft and the sweet smell of the perfumed water still lingered on her skin. It was so very different from the feel of Stephen's firm flesh, yet it was still surprisingly pleasant.

'But you said that you did not like bedding your husband, so I must surmise that if you say kissing is delightful, then you have kissed other men?' Berengaria smiled and ran the tip of her pink tongue over her full bottom lip. 'Have you perchance kissed the Comte?' This time it was Edwina's turn to blush and, when she did not reply at once, Berengaria gave a soft laugh. 'Then you have.'

'You do not approve?'

'Approve?' Berengaria gently touched Edwina's trembling lower lip with her fingertip. 'Stephen is handsome and you are no longer married, so it is not wicked at all, is it?'

Edwina suddenly found that she couldn't move. There was a strange bond between her and Berengaria; an intimacy she could not, or would not, even begin to understand, let alone explain. 'Whether wicked or not, kissing him is wonderful, especially when he puts his tongue in my mouth and twines it caressingly around mine.'

'His tongue?' Berengaria moved her head until it was level with Edwina's. 'I don't understand – you will have to show me.'

'You mean kiss you?' Edwina asked in surprise. Yet in truth she was not entirely sure whether she was surprised or even concerned by the suggestion. Part of her was intrigued by the wild notion as she wondered what it would feel like to have a woman's lips touch hers and share something as intimate as a kiss with someone of her own sex.

'My priest has warned me against all sins, even listing them for me. Yet he has never said that a kiss between females is sacrilegious. Is it not just a sign of affection between friends?' Berengaria moved closer until their lips were almost touching. 'Show me what a kiss is like.'

Berengaria's warm breath mingled with hers and almost without thinking Edwina moved a fraction closer until their lips made contact. She immediately felt a dart of something inexplicably strange slide insidiously through her body. The treacherous delight made her press her lips closer until their mouths were conjoined; hot, warm, moist lips pressed passionately together in a gesture purely of friendship, nothing more. Berengaria's tongue moved first, the tip tantalisingly caressing Edwina's tongue, twining around it like a warm pleasure-giving serpent. It brought with it a wild dissolute emotion that turned Edwina's perceptions upside down and around and around. She found herself sharing with Berengaria a kiss as passionate and unforgiving as that between a man and a woman.

When Berengaria breathlessly pulled away, she stared incredulously at Edwina, her hazel eyes full of puzzlement and awe. 'That was extraordinary. It has made me feel strange and full of a wild excitement. My heart is beating so fast.' Pulling back the sheet, she took hold of Edwina's hand. 'I feel as if my insides are melting and I am warm and hot just here.' She innocently pressed Edwina's palm against her lower stomach. Unconsciously Edwina moved her fingertips and, as they tantalisingly brushed the sensitive flesh of her belly, Berengaria gave a soft groan. 'Why should that be?'

'I am not sure,' Edwina said, conscious that she was also breathless and shared the same treacherous heat in her stomach. She was still confused as she was experiencing something like desire, a feeling more akin to the sensations Stephen aroused in her when he made love to her. How could her body be consumed by this faithless fire when she wasn't being seduced by the man she adored? It was as incomprehensible to her as it appeared to be to Berengaria. 'It must be uncertainty, concern for what is happening.'

'Yes, uncertainty,' Berengaria agreed. 'In that case should we not try to comfort one another?' She plucked at the towel tangled around Edwina's hips. 'That must be most uncomfortable. Remove it and then we can go to sleep.'

'Very well.' The remaining candle was burning low now, the wax melting swiftly. It flickered unsteadily, making it difficult for Edwina to see Berengaria's expression in the dim light. Rather awkwardly, she struggled to free herself from the towel's constrictions and tossed it by the side of the bed.

'Come. Lie down now and relax,' Berengaria said softly, but Edwina detected an underlying tension in her words. She understood why, she also felt the tension and her heart was still beating out of control as she snuggled down on the pillows with Berengaria next to her. Rolling onto her side to face Edwina, the princess added, 'Before we sleep you can tell me what happens next, after the kisses. Which I would like to practise again when you will permit me.'

'Again?' Edwina repeated, conscious that her entire body felt weak now as if her limbs were melting like the candle wax. Cautiously, she laid her hands on Berengaria's full bosom. 'Well, apart from kissing you, he will no doubt touch you here. Men appear to like breasts,' she said, feeling as though her whole body were on tenterhooks. The princess's breasts were fascinating to touch, so soft and malleable in contrast to her own which were small and firm.

Edwina was so enthralled that she barely heard Berengaria's indrawn hiss of breath as she caressed the soft globes. 'That feels so good,' Berengaria gasped, trembling as Edwina's fingers, almost of their own volition, suddenly moved to her nipples. The princess's teats were larger than she had expected and already stiffly erect. Recalling how Stephen had pleasured her, Edwina rolled the nipples between her fingers and thumbs, pulling at them gently until Berengaria whimpered with delight. 'They lied to me, they told me that women did not enjoy this,' she said hesitantly. 'Edwina, there is a strange unfamiliar ache between my thighs.'

'Desire makes you feel like that,' Edwina told her, still continuing to caress her because in truth she did not want to stop. She was unable to comprehend this strange conundrum. She loved such intimacies with Stephen, but had loathed them with Hugh. She had always believed that she only enjoyed them because she loved the man who gave her so much pleasure. Yet that was not the case here; she was enjoying fondling a woman.

For a moment Edwina did pause to wonder if this might be considered sinful, but even in Hugh's disreputable household she had never heard such matters ever mentioned. He had always been crude in his conversations and disgustingly frank at times and she had often heard him speak with derision about men who performed sinful sexual acts on one another, but he had never in such conversations mentioned women. It appeared that the Church did not even acknowledge such a likelihood, let alone speak of it at all, so it was logical to presume that this was not wrong.

Tossing all concerns aside, Edwina gave herself up to the wild temptations, telling herself that she was just helping Berengaria. She was teaching her about the intimacies she would be expected to share with her husband. Now, she would not go to the marriage bed without the necessary knowledge about matters of the flesh.

'What happens next?' Berengaria prompted breathlessly.

'Perhaps this.' Edwina couldn't resist kissing one of the temptingly stiff pink nipples. She pulled it between her lips and gradually drew it deeper into her mouth.

The pulsing heat between Edwina's thighs increased as she sucked hard on the sweet little nipple until it began to turn scarlet. All the while she continued to pull and tweak the other teat until the princess's entire body was trembling with desire.

It seemed prudent now to let the lesson continue and show Berengaria the full measure of what happened between a man and a woman. Rather cautiously, Edwina's hand slid lower, over the quivering belly, aiming for the core of Berengaria's womanhood. She slid her hand between the plump thighs and brushed her fingers against the crisp pubic curls.

Marvelling at the many differences between a man and a woman, Edwina slid her fingertips between the cleft of flesh, finding in the interior a seductive smoothness and a moist warmth that prompted her to explore further. How soft and velvety the valley of a woman's sex felt. She found the small nub that had always given her so much pleasure when Stephen touched it. She heard Berengaria's loud gasp of surprise and felt her entire body tense. 'Do you want me to stop?' Edwina whispered in the darkness, as by now the candle had flickered and died.

'Please, no,' Berengaria whimpered. 'Touch it again. It feels so delightful, like nothing I have every experienced before . . .' Her words descended into a moan of pleasure as Edwina circled the tiny bud, then stroked and teased it until it began to grow and stiffen much like Berengaria's pinkly abused teats.

The velvety soft tissue gradually became slippier beneath her fingertips as more moisture filled the pink valley. Flesh moved slickly against flesh until Berengaria was shuddering with bliss.

'Don't be afraid.' Edwina's voice had suddenly become huskier and she pressed her thighs together, trying to increase the pressure on her own hungry, aching sex. Gently, she slid two fingers into the princess's vagina, knowing she had to be cautious. She could not venture too deep, she had to retain the proof of Berengaria's virginity.

It didn't appear to matter too much about the lack of depth because by now Berengaria was moaning with pleasure. 'Do not stop,' she begged.

Edwina continued to gently move her searching fingers, while teasing the princess's clit with her other fingers and caressing the quivering mound of the princess's stomach with her lips. Soon Berengaria was moaning softly, overcome by erotic delight. Then, she suddenly gave a sharp scream of bliss, her entire body wracked by convulsions as her climax came.

As the trembling of her limbs ceased, Berengaria gently pushed Edwina back against the pillow. 'That was wonderful but there must be even more to this. Let me try it on you.' Her soft lips clamped over one of Edwina's already stiffened teats, while a cautious hand slipped between her aching thighs. Relaxing, Edwina sighed, prepared to let the princess do anything she wished to her.

Edwina stood by Berengaria's side as they both stared at the small insignificant man, dressed in outrageously ornate garments. Emperor Isaac Comenius was short and incredibly skinny and even the kindest person would not have been able to call him attractive. With his large misshapen nose and pockmarked skin he was, in truth, remarkably ugly. Edwina thought that compared to the Emperor of Cyprus, the ill-favoured King Philip of France was an attractive man.

Isaac's manner was imperious and rather condescending, as if Berengaria was of little consequence compared to him. This angered Edwina, especially as Berengaria had been as polite and charming as she could be in these difficult circumstances. There was no way this insolent upstart should speak so disrespectfully to the future Queen of England.

'So you will both be allowed to move around the palace unhindered,' Isaac ended his long diatribe, 'at all times, while you are here as my guests.'

'We are very grateful for your kind hospitality,' Berengaria said in a surprisingly calm voice, appearing untroubled by the fact that she was forced to stand here while Isaac lounged dissolutely in his carved, throne-like chair.

Edwina admired her self-control at this moment in time. It couldn't be easy maintaining a regal demeanour while dressed in garments more befitting a courtesan than a princess. Whether their own garments had been washed or not, she had no idea as they had never been returned to them. Instead they had been provided with low-cut undershifts of a thin clingy silk and dresses of a similar, slightly thicker fabric, which clung suggestively to every curve of their bodies. The buttercup-yellow gown Edwina had been given fitted quite well considering, but Berengaria's red gown was far too tight around the bust, which forced her full breasts to spill obscenely out of the low neckline. In an attempt to preserve the princess's modesty, Edwina had fastened the thin white veil, which should have covered her head, around Berengaria's neck to cover her bare breasts. Now she was forced to stand before the emperor bareheaded, which increased her discomfort even more.

'I think perhaps that your future sister-in-law, Queen Joanna, might also like to benefit from my hospitality?' Isaac continued in thickly accented French.

'Regretfully, I think not,' Berengaria replied.

Edwina knew full well that Joanna would not be so foolish as to go against the advice of others on board their ship as Berengaria had.

'A pity,' said Isaac with a troubled frown.

Berengaria cleared her throat rather awkwardly. 'I think, in the circumstances, despite all the kindness you have extended, that I should return to my ship. No doubt King Richard has sent out search parties to locate us, and will soon be sending some of his forces to escort me safely back to the fleet.'

'I would prefer that you did not.' Isaac paused and then added, 'So you do not think that this magnificent Lionheart would wish to accept the hospitality of a fellow monarch?' He stared with dark penetrating eyes at Berengaria.

'He wishes to reach Acre as soon as possible, to strengthen the forces already besieging the city,' she replied. 'So no doubt he would be forced to refuse your honourable invitation.'

'Then it is a pity he lingered so long in Sicily, at least six months, I understand,' he challenged her. 'He does not appear to be in that much of a hurry, does he?'

'It was a military decision. I would not think to question that.'

'Military.' Isaac clasped his hands together and leant forwards intently. 'Such decisions include bringing together the necessary equipment and money to pay for his vast army. He will have a little less of both now, it appears. Are you aware, Princess, that one of the king's dromons was wrecked on the rocks of Aphrodite?'

Berengaria nodded sadly. 'That is partly why my men came ashore, to send out a search party to look for survivors.'

'There were none. We have not even had any bodies from the wreck washed ashore as yet.' He relaxed back in his chair. 'It was a pity there were no survivors of the tragedy. Word has just come to me that another of your vessels was also sunk. One of my ships spotted the wreckage of a dromon further south.'

Berengaria tensed and glanced worriedly at Edwina for a moment. 'I was not aware of that.'

'You were lucky to survive the storm, were you not?' Isaac said with a smirking grin. 'Perhaps God is on your side, Princess, even if he was not on the side of the occupants of the other vessels.'

'I would not presume to questions his motives for saving us, I am just thankful that he did.' Berengaria's hands automatically reached for the rosary she usually wore around her neck, which was of course not there. The gift from Richard was worth much and Edwina was relieved that the princess had been wise enough to leave it onboard ship. Otherwise, no doubt, if she had brought it with her, the emperor would have taken it from her. Edwina wondered about Isaac's motives; perhaps he thought that he could force a ransom out of King Richard to free his betrothed.

'As I am grateful too, noble lady.' Isaac stood up. 'Now, I am afraid I must leave you. I have many matters of state to attend to,' he said brusquely.

'One moment,' Berengaria said in a very regal manner. 'The men who brought me to shore, you hold them captive, I think.'

'They were indeed captives for a short while,' he

conceded, 'but they have all been sent back to the dromon. They carried a message to the captain telling him that you have decided to avail yourself of my hospitality.'

'Oh, Edwina,' Berengaria gasped, her naked, perspiration-covered body trembling violently as she reached a climax. Rolling over, she pressed herself against Edwina, breasts to breasts, stomach to stomach. Their soft forms melded together as her lips sought Edwina's. They kissed with a passionate ferocity, which belied the more restrained relationship that existed between them during the hours of daylight.

Darkness somehow changed them into far more sensual creatures, with little or no inhibitions. They had been here for almost a week and there was no modest reluctance between them now as Edwina continued teaching the princess all she knew about lovemaking. They both still spoke of their encounters as lessons but deep down they knew it was far more than that: a relationship that defied all they knew and travelled beyond the boundaries of accepted relationships, venturing into territories that neither of them knew let alone understood.

Berengaria, the formerly modest pious princess, had surpassed all expectations, revealing a passionately sensual creature trapped beneath the outwardly innocent, highly moral exterior. It was a combination that Edwina thought would fascinate most men, as she returned Berengaria's kiss with equal enthusiasm.

As Berengaria pulled away, she said breathlessly, 'When we return to our former existence, I do not think that we should think of, let alone tell anyone about this.'

'I would never speak of it to anyone,' Edwina replied as they lay side by side, letting the night breeze, which was blowing in through the open window, cool their weary sex-satiated flesh.

'So you will not even tell Stephen?'

'I think not.'

'Do you think that Richard might wonder on our wedding night where I acquired such skills?'

'From what I know of men, he will not think to question it. He will just be thankful that he has wed a woman who enjoys sex. Nevertheless, perhaps it might be wise to appear a little less skilled when he first takes your maidenhead,' Edwina said, having always been careful during their sensual encounters that the proof of Berengaria's virginity should remain intact; it had not appeared to blunt her pleasure by doing so.

'This cannot continue when we return to our former lives.' Berengaria sounded sad. 'So we must enjoy this while we can.' Berengaria's hand fluttered over Edwina's stomach, trailing down to the golden mons.

Edwina was so tempted to part her legs as the tantalising fingers slipped between her thighs. 'We cannot,' she said as she reluctantly pulled away. 'It is time for me to see what I can find out.'

'You will be careful?' Berengaria said with concern as she sat up and watched Edwina slide from the bed.

'Of course I will.' Edwina rummaged beneath the bed and pulled out a plain blue dress which she had stolen from a linen press. Dressed like all the other maidservants she could hopefully creep around the castle unhindered. She slipped her feet into soft leather slippers. 'I won't be long,' she promised as she hurried out of the door, then pulled it shut behind her.

The long passageway was dark, lit only by a couple of flickering lamps at the far end. Thankfully, there appeared to be no guards on duty. Edwina knew the layout of the castle well as she and Berengaria had walked around it often. During their imprisonment they'd had little to occupy their minds; nothing to read, no needlework to keep them busy, so she and Berengaria had talked endlessly. Three times in all they had been allowed outside in the gardens but only with an omnipresent escort of three sullen-faced soldiers.

Despite Isaac's claim to the contrary, Edwina wanted to find out if he was still holding the men who'd arrived with them on the longboat prisoner. At first, under Berengaria's persuasion, she had done nothing, as the princess was convinced that one day soon Richard's war galley would sail majestically into the harbour to rescue them. But as the days passed, Edwina had decided to take matters into her own hands.

Taking a deep breath, she hurried along the corridor and almost ran down the wide stone staircase. All was silent but, as she got closer to the Great Hall, she heard shouts and sounds of laughter coming from within. She had hoped that everyone would have retired by now but presumably Isaac dined late and he and his friends were still feasting.

She had been prompted into action tonight because of what Berengaria had seen yesterday when she had insisted on an audience with the emperor in order to complain about being denied access to the chapel. When Berengaria had entered Isaac's private chamber, she had noticed Richard's royal seal, which usually hung around the neck of the king's vice chancellor, lying on the table, before he had swiftly concealed it. The vice chancellor had been a passenger on the wrecked dromon but Isaac claimed that there had been no survivors and no bodies recovered so how, Berengaria had wondered, had he got his hands on such a precious item?

Following the corridor that led past the Great Hall, Edwina made her way towards the kitchens. There was no sign of any guards so hopefully they were more intent on filling their stomachs than taking account of the movements of a maidservant. She entered one of the storerooms and picked up a pitcher of wine, which had been left with a number of others on a tray ready to be carried into the hall. Then she helped herself to a loaf of bread, which was still warm from the oven.

The delicious odour made her feel a little hungry herself as she slipped out of a door at the side of the keep. The bailey was eerily quiet at this time of the night, apart from the distant barking of a couple of the emperor's hounds. Edwina hurried down the steps that she was certain led to the dungeons. To her surprise, the passageway was not cold and dank but dry and reasonably warm, appearing to have been carved out of the rock on which the castle was built. Lamps lit the gloomy interior at fairly regular intervals and she turned a corner, expecting to be challenged by a guard, but fortune had smiled upon her and he was fast asleep, sitting on a chair in front of a small table, his head lolled forwards, snoring loudly.

Putting the bread and wine on the table, because it had supposedly been for the guards and her excuse for coming here, she tiptoed past the sleeping man. There were a number of cells with heavily barred doors but they were all open so they must be devoid of prisoners. Further on were different cells that had been carved out of solid rock, with barred fronts that looked more like cages. She thought they might have once housed animals because there was a distinctly feral musky smell in the air.

The first couple of cages contained a number of scruffy-looking men who looked to her as though they might be Frankish sailors. Most were fast asleep, lying on the skimpy piles of straw that served as their beds. However, the next cage did contain men she recognised: the sailors who had been captured on the beach and four of the men who had crewed the longboat. A couple of them opened their eyes wearily as she walked past but clearly they did not recognise her dressed as a maidservant.

Where was Martin? Had he been captured as well? She found the answer in the last cage and she was overcome with anguished concern when she saw him lying motionless on the cell floor, chained hand and foot, clad only in a tattered pair of breeches. His back was criss-crossed with angry red weals, which could only be the result of a whipping, and what she could see of his face and arms was bloodied and bruised.

At first she thought him dead but relief flooded through her as she realised that he was still breathing. Not sure if he was conscious, she pressed her face to the bars. 'Martin,' she called in a low voice. He didn't respond so she tried again, this time a little louder. 'Martin, it is me, Edwina.'

The sound of her name seemed to rouse him a little and he opened his swollen lids and painfully turned his head towards her. 'Edwina,' he gasped between cracked lips, his voice so faint she could barely hear him.

'Martin.' Tears welled up in her eyes. 'Speak to me, please,' she begged.

'Edwina,' he managed to mumble. 'I am all right.'

His chains rattled as he struggled to his knees and crawled painfully towards her. Eventually, he collapsed limply against his side of the bars and she realised that his wounds were crusted over and were most likely a couple of days old, while the bruises were darkening and turning more yellowish in colour.

'What did they do to you?' Falling to her knees, she reached for him through the bars.

'It was my fault. I tried to escape,' he said in a strained voice, as he attempted a wry lopsided grin.

'Previous to that they hadn't really harmed me but after my failed attempt they whipped me as a warning to the others.'

'But what about all the cuts and bruises, the swelling?' she asked, gently touching his abused cheek. 'Did they beat you as well?'

'No.' He tried to laugh but it came out more like a painful cough. 'In my eagerness to escape, I did not take account of the fact that half the garrison would try to stop me. They were rather overzealous when they caught me.' He winced as he struggled into a more comfortable position.

'We were told that you had all been sent back to the ship.'

'Are you surprised they lied?' He ran his tongue over his cracked lips. 'No doubt they also lied to you about the survivors from the wrecked dromon. They are in the first cells. They told me that the vice chancellor was still alive when they reached the shore, but he is not here now so I can only presume he is dead.'

'The emperor has King Richard's royal seal; Berengaria saw it.'

'The bastard,' he faltered. 'Forgive my use of such a word, my lady.'

'Martin,' she said softly, wishing she could get inside the cell and tend his wounds. 'In your present state, I'd forgive you anything.'

'Regretfully, I fear I do not have the capability,' he said with a teasing, still crooked grin. 'Do you have any water?' He awkwardly licked his dry lips again. 'I am parched and they are rather remiss in providing even the basic needs of life in here.'

'I can do better than water.'

Rising to her feet, she hurried back to the guard, praying that he was still asleep. Fortunately he was, so she grabbed the bread and wine and carried it back to

Martin. 'Here.' She knelt and passed the jug through the bars but she had to break the loaf in half to squeeze that through as well.

The delicious scent of fresh bread filled the air and she was afraid that his fellow prisoners would wake and demand their share. 'It is little enough. I would have brought more if I had known. Once you have eaten and drunk you can share the rest, but do not deny yourself as you need to keep up your strength.'

6

Feeling very upset about Martin's terrible condition, Edwina made her way back into the castle, knowing that she had to find a way to somehow help him. As she moved along the passageway, she could still hear sounds of revelry coming from the Great Hall, but it was not far to the stairs now and the safety of her room. Suddenly, the noise from inside grew louder as a door was flung open and she shrank nervously back into the shadows. Isaac stepped into the corridor only a few feet in front of her and she held her breath, fearful she would be discovered, but fortunately for her he seemed too deep in thought to notice anything as he walked into his private suite of chambers.

She gave a faint sigh of relief as the door to the Great Hall was slammed shut, blocking out the noise again. Anxiously, her heart beating far too loudly in her chest, she went to creep past the door of Isaac's room. It was then that she realised he had left it slightly ajar. Curiosity made her ignore caution for a moment, so she tiptoed forwards and peered through the crack.

Isaac was not alone, he had visitors – two dark, heavily bearded men in Saracen robes. Edwina stiffened anxiously; she was very aware of how important this discovery might be as she heard the emperor greet them. '*Salamou alaikum,*' he said.

'*Wa alaikum el salam,*' they replied.

It appeared likely to Edwina that Isaac was indeed in league with Salah ad-Din, or was at least considering the notion. Why else would two Saracens be here?

Stephen had been teaching her Arabic and she knew a fair number of words and phrases, so she listened intently to what was being said, rather surprised that Isaac seemed able to speak the language so fluently. She heard Salah ad-Din mentioned as well as Richard and the city of Acre. There were other words she recognised, which all led her to the conclusion that they were perhaps discussing using Cyprus as a Saracen base. Whatever this all meant she knew that it might have serious repercussions for the Christian cause.

Scared that she might be spotted if she lingered here much longer, Edwina crept past the door and hurried towards the stairs, wishing that she had understood more of the conversation. Maybe in the circumstances she wasn't paying full attention to her own safety because, before she even realised there was someone creeping up behind her, she felt a hand grab hold of her arm. She was swung violently around to face the captain who had discovered her and Berengaria on the beach.

'What are you doing spying on your master?' His expression changed from anger to surprise. 'Lady de Moreville, dressed like a servant!' he exclaimed. 'Why should that be?'

'My mistress was hungry,' Edwina lied. 'She bade me find her something to eat. They take our clothes away at night so I was forced to steal this from one of the maids.'

'Not bad, I might well have believed you,' he said with a cynical smile as he tightened his hold on her. 'If I hadn't seen you spying on the emperor and his guests.'

'Me spying?' she said innocently. 'I have no idea what you mean.'

'I stood here and watched you, my lady,' he said, his fingers digging cruelly into her arm. 'You seemed mightily interested in the conversation.'

'I did not,' she countered. 'I do not happen to speak Arabic.'

'If you were not interested, then how did you know what language they were speaking?'

'I just presumed it was Arabic as it sounded so different from other languages I've heard.' Summoning all her strength, she glared at him boldly. 'Now unhand me.'

'Not until you tell me why you were spying on the emperor.'

'I just happened to pass his room and couldn't help noticing that his guests were Saracens. At least they looked like Saracens, although to be truthful I have never actually laid eyes on one before.'

'You are a guest here, my lady. You should not spy on your host and abuse his hospitality.'

'Hospitality,' she repeated with derision. 'The princess and I are under no illusions, we are prisoners here.'

'Prisoners? What a foolish notion,' he growled.

'We are watched constantly, never allowed to go outside unescorted.'

'Purely all for your own safety.'

'How safe are we when you take our clothes away at night so that we cannot leave our room?'

'I've had enough of this.' His fingers dug like sharp claws into her flesh, making her whimper with pain, as he dragged her along a passage and flung open a narrow door, which led into a small room packed with casks of wine. 'You can wait in here until I have spoken to the emperor.' He shoved her inside and slammed the door shut, leaving her alone in total darkness.

Edwina couldn't even begin to guess how long she had been sitting on the stone floor, her back supported rather uncomfortably against a cask of wine. It might well have been hours. Not even a glimmer of light seeped into the room and she was now feeling stiff and rather chilly. She had dozed for a while but her thoughts kept returning to what faced her; she had no idea what Isaac would decide to do with her. It was not as if she could tell anyone what she had found out, she reassured herself for the umpteenth time. So he could not think that what she had discovered could harm him in any way.

Her mind was still going around in troubled circles, when she heard the grating sound of a bolt being pulled back. The door was pushed open and a bright light washed over her. She blinked, realising that it was a beam of sunlight streaming through a window on the other side of the corridor. So it was morning already, she thought uneasily, as she tried to focus on the tall figure standing in front of her.

'Up,' the captain said, grabbing hold of her and hauling her to her feet. She staggered a little, her legs stiff from sitting so long, as he dragged her out of the storeroom.

'My mistress will be concerned,' she said as she was marched along the corridor towards the room where she had seen the Saracens, 'that I have not returned.'

'That does not interest me. From now on the princess will do exactly as she is told,' the captain said grimly as he thrust her into Isaac's chamber.

The emperor sat there staring at her coldly. The captain pushed her forwards, and then stationed himself behind her, his hand clamped to her shoulder so that she could not move. 'So Lady de Moreville, you thought to spy on me?' the emperor said.

'This is all a mistake.' Straightening her spine, she did her best to stare quite calmly at him.

'Mistake?' Isaac chuckled menacingly. 'Yours, not mine it appears. Now tell me what you gleaned from my meeting?'

'Nothing as it happens. Unlike you, I do not understand Arabic. If that was the language you were speaking,' she said, widening her eyes and looking at him innocently.

'You lie,' he hissed. 'Just admit that you were up to no good. I have recently been told that a prisoner of mine was discovered with a pitcher, which had contained wine from my very own cellar. How do you think that came to be?'

'Prisoner,' she replied, trying to maintain a look of pure innocence. 'I do not know what you are talking about. Nevertheless I am a little confused, sire, by the fact that you entertain Saracens in your castle.' She smiled coyly. 'That is if they were Saracens, of course; as I told the captain I have never seen one before.'

'If they were, then would it not be wise of me to ensure that no one lives to speak of their presence here? Speaking quite hypothetically, of course,' he said with a chilling smile.

'You dare not harm me,' she stuttered as icy fingers of fear slid insidiously down her spine.

'Dare not?'

'I am a lady-in-waiting to the future Queen of England.'

'"Future" is the word we should consider, is it not?' he said with cold menace. 'She is not yet queen and her betrothed seems inordinately slow in coming to look for her.'

'He will come, you know that.'

'Even if he does, do you think the great Lionheart is going to concern himself about the fate of one insignificant lady-in-waiting? Princess Berengaria brings him land and power while you, my lady, are a minor inconvenience, nothing more.'

Her concern was increasing as this troubling conversation continued. 'I am not that unimportant as it so happens,' she challenged, fearing now that her life was definitely under threat. 'My late husband was an important English lord and my betrothed is one of the king's most trusted lieutenants.'

'How can you be betrothed when you are officially still in mourning? The princess told me that you had recently lost your husband. The lies trip off your traitorous tongue far too easily. Now I want the truth. All of it!'

Edwina stiffened anxiously as she felt the cold blade of a knife suddenly pressed to her throat. Yet it didn't pierce her flesh, it just cut her garment from neck to hem in one smooth movement and her dress was ripped from her body, leaving her standing in front of the emperor stark naked.

'How dare you,' she gasped, as humiliation and embarrassment joined with the terror she was now experiencing.

'I dare,' hissed the captain as he clamped his hand across her breasts. Sliding his other arm around her hips, he rested his warm, rather sweaty palm on her bare stomach. 'The truth now!'

'Truth,' she repeated, unable to hide her apprehension as she felt his hand move downwards until it was pressed uncomfortably against her pubic mound.

She swallowed anxiously as he jerked her back against his muscular form. Even through his uniform, she could feel the hard line of the captain's cock digging into her buttocks. Her heart began to hammer in her chest and her mouth went dry with fear as his loathsome hand moved lower until his fingers were inching intrusively between her trembling thighs. She could see that the emperor was watching the captain's every move. His dark beady eyes were focused on her sex, and he was clearly enjoying every moment of her obvious distress.

'You know that I would not baulk at having you killed,' Isaac remarked as he moved aside some papers and picked up an object that had been concealed beneath them. 'King Richard's vice chancellor was reluctant to give up this royal seal. Far too reluctant it appears for his own safety.'

'You killed him?' she gasped, wincing visibly as the captain's fingers invaded the slit of her sex.

'I might have.' Isaac's smile was pure evil.

'Then not only are you a traitor to Christendom, you are a murderer as well.' Edwina forgot all thoughts of caution for a moment as she added, 'You have imprisoned the survivors of the wrecked ship and the crew who brought the princess and I here. You have beaten a noble Hospitaller near half to death. And it appears you are in league with Salah ad-Din as well. Your sins are endless, are they not? God will punish you for them all, I have no doubt of that.' She gave a faint gasp, her entire body trembling as the captain's fingers slid inside her.

'You are foolish,' her tormentor said softly, his voice pitched just loud enough for Isaac to hear. 'You have just sealed your fate, my lady. Contrition might have been a better move. However your body is so soft and moist, eagerly welcoming me into its seductive depths.' She gritted her teeth, trying to ignore the humiliations he was forcing her to endure as he added, 'If you want to live then I will ask the emperor to give you to me instead. It would be a delight to have a willing woman to warm my bed at night.'

'A fine offer,' Isaac commented, clearly enjoying watching the captain sexually abuse her.

She felt the man's engorged cock rubbing lewdly against her buttock cheeks and she grimaced and hissed with disgust, 'I'd rather die than couple with scum such as you.'

'Death is not the only option for a beautiful woman,'

Isaac Comenius pointed out as he snapped his fingers at the captain. To her intense relief, the man immediately withdrew the offending digits and stepped away from her. 'You, my dear lady,' the emperor continued, 'are worth far more alive.'

The two Saracens must have entered the room at some point, because they suddenly moved into her line of vision. One stepped closer and looked her up and down quite dispassionately as if he were examining a piece of merchandise. He reached out his hand and touched her breasts. 'You want us to take her?' he asked in surprisingly good French.

'Yes, far away from here where she can do no harm,' Isaac agreed. 'She is far too curious and strong-willed for her own good.'

'Buyers like spirited women, it amuses them to spend time taming them.' The Saracen turned to look at Isaac who was now smiling with cruel delight as he witnessed Edwina's confused consternation.

'What are you doing to me?' she asked, her voice shaking with terror as cold fear clawed at her heart.

'You, Lady de Moreville, are destined for the slave market in Damascus,' he said with a satisfied grin.

The captain leant forwards until his mouth was pressed to her ear. 'Slavery is a living death, you would have done better to have chosen me.'

'She will no doubt bring a good price with her golden hair and beautiful face,' the Saracen who'd examined her said matter-of-factly. 'But she is far too thin. We will have to fatten her up.'

The smooth warmth of the leather saddle against her naked sex felt strange. Edwina's sensitive flesh was being stimulated by every movement of her mount as she clung onto the pommel with her bound hands. The pressure on her most intimate parts grew stronger as the man leading her horse by a long rein kicked his mount into a fast canter, forcing hers to follow suit, taking her away from Limassol and closer and closer to the fate she now feared, perhaps more than death itself. Slavery! The word pounded in her head as her horse's hooves pounded against the hard-packed soil of the road.

Edwina wore nothing but a ragged shift. It barely reached her thighs and left her arms uncovered, but her Saracen captors had already told her that when she reached their ship, which was anchored further along the coast, she would be forced to wear an all-concealing burka, which would modestly cover her from head to foot and keep her hidden from the eyes of the Moslem crew. She suspected that they had not planned on leaving Cyprus with a female Frankish captive. They seemed rather irritated by her presence, as if she were an inconvenience, nothing more.

She had no intention of letting herself lose all hope just yet. After all she was still on Christian soil, albeit in a land ruled by a tyrant who appeared to be thinking of allying himself with the Saracens. Even so, she knew that if she wanted to try to escape she must act soon. Once she was onboard the vessel all would be lost and she would probably be destined to spend her life in one of the harems that Stephen had told her about. There she would probably be used and abused sexually by her new Saracen master.

Determined not to let that happen, she tried to think of a way to escape, as they travelled further away from Limassol. Yet thinking of anything was not that easy, especially now that the unending stimulation of the leather saddle rubbing constantly against her uncovered sex was becoming rather uncomfortable. She glanced around her; the road was narrower here and they had left all signs of habitation far behind. All she could see was rock-strewn ground and scrubby grass, baked brown by the heat of the sun. Just ahead, however, the road began to climb up into more mountainous country, turning into little more than a track zigzagging through a forest of tall pines.

In wild desperation, she considered throwing herself from her mount, but she was afraid that she might hurt herself as she fell and she had to be able to jump to her feet and flee quickly if she were to have any chance of getting away from these men.

The sun was rising higher in the sky now and Edwina could feel the intense heat of the rays beating mercilessly down on her body. Soon she feared her exposed flesh would gradually turn scarlet and burn.

As the incline grew steeper the horses slowed their pace and, through the trees, she caught a brief glimpse of blue in the distance to her right. She knew that the sea could not be that far away. Just ahead the track split in two, one branch turning towards the mountains, the other towards the coast. No doubt the Saracen ship was not far distant from here, so she had to act soon.

Edwina bent forwards over the neck of her mount and gave a loud groan. When she received no response, she groaned even louder and eventually the man leading her horse slowed his mount to a walk, while the other Saracen guided his horse closer to hers.

'What?' he asked irritably.

'I need to . . .' She groaned again, then shook her head. 'I have a pain in my stomach, I have to relieve myself.'

'You can wait,' he said curtly.

'I cannot,' she gasped. 'I am unwell.'

He made an irritated clicking sound in his throat and then called out to his companion, who immediately steered her horse onto the narrow band of rough grass that lined the road. All three horses stopped and bent their heads to nibble at the grass, which was a little greener and more succulent looking under the shade of the tall trees.

Before they could move to help her, Edwina slid rather awkwardly from her horse and stepped over to the Saracen who had ridden beside her. She held out her bound hands. 'I cannot do it with my hands tied,' she said, lowering her eyes as if embarrassed by her request.

He shrugged his shoulders and ignored her until his companion spoke to him rather curtly, whereupon he sighed heavily and then untied the rope that bound her wrists together, looping it carefully so that it could be used to bind her again. 'There.' He pointed to a large pine tree. 'Relieve yourself there and be quick about it.'

Edwina hurried across the stubbly grass and stepped behind the wide trunk. Crouching down, she waited until they turned away and began conversing with one another. Immediately, she straightened and fled into the forest. Fear made her fleet of foot and helped her ignore the pain as the rough ground and stones tore at her bare feet. In her desperate bid for freedom, she made for a steep incline, which she hoped would be difficult, perhaps near impossible, for horses to climb, knowing that she had more chance of escaping if they could only pursue her on foot. She scrabbled desperately up the steep bank, not even aware that her battered soles were leaving bloody footprints on the smooth surfaces of the stones. By now her heart was hammering in her chest and every breath was tearing at her throat but she kept going until she reached the top, never even daring to look back and see how close her pursuers might be.

At last she allowed herself a brief glance and saw the two dark-robed figures darting through the trees towards the incline. There was a fair distance between her and them. She ran into the forest. The trees appeared to be thicker here and she prayed that she could find somewhere safe to hide. Edwina knew that it would be impossible to keep up this fast pace much longer as the pain in her battered feet was getting worse and worse. She stumbled as her toe hit a sharp rock and the searing agony ripped up her leg, making her pause for a moment. With a determination she had never known she possessed, Edwina staggered onwards, keeping her eyes fixed on the ground now to avoid the worst of the rocks and stones. Not looking where she was going, she ran straight into a tall dark form. She gave a yelp of terror as she was gripped in a vicelike embrace.

'No, please,' she moaned, beating her hands against the hard chest of her captor.

The man, who was clad from head to foot in dark robes with only his eyes uncovered, swung her into his arms. Before she really knew what was happening, he had carried her into a narrow entranceway between two rocks, which led into a cave. The interior was cool and almost pitch black. As he set her down on her battered feet, she tried to dart away from him. He made a grab for her but the small stones beneath her feet slipped and gave way. She felt herself falling but even before she hit the ground the darkness had swallowed her up completely.

Edwina looked towards the door of the cabin as it was pushed open. This time it wasn't the rather exotic-looking foreign woman who had tended her wounds a few moments ago, it was Stephen who entered the large stateroom. He was still wearing the long black Saracen robes that had terrified her so much when she had cannoned into him in the forest.

'Edwina.' He appeared anxious. 'Are you recovered?' he asked, stepping cautiously towards the bed on which she lay.

'I would feel better if you removed that garment,' she replied with a rather wobbly smile as she clutched the bedclothes to her chest. 'At least that turban and the scarf across your face have gone. I didn't recognise you when you grabbed me so unexpectedly. I thought you were another Saracen from my captors' ship.'

'I gathered that,' he said with a wry grimace as he tore off the long black robe and threw it aside. 'I didn't have time to explain. I had to hide you from your pursuers.'

Edwina nodded. 'I realise that now.' She had regained consciousness to find herself safely cradled in Stephen's arm and being carried through the forest towards a beach where a longboat was waiting to take them to the royal galley anchored offshore. She had been so relieved to discover it was him that she had not even asked if they had evaded her pursuers or if Stephen had been forced to kill them. Frankly she didn't even want to know.

'It was fortunate I came upon you – if I had not –'

'I might have been on my way to a slave market in Damascus by now,' she finished for him. Edwina could see that he was deeply troubled by that thought. 'Really, Stephen, I will be fine,' she assured him. He was now dressed in only a pair of loose-fitting black trousers and, to her, he looked quite magnificent, the muscles of his powerful arms and shoulders moving smoothly under his golden skin as he stepped towards her.

'I just thank the Lord that when we arrived we spotted the Saracen vessel. It was Richard who decided that I should go ashore in disguise so that I could find out all I could before we decided on a plan of action. If I had not chosen to keep close to the path that led from the bay where the Saracen ship was at anchor, we might never have found each other. Destiny was clearly on our side, Edwina.'

She knew how right he was but she couldn't think of all that at this moment, as she had other matters on her mind. 'Is the king onboard?' she asked, well aware that she was in Richard's stateroom: the woman who had tended her had told her she was honoured to have been given the king's private quarters. She had no wish for them to be disturbed as her heart had begun to beat faster at the mere sight of Stephen's naked chest. She desired him so much, desperate now to feel his strong arms around her once again and to lay her hands on what was hidden beneath his black silk breeches. 'Where is he now?'

'In Limassol, no doubt.' Stephen sat down on the bed beside her. 'He and his knights landed less than a mile from the emperor's castle and rode to rescue the princess. While at the same time at least a dozen English war galleys sailed into the harbour. I just received word that, not surprisingly, Isaac Comenius fled in terror when he heard that King Richard approached.'

'And Berengaria and the Frankish prisoners?' She knew that she should feel more concerned about them, but all she could think of was Stephen's close proximity and his hungry gaze raking her body.

Gently, he eased the sheet from her clutching fingers and let it fall to her waist. As his eyes focused on her bare breasts, she heard him draw a ragged breath before he answered. 'They are all safe. No doubt none of them suffered as much as you, my love.'

She could see that he was confused and concerned by what he thought she might have been forced to endure. As they had travelled back to the ship there had been little time to ask her what had happened in any detail. But at least she had been able to tell him the whereabouts of the princess and the Frankish prisoners, so that the king immediately started making plans to rescue them. She shivered with excitement, almost able to experience the feel of his eyes on her naked flesh, as her skin began to tingle and her nipples stiffened.

'I endured nothing in contrast to your friend Martin, the Hospitaller. He is in a terrible state. The emperor had him whipped and beaten up by the guards.'

Stephen's green eyes darkened in fury for a moment. 'When Isaac is captured he will be punished for his crimes – there is no doubt about that.' Gently he put his hand on her chin and tipped it to force her to look directly at him. 'Edwina, what did he do to you?'

'Nothing of consequence, Stephen.' She smiled reassuringly, knowing that he feared she might have been raped. 'We can discuss it later.' Consumed with thoughts of making love to him, she stared at his muscular chest, then slid her eyes downwards to focus on the telltale bulge between his strong thighs. 'There are other more important matters to attend to, are there not?'

This was the first time she and Stephen had been together for almost three weeks and she intended to take full advantage of the opportunity. A shiver of anticipation travelled through her as she kept her eyes glued to the fascinating bulge of his manhood, hidden by only a thin layer of black silk. Unable to resist it a moment longer, she touched the tempting mound.

Stephen gave a strangled groan and his hands reached for her breasts, while his lips swooped down to take possession of her mouth. He kissed her with rough intensity, the kiss fuelled by raw desire and angry concern as his tongue eased its way into her mouth. Tongues entwined and lips melded to lips, the sensual gestures exposing the true depths of their feelings for each other that words somehow failed to fully convey.

Sword-roughened fingers stroked her nipples and pulled at them teasingly until they turned into rigid peaks. Then his fingers were replaced with his hot moist mouth, sucking and nibbling at the taut buds until she wanted to cry out with pleasure. Yet she bit her lips and held back, having no wish to let anyone on the vessel know that she and Stephen were having passionate sex in the king's bed.

Stephen lifted his head and smiled lovingly at her, before he jerked back the sheet to reveal her nakedness to his gaze. He sprang to his feet and hurriedly pulled off his loose trousers. Edwina watched with wild excitement, her sex feeling warm and moist with desire as his tumescent cock reared from its silk covering. He took hold of her hips and eased her down the bed, sliding her off the pillows that had supported her until she was lying prone on the soft feather mattress.

Then, carefully, so as not to touch her bruised and battered feet, which were now covered with sweet-smelling unguent and bandaged securely, he nudged her thighs apart and knelt between them. As he looked down at her, his expression suddenly turned very intense. 'They didn't . . .'

'Defile me,' she spoke the words he could not. 'No man has ever had me but you and my late husband,' she assured him.

His expression changed to one of relief. 'Edwina.' He tenderly cupped her sex with his large hand. 'I was afraid for you,' he admitted. He slid his fingers along her soft moist valley. 'You're wet already,' he said, his voice turning husky with desire.

'Just looking at your naked body does that to me,' she said with a sensuous smile. She lifted her hips, desperate to feel his fingers venturing inside her, or better still the entire length of his delicious cock. 'I want you now!'

She had barely finished speaking when he lunged forwards, the weight of his body bearing down on her. Supporting himself on his forearms, he thrust his rigid shaft deep inside her. It felt deliciously hot and thick and as solid as steel as it penetrated her moist depths.

With a soft gasp of pleasure, she lifted her hips, pressing them hard against his groin so that he could penetrate her as deep as possible.

She waited, nerves afire, senses finely attuned, as she experienced the pleasure of being filled by him completely. He withdrew, then thrust and filled her once again, and the sensation was wonderful beyond belief. The weight of his body bore down on hers and she clutched onto him, her fingers digging into his warrior-hard muscles as he rammed into her with long smooth strokes. In this time and place she existed just to be pleasured by him. She was a willing vessel for his desire as he pounded into her body, even harder and faster, his breath now coming in short urgent gasps. Edwina arched her back, grinding her pelvis harder against his groin and savouring the feel of his body spearing hers as the climax built inside her.

All of a sudden he moved, angling his hips so that each time he thrust into her, his rigid shaft brushed teasingly against her aching clit. She shuddered, her senses reaching fever pitch until a sweet tension gripped her body and the powerfully intense climax flooded over her – even more wonderful and more powerful than it had ever been before.

'Do you think they will be happy?' Edwina whispered in Stephen's ear as she looked over at Richard and Berengaria sitting side by side, ostensibly enjoying their wedding feast.

Five days had passed since the king had arrived in Cyprus and now a large part of the island was under his control, although he had yet to capture the emperor and his steadily dwindling army. They were in retreat, marching towards the south of the island where Isaac had a number of fortified castles set among high mountain peaks.

'To be honest, Edwina, I do not know.' At this moment in time Stephen appeared far more interested in sensually caressing her leg through the thin silk of her gown than in the future happiness of the king and his new bride. 'Did I tell you how beautiful you look tonight?'

'Many times.' She gave a soft laugh. She did indeed feel beautiful this evening in the new cream silk gown Stephen had given her. It was heavily embroidered and decorated with seed pearls at the neck and sleeves. She wore no veil. Her blonde hair was plaited and twined elaborately atop her head like a coronet and instead of a headdress one of the maids had woven small white star-shaped jasmine flowers in her hair. Every time she moved she was enveloped in a sweet cloud of their evocative scent. 'And did I tell you how handsome you look, my lord?'

Stephen, unlike most of the Frankish knights who wore ceremonial battledress, had chosen Eastern-style garments and the long dark-blue tunic, liberally embroidered at the slashed neck and hem in silver thread, suited his colouring. The endless sunshine in Cyprus had turned his skin a deep golden brown, which made him look even more handsome with his near jet-black hair and piercing green eyes.

'You did tell me.' Stephen smiled at Edwina. 'This is a good day for us all. Everyone looks happy tonight.'

Edwina glanced again at Berengaria. The new Queen of England looked positively radiant in a deep-pink silk gown. Her cheeks were flushed, her eyes sparkled and her long brown hair lay in loose curls around her shoulders, while on her head was a delicate gold crown embellished with precious stones. Berengaria was deliriously happy because she was at last marrying the man she had convinced herself that she loved. Yet Edwina feared that Berengaria's feelings were coloured by a multitude of different emotions. She felt that her friend didn't know her new husband well enough to truly love him as yet. Nevertheless, Edwina was relieved that Richard was making an effort to be especially attentive to his new bride, feeding her tempting morsels from his plate and constantly whispering words in her ear which were making her blush coyly.

'This castle seems so different now,' Edwina said.

She had seen how the people of Cyprus had enthusiastically welcomed Richard and his men, happy that their cruel emperor had been defeated. Even the servants in the castle seemed to her to be more relaxed and light-hearted as they made preparations for this wedding and decorated the Great Hall with a multitude of brightly coloured flowers. Isaac, in his hurry to depart, had left all his treasures, including a large amount of silver and gold plate, behind. This now covered the long tables along with the gold goblets and plate owned by the king, so there was an especially magnificent array of wealth on display.

No more courses were due to arrive and the banquet was all but finished, so it was time for the entertainment. Richard's personal troubadour, Blondel, was about to sing a song he had composed especially for the wedding. After that, she'd heard that there would be mummers and jesters as well as dancers and acrobats.

'It is warm in here now, is it not?' Under the cover of the table Stephen's fingers slid up to her leg and pressed tantalisingly against Edwina's sex.

Edwina bit back her gasp of pleasure, blushing slightly as the warmth of desire suddenly flooded her body. 'Stephen, you forget yourself!'

'No, I do not,' he said softly. 'I think about having you all the time. Perhaps we should walk a while and find somewhere cooler to sit.'

'As you wish, my lord,' she agreed, so wanting to be alone with him again.

Stephen sprang lithely from his bench and extended his hand to help her to her feet. Then she placed her hand demurely atop his and accompanied him along the side of the room and through an open doorway. Once outside the hall, the air was a little cooler to her relief.

'We could go to your room,' Stephen said softly so that no one close could hear.

Berengaria had favoured her by giving her separate quarters from the other ladies-in-waiting so that she could spend time alone with Stephen. Although Edwina was now recovered from her ordeal, and her feet were all but healed, Berengaria had only allowed her to return to her duties yesterday and only then because the wedding was so close.

'You know we cannot retire before His Majesty and his new bride,' she reminded Stephen. 'No doubt the queen will want me to help her to prepare for bed. The king may require your presence also.'

'Perhaps to bolster his resolve?' Stephen said rather cynically. 'He confessed that he is not overly looking forward to bedding her.' He drew her into a wide window alcove where they could converse with more privacy. 'The queen is so pious and modest, not the kind of woman a man of lustful appetite wants in his bed.'

'Your friend may well be surprised,' Edwina said with a knowing smile. 'Berengaria is not all that she seems.'

'How so?' he asked.

Edwina wondered if she might have said too much, so she felt a little relieved when two people walked into the same alcove, perhaps wanting to partake of the cool breeze, which was drifting in thorough the high arched window. It was Richard's sister Joanna, the Dowager Queen of Sicily, looking very attractive in a gown of scarlet velvet. She was accompanied by a man that Edwina did not recognise. Yet he must be important because he was very finely dressed in cloth of gold and cream velvet. Although, his richly embroidered surcoat edged with white fur looked a little inappropriate for the warm climate.

'Your Majesties,' Stephen acknowledged as he bowed and Edwina curtsied.

'Have you met the Comte de Chalais, one of my brother's most loyal knights, King Guy?' Joanna smiled sweetly at the dark-haired, bearded man by her side. 'And his companion, Lady de Moreville.'

So this was Guy de Lusignan – once King of the Latin Kingdom of Jerusalem, now bereft of a kingdom. Edwina had been busy attending Berengaria yesterday, but she had heard that he had unexpectedly arrived from Acre late in the afternoon accompanied by a large contingent of Templar Knights.

'The Comte and I are acquainted.' Guy acknowledged Stephen with a nod of his head. 'However, this lovely lady and I have not met,' he said, smiling sensually at Edwina.

Beside her, Edwina felt Stephen tense, leading her to believe that he did not like the way Guy de Lusignan was looking at her. Yet she couldn't help but be just a little flattered by having a king display so much interest in her. She blushed as Guy took hold of her hand and kissed it, his lips lingering far longer than necessary on her skin.

'Your Majesty,' she acknowledged shyly. She wouldn't have classed him handsome but he was quite an attractive man, most probably a fair few years older than Stephen and definitely a few inches shorter.

'I am delighted to make your acquaintance, my lady,' he said, his brown eyes looking her up and down with way too much interest. 'Your husband?' He lifted his rather bushy eyebrows. 'Will I have the pleasure of becoming acquainted with him as well?'

'Unfortunately not.' Stephen's tone and manner were stiff, almost to the point of rudeness. 'He died quite recently in Sicily.'

'My commiserations,' Guy said coolly, although the look he gave her was far from cool. She quailed under his seductive gaze, feeling a little troubled by the hint of lechery in his brown eyes. 'A sad loss.'

Joanna, in Edwina's considered opinion, seemed as troubled by Guy's interest in her as Stephen clearly was. 'We should leave,' Joanna said curtly. 'I have to present a wedding gift to my brother – a gift that you might be interested in, Guy.'

'Really?' He at last drew his eyes from Edwina and focused on Joanna.

'One of my most noted historians has drawn up an ornate and detailed Plantagenet family tree. You may not be aware of it but my brother is very interested in genealogy. Did you know that your late wife, Sibylla, is distantly related to my family?'

'I believe she did mention that on occasions.' Guy looked back at Edwina. 'Excuse us, will you? I trust that we will meet again soon, Lady de Moreville?' he said, smiling charmingly at her but ignoring Stephen.

As they walked away, Stephen said softly and with so much anger that his voice shook, 'I did not like the lecherous way he was looking at you.'

'He is a king,' Edwina said soothingly. 'They consider themselves above common courtesy.'

'A jumped-up upstart of a king,' Stephen replied venomously. 'Guy de Lusignan was a minor nobleman who was forced to flee France after he and his brother ambushed and murdered the Earl of Salisbury. His only right to the throne was through his wife. Why Sibylla allowed her mother to persuade her to marry him I'll never know.'

'You speak as if you knew Queen Sibylla?'

'I did,' he confirmed. 'She was beautiful and charming. In our youth we were friends. I considered her brother, Baldwin, the late king, my friend also. I doubt that we would have lost control of the Holy Land if he were still alive. It was Guy's stupidity and his disastrous decisions at the Battle of Hattin that did that.'

'King Baldwin,' she reflected. 'He died in his early twenties, did he not?'

'Yes,' Stephen said sadly. 'As a result of the leprosy he contracted when quite young. He was a brave man. His stepsister, Isabella, should, in my opinion, be queen now that sadly Sibylla is dead.'

'I never knew the situation was so complicated.'

'Complicated, yes,' Stephen agreed. 'I trust that once we have wrested the kingdom from Salah ad-Din's hands the matter can be settled once and for all. Most of the surviving barons of the kingdom want Isabella as queen but at present Guy has the full support of the Knights Templar and they are a force to be reckoned with. It seems wiser at present to leave the situation as it is.'

'My lady,' Edwina heard a youthful voice say breathlessly. She turned to look at the boy hurrying towards her, who appeared very agitated. 'I have been looking everywhere for you, Lady de Moreville. The queen requires your presence.'

Edwina smiled reassuringly at Berengaria as she readjusted the lace-edged pillows behind the new queen's head. Berengaria was looking far less relaxed now than she had earlier in the evening. The maids had all been dismissed, as had the other ladies-in-waiting, and now she and Edwina were alone. 'Everything will be fine, Your Majesty,' Edwina said as Berengaria nervously clutched hold of the sheet.

'Not "Majesty" to you, Edwina,' Berengaria said, smiling nervously. 'In private you must always use my given name – we are friends, are we not?'

'Yes, friends,' Edwina replied as she sat down on the bed beside her royal mistress. She patted Berengaria's hand. 'Always friends.'

'Then tell me as a friend that everything will be all right.' Berengaria flung her arms around Edwina. 'I only wish to please him.'

'Please him you shall.' Edwina hugged her back and then gently disentangled herself from the queen's embrace. 'You know exactly what to do to please him, do you not?'

'Because of you I do,' Berengaria replied, still appearing anxious. 'But it seemed so much simpler when it was just you and I alone in that room.'

'That can never be again,' Edwina said. She had put that rather unrestrained part of her life behind her now and Berengaria must do the same. No one must know of the intimacies they had shared for both their sakes. She had kept that brief interlude of illicit passion to herself, not even daring to broach the subject with Stephen as she had no idea what his reaction might be. 'You are a queen, you are King Richard's wife.'

'It is just that the thought of what we will do makes me nervous.' Berengaria grabbed hold of her hand, still appearing to want some kind of reassuring physical contact. 'Do you think that he will desire me as I desire him?'

'I have no doubt that he will.' Edwina couldn't be entirely sure but she hoped he would find Berengaria far more attractive clad in this low-cut thin lawn garment that she had persuaded her to wear. It displayed her generous breasts to perfection and was far more flattering to her than the voluminous nightgowns she had always worn before. 'Don't forget a little coyness at first. But as soon as you are in his arms become the passionate woman you were born to be.' She leant forwards to kiss her friend on the cheek but Berengaria moved her head unexpectedly and she ended up kissing her full on the lips. Edwina was surprised at how pleasant it still felt as Berengaria's mouth immediately softened and opened. Before the kiss could deepen into something far more sensual Edwina pulled away. Perhaps that had not been a wise move, she told herself, as she rose to her feet.

It was fortunate that she had acted when she did, for at that very moment the door opened and Richard stepped into the bedchamber. Edwina curtsied, relieved to see that the king was alone. Stephen had wisely suggested that, for the sake of his new wife's modesty, he forgo the usual rather ribald bedding ceremony and it appeared that Richard had taken that advice.

He smiled and Edwina thought that he looked remarkably attractive and far more approachable dressed in just a loose-fitting brocade robe.

'Lady de Moreville.' Judging by the way he slurred his words, it was apparent that he had imbibed a fair amount of wine.

'Your Majesty.' She flashed an encouraging smile at Berengaria. 'I bid you both goodnight,' she said and then walked towards the door, hoping that the king was not too drunk to be able to perform tonight. Berengaria would be mortified if she was still a virgin when she awoke tomorrow morning.

7

Edwina looked in total awe at the city of Acre, which had once been the major port of the Latin Kingdom. It was far larger than she had expected it to be and shaped like a huge triangular shield with two sides fronting the sea, while the eastern side was protected by massive crenellated walls.

A group of knights had greeted them on the beach when they had landed and were now escorting Berengaria along with Edwina and the queen's ladies through the Christian lines. Edwina had never even been near a battlefield before and she found it was a troubling sight, regimented yet chaotic, and terrible yet magnificent, all at the same time. King Guy had arrived here with only a small force over two years ago and he and his men had been blockading the city all that time: now these few knights and soldiers had swelled to a besieging army of unimaginable proportions. She could see a near endless sea of tents and thousands of knights and soldiers. Huge siege engines fronted the Frankish lines and she knew the names of some of them – trebuchets, mangonels and onagers. They all looked imposing but she wasn't knowledgeable enough to be able to distinguish one huge catapult from another. Nevertheless, she could distinguish the awesome and terrifying clattering and crashing sounds as the huge stones they projected constantly pounded the walls of the city.

'How do they endure that day after day?' Berengaria said to Edwina.

Just in front of them a group of weary, dust-covered

soldiers trooped past carrying stretchers on which lay wounded men covered in blood, some terribly mutilated and crying out in agony.

'Do not look, my lady,' Edwina said and Berengaria averted her eyes. Yet Edwina was unable to draw her gaze from the pitiful sight. 'Where are they taking them?' she asked the knight who walked by her side.

'There are a number of medical facilities run by the Hospitallers at the rear of the lines. They will be well cared for,' he replied in a calm matter-of-fact way as if the sight of them hadn't troubled him at all.

Could one eventually become accustomed to so much suffering? Warriors must have to do so. For once, Edwina was relieved that she had not been born a man.

Edwina did find it difficult to understand why the king had decided to bring his new wife to this terrible place, but perhaps he'd had little choice. After leaving Cyprus they had sailed straight for Tyre, which was further north along the coast from Acre. Tyre was one of the few cities of the former kingdom that was still in Christian hands. It was controlled by Princess Isabella's husband, Conrad de Montferrat, and it was he who had stubbornly refused the king and his followers access to the city. In Tyre, as the king had planned, Berengaria would have been safe and comfortable, but now instead she and her ladies would have to live in the middle of a war zone.

By now they had passed through the French lines and were in English territory. The soldiers here seemed much more cheerful, greeting the ladies with smiles and cheers – it appeared that the queen's arrival was considered a propitious event. Edwina could only presume that they believed that if the king had been confident enough to bring his wife here he must be equally confident of victory.

There had been even more enthusiastic celebrations

when Richard had landed three days ago but she and Berengaria had been forced to watch those from onboard the royal galley as the king did not want them to land until suitable preparations had been made for the queen. Edwina was proud to know that her king's reputation as a formidable warrior was renowned far beyond Christendom. Rumours were rife among the fleet and she had heard it said that the Saracens feared and respected him above all other Christian leaders as they believed that he was the one man who could lead the Frankish forces to victory. Not surprisingly, when the Lionheart had first stepped ashore he had been greeted by frenzied shouting and cheering. Even from the ship anchored in the bay, she and Berengaria had been able to see the huge celebratory bonfires they made on the beach and hear the men's voices raised in joy as they sang rousing Crusader hymns.

'The men are all convinced that Acre will be ours in days now that the great Lionheart is here,' the knight at Edwina's side said with pride.

'Let us hope that comes to pass,' she replied.

Judging by the banners she had seen fluttering above the tents just about every nation in Christendom was represented here and it heartened her to know that so many different people shared the same noble cause. In fact this camp greatly resembled a small city. They walked past lines of tents and many rows of tethered sturdy warhorses, which were used by the heavily armoured knights. She saw pavilions filled with weapons and supplies; another medical facility, staffed by Hospitallers; and even a small smithy. Somewhere, she knew, most likely some distance away from the military personnel, would be the washerwomen and ubiquitous camp followers who provided far more personal services for the men.

It was at this point that she caught sight of Stephen

striding towards her and Edwina's heart leapt in her chest. He looked so magnificent in his armour and his chiselled features were breathlessly masculine. She sometimes forgot for a moment how handsome he was and she knew that she loved him more deeply now than she had before. It was a love that had survived many tribulations and would never die.

They had barely spent any time together recently apart from those few halcyon days in Cyprus before the royal wedding. The very next morning Stephen, Richard and King Guy had set out in pursuit of Isaac Comenius. It had taken nigh on two weeks, but eventually the emperor had been captured. She had stood with Berengaria on the steps of the castle and watched as the captive was returned to Limassol. Appearing terrified, Isaac had prostrated himself before Richard, begged for forgiveness and pleaded for mercy. She had been told that, because of a past imprisonment in his youth, he was terrified by the thought of iron chains. The former emperor had been visibly relieved and thanked Richard profusely when the king had magnanimously promised not to put him in iron chains. Nevertheless Richard was not that forgiving a monarch, and he had then beckoned forwards a servant carrying a basket. Richard had kept his promise: there would be no iron chains because inside the basket were specially wrought chains of pure silver. For a brief moment, Edwina had even pitied the broken man Isaac became as he collapsed sobbing on the ground.

'Your Majesty, welcome.' Stephen bowed to Berengaria as he reached them. 'Quarters have been prepared for you.'

'Stephen.' Berengaria acknowledged him with a warm smile. 'Edwina and I are pleased that you are well. I should like to be conducted to the king straight away.'

'Regretfully the king is unable to see you right at this

moment, Majesty. He suggests that first you rest a while.'

Edwina could see that Berengaria was disappointed even though she tried to conceal it. Despite the king's apparent drunkenness their wedding night had been a success. Now that the queen had tasted the pleasures of her husband's bed, she had told Edwina that she was eager to repeat the experience as often as possible but she had barely seen Richard since that night.

'The queen would like to bathe,' Edwina told Stephen.

'A bath will be provided if necessary. However,' he said worriedly, 'water is difficult to come by here, would washing suffice?'

'It will,' Berengaria interjected regally.

Unfortunately, Edwina's enthusiasm for bathing had not rubbed off on the queen. Edwina was constantly troubled by the fact that few people she came across even washed on a regular basis and, despite the fact that she should be well accustomed to it by now, she still found the strong body odours of some of the other nobles rather stomach-churning at times.

'Is the royal compound near?' Edwina asked Stephen.

'The king has had a special compound constructed for the ladies of the court,' he told her. 'It is in the safest part of camp and will be well protected at all times.' He glanced back at the massive earthworks along the entire rear of the camp. 'Our spies tell us that Salah ad-Din and his men are camped in those hills in the distance so the earthworks are there to stop them trying to break though our lines.'

'Why did the king not greet Berengaria when she landed?' Edwina asked as Stephen led her into his tent. 'She is upset at his reluctance to see her.'

To be brutally honest Stephen had other matters on his mind at this time, which were much more important to him than the romantic notions Berengaria held about her new husband. He wanted Edwina, needed to strip her naked and make love to her right now. Yet he had to force himself to hold back on his lustful urges. She deserved to know the truth and he hoped then when she learnt it she would be able to explain the situation to the queen in a thoughtful and tactful manner.

'He is not reluctant to see her.' Stephen couldn't resist pulling Edwina into his arms. He held her close, her breasts pressed against his armoured chest. Tenderly he kissed her cheek, knowing that once his mouth made contact with hers he would lose all sense and reason in the height of his desire for her. Forcing himself to hold back, he contented himself with brushing his lips against her jasmine-scented hair. 'Richard is ill – he fears his condition may upset Berengaria.'

'Ill!' Edwina exclaimed, tipping back her head so that she could see into his green eyes. 'Not seriously so, I trust?'

'It is bad but not life-threatening.'

'Bad, how bad?'

'He will recover, given time. The illness is called Arnaldia. The King of France suffers from it as well but to a lesser degree.'

Taking her hand he led her deeper into the tent, hoping that she would notice the latest addition to his furnishings. Half hidden behind the curtain, which gave some privacy to his sleeping quarters, was a wide divan covered with a brocade counterpane and scattered with brilliantly coloured silk pillows. During warfare his lodgings were usually quite spartan but he had added more comforts in order to please Edwina. He hoped that she would be able to discreetly share these quarters with him when the queen did not require her presence.

'Arnaldia?' Edwina queried. 'I've not heard of it.'

'It is not that uncommon in the Holy Land. Some

physicians say it is caused by the Frankish diet which, coupled with heat, upsets the balance of humours in the body.' Stephen did not think it wise to tell her of the symptoms. The sudden high fever and soreness of the mouth and gums were bad enough, but the king had coped with that without complaint. However, Richard was vain about his looks and he had looked at Stephen in horror when the physician had warned him that his hair might fall out and his nails loosen. 'He will recover in time and with the right treatment, especially now that I have persuaded him to allow an Arab physician to treat him.'

'A Saracen?' she asked worriedly. 'Is that wise?'

Stephen smiled reassuringly. 'He will not harm Richard. In fact his treatments are more to be trusted than those of Frankish physicians. Doctors from the East are far more knowledgeable and this man is a devout Christian.'

'Are there many Christians among the Arabs?' Edwina looked confused.

'Why should there not be? This land is the birthplace of Our Lord and he was an Arab or more precisely a Palestinian. Christianity is nearly twelve hundred years old while the Moslems' great prophet Mohammed preached less than six hundred years ago.'

'For some reason I always thought their religion far older than ours. How do you know so much about it, Stephen?'

'In truth, I do not know that much. Nevertheless, my godfather encouraged me to read Arabic literature and I have even studied parts of their holy book the Qur'an.'

'It appears that I have much to learn about this land.' Edwina's eyes at last alighted on the divan. 'That looks comfortable.'

'It was recently liberated from a Saracen caravan. I thought that you might appreciate the luxury, as opposed to a hard soldier's pallet. I doubt that you will have much privacy in the queen's compound so I could not possibly visit you there at night.'

'Berengaria relies on me. If it were not so I would move in here with you and not care one jot for the scandal it caused.'

'Life here may be less regimented than at court but we will still be expected to maintain at least an air of morality and I have no wish for your reputation to be compromised. We have many years ahead to be together, do we not?'

He saw concern in her blue eyes for a moment before she managed to conceal it and he knew that she feared he might perish in battle. Life as a knight could be dangerous and death was always a possibility. He could not in good conscience lead her to believe otherwise. He would go to Richard and beg permission to marry her right now if he could but, despite the fact that she had loathed Hugh, she still had to maintain the necessary period of mourning before she took a new husband.

As Stephen looked lovingly at Edwina he was reminded of the last time she had been in his bed, her lips swollen with kisses, her blue eyes languorous with desire, those luscious breasts and sweet cherry-coloured nipples. Lust and love entwined like the strands of a rope, binding her even more securely to him than a wedding ring ever could. Just thinking of her, remembering the last night they had spent together and the passion they had shared, turned his cock rock hard. He could feel it pressing against the heavy constriction of his chainmail leggings.

'I pray that we do have many years ahead of us after this war is over,' she said softly.

'And in the meantime this tent can be our own private refuge from the constraints of court life and the rigours of warfare.' Tenderly he drew her towards the divan.

'Have we time?' she asked with a teasing smile.

'I will make time. While his illness prevails, the king has left me in charge of his army, much to Guy's disgust. So everyone else will have to wait for me, will they not?'

'I will have to help you out of your armour.' Edwina eyed his second-best surcoat. He had not worn the old one because it was spattered with blood and he did not want to upset her feminine sensibilities. 'I used to help my brother Fulk when he attended tournaments in his youth.'

As Stephen flung off his surcoat, she sank to her knees and began to unlace his chainmail leggings, but not surprisingly she was a little more clumsy and slower than his squire would be. Once she had undone the complex laces, she let the heavy leggings fall to the ground.

Straightening, Edwina reached for the buckles of his hauberk and unfastened them but she wisely did not try to help him remove the weighty garment. Stephen struggled out of it and placed it on its wooden stand. Beneath the mail he wore a thickly padded gambeson, a shirt, breeches and boots, which he removed swiftly, eager now to get her into bed.

As he tossed aside his sweat-soaked garments, he was all too conscious of the seductive way Edwina was looking at him. 'I hope I don't stink too much,' he said anxiously as he resisted the temptation to crudely sniff his armpits.

'Even at your worst, my love, compared to other noblemen you smell like a garden of flowers. At least it is the honest sweat of battle and not the stink of months of unwashed skin,' she said as she tore off her modest silk gown, followed by her shift.

Stephen's eyes hungrily roved Edwina's body as she sank down on the divan. Never had she looked more beautiful to him. Her curves were returning now; he could see it in the splay of her hips below her narrow waist and in the extra fullness of her creamy breasts. 'You are so lovely,' he said huskily. 'Lovelier than any woman I have ever laid eyes on.'

'If you say that often enough I might come to believe it,' she said as he stepped towards her.

Stephen threw himself onto the divan, feeling it give a little under his weight. He pulled her into his arms and, as their lips made contact, a fiery spark of desire travelled down to his belly and into his cock, which was already achingly hard. Her mouth softened and opened and their tongues entwined, causing the spark to burst into flames, whipping his desire like the hot desert winds into a sirocco of lust. He kissed her hard and deep, wanting to place his own possessive mark on her forever.

Catching her lower lips between his teeth, Stephen nibbled the soft flesh seductively, then kissed her again, long, slowly and languorously until she was gasping for breath. His lips made love to her mouth while his hands moved over her beautiful body. Roughly palming her breasts, he kneaded them, tugging at her nipples until they stiffened into firm peaks.

His hot breath brushed her cheek, slid down her neck and took possession of one of those sweet little teats, sucking and nipping at the rosy bud until she gave a moan of pleasure. Stephen could not resist the temptation a moment longer; he brushed his sword-roughened fingers against her sex and pressed the heel of his hand against her pubic mound. Her breathing quickened and her thighs rolled open, inviting him to enter the most seductive, sacred part of her body. Desire washed over him, hot and powerful as the sun, as he explored the valley of her sex and slid his fingers into her velvety sheath. It seemed to swallow him up, urging him to venture deeper, as Edwina moaned again, pressing her hips demandingly against his hand.

By now Stephen was so aroused that he feared he might climax just by touching her and that was not his aim; he wanted to come inside her and experience the pulsing heat of her vagina as she too reached fulfilment

'Not this way,' he said, his voice husky with need. Her body was pliant and willing to obey his commands as he rolled her onto her stomach. 'I promise you this will be good, my love. Crouch for me on your hands and knees.'

He had never taken her this way before but she made no protest and did as he asked. As he positioned himself behind her, she glanced invitingly back over her shoulder at him and waggled her perfect heart-shaped buttocks.

Stephen made a strangled sound, consumed by an overwhelming need for this woman. Everything else receded: the interior of the tent, the noise of the trebuchets pounding the city walls, all the familiar noises of the camp. All he could hear was his own laboured breathing and his heart pounding out of control in his chest. Carefully he positioned himself, easing his cock slowly into her vagina.

'Push harder,' she begged, pressing her buttocks provocatively back against his invading flesh. Unable to hold onto his sanity a moment longer, he rammed his shaft inside her, hearing her soft gasp of surprise at how deeply he had penetrated her, perhaps deeper than ever before.

'I'll not hurt you.' He slid one arm around her waist, while his other hand reached for her breasts, which dangled temptingly downwards, easily within his reach. He caressed them roughly as he began to thrust, pumping into her, grinding his hips in circles to increase the sensations they were both experiencing. Edwina arched back against him, panting slightly as his thrusts became harder and faster, the tempo increasing as he felt his pleasure begin to grow and peak.

The tension built even more strongly inside him as his fingers pulled teasingly at her nipples. 'Touch me, down there,' she begged and he reached downwards, his searching fingers seeking out the small bud of her clitoris. He drove harder, the heavy weight of his testicles slapping against her creamy buttocks as he touched the bud, teasing and tantalising it with steadily mounting pressure. He felt her body quiver beneath his and thrust even harder, increasing the stimulation on her clit until he felt her come, her insides contracting around his cock in powerful waves.

After her climax, she went limp, just managing to weakly gasp his name. At that self-same moment he peaked too, with a pleasure so intense that his entire world was shaken by the strength of his orgasm.

Armand de Mirabel slunk silently into Guy's tent.

'No one saw you come in here, I hope?' Guy de Lusignan asked anxiously as he caught sight of the intruder.

'I was careful, as I always am.' Armand's manner changed when he saw that Guy was alone. Walking over to the table, he casually helped himself to a goblet of wine.

Guy stiffened resentfully. Armand had no respect for his king, always making himself at home here without even a 'by your leave'. Yet he dare not complain about his attitude. Armand was stubborn and could just as well refuse to continue helping him and give all his loyalty to the Lionheart instead.

'Sit,' Guy said before Armand could do so without

asking permission. 'How fares Richard?' he asked as he flung himself down on the nearest chair and stared enquiringly at his young visitor.

'He is all but recovered so I am told.' Armand said, taking the chair opposite Guy.

Guy couldn't help noticing that Armand grimaced when he took a sip of the wine, but he tactfully did not point out that it was uncommonly sour. All Guy's decent wines had been exhausted and he was left with a couple of barrels that had come from southern France. Unfortunately they had not travelled at all well. 'I hear that the queen has been nursing him herself.'

'She has,' Armand confirmed but did not elaborate. Sometimes he kept way too much to himself and Guy had to force it out of him, which he found highly frustrating. 'What is amiss?'

'Nothing.'

'Really?' Guy crossed his legs and stared expectantly at Armand.

'Of late I am finding the king's manner irritating. Since I joined him in Sicily, I have tried so hard to become his friend and ally.' Armand frowned. 'He allows me so close.' He demonstrated with his fingers. 'Yet no closer. He still favours the Comte de Chalais above all others and he will not even see me at present. Stephen is one of the few knights who have been allowed to visit him while he is on his sickbed.'

Guy knew little of what had been going on recently as, ever since the queen had arrived, he had been very pointedly staying away from all the battle strategy meetings. To be frank he did not like Stephen suddenly being placed in charge of the Lionheart's army, especially when the young man had the gall to disagree with Guy's every suggestion. Eventually he had decided it was easier and less humiliating to stay away until Richard resumed command, but a week had already passed and the Lionheart appeared to be taking an uncommonly long time to recover. Even so Guy hated not being in the centre of all that was happening and this uncomfortable situation was getting him down. He had to rely solely on Armand, who fortunately had been allowed to attend these meetings, but this meant Guy had to hear everything second-hand. He was never quite certain if Armand was lying, leaving things out or embellishing the truth at times.

He looked thoughtfully at Armand. There was something about the young man that troubled him. So far he had been loyal but Guy still couldn't bring himself to wholly trust the clever but rather devious young knight. Despite his concerns he'd been forced to select Armand for this special assignment as his choice of candidates had been limited. A number of things had made Armand stand out: he was ambitious, charming and stunningly good-looking while his rapacious sexual appetites were renowned and he appeared not to care what gender his partner was – pleasure crossed all boundaries for him.

Once Guy had learnt that Richard planned to leave his winter quarters in Sicily and set out for the Holy Land, he had decided to send Armand to join him, believing that it would be wise to have one of his own followers in a position close to the king. At that time he and Richard had not met, but he had heard a few unpleasant rumours about the king's sexual leanings. He had hoped that Armand, who was a skilful seducer, might be able to lure the Lionheart into a sinful relationship, which could then be used to their advantage. However, although Richard had befriended Armand and appeared quite fascinated by his charm, looks and rather obvious sexual ambiguities, he had never treated him as anything other than a friend. Guy had now come to the conclusion that the rumours about Richard were just an attempt by his enemies to blacken his name. Now, however, Armand had to find other ways to get even closer to Richard but it appeared that Stephen was one barrier he had been unable to cross.

'Why can the Lionheart not resume control of his army?' Guy said frustratedly. 'That upstart Stephen puts me down at every turn, even having the gall to disagree with me – a king! And he does not have even one drop of royal blood in his veins.'

'Did your marriage somehow change your blood to that of royalty?' Armand asked with a cynical smile.

Guy curled his lip in disgust. Guy liked to believe that he was as blue blooded as any other royal monarch, yet he could not deny that Armand was correct and that his kingship came only from his union with Sibylla. Armand was far too aware of how fearful Guy was about his situation at present. Philip of France was related to Conrad de Montferrat, so he favoured Guy's young sister-in-law, Princess Isabella, becoming queen. Currently Richard supported Guy's right to be king, but that situation could change in an instant, especially now that the Baron of Ibelin had unexpectedly arrived on the scene.

Balian of Ibelin and Stephen's godfather Raymond of Tripoli had been Guy's greatest adversaries at the royal court of Jerusalem. It was those two men who had spoken out so vehemently against his plans to march the army out of the city and pursue the Saracen forces into the barren waterless countryside near the Horns of Hattin. They had argued that it would be far wiser to wait for Salah ad-Din to come to them. Unfortunately they had been proved right: his army had been decimated, Jerusalem had fallen and he had been imprisoned by Salah ad-Din for nigh on a year.

'No doubt King Richard will take charge again soon. Rumour has it that he is planning a massive assault on the city. He has been closeted with Stephen and Balian for many hours at a time in the last few days.' Armand paused and frowned. 'Stephen I can understand, Richard depends on his opinions way too much for your liking. But why do you hate the Baron of Ibelin so much?'

'It is not your concern,' Guy snapped.

He had no intention of telling Armand that Balian had been one of the barons who had done all he could to prevent Guy from becoming king. When King Baldwin was close to death he had asked Raymond and Balian to try to persuade his sister, Sibylla, to divorce her husband immediately. Baldwin had never liked or trusted Guy and for some ridiculous reason had thought that he would not be a good ruler. Fortunately, the plot had not succeeded because he'd been in a position to be able to force Sibylla not to give in to their outrageous demands.

Now that he was king, regardless of what happened, he had no intention of ever giving up his crown. Unfortunately, however, Balian was very influential and he had made it very clear to all and sundry that he favoured Isabella's right to become queen. Guy feared that Balian would try to persuade Stephen to side with him and they might well convince Richard to join them. Without the Lionheart's open support and influence, Guy could lose his throne.

'I apologise for even presuming to ask,' Armand said, still eyeing him curiously.

Guy decided it might be wiser to change the subject. He had been formulating a plan for the last few days which should please Armand almost as much as it pleased him. 'I was thinking that it would be fortuitous for both you and I, if the Comte de Chalais were to disappear for a while.'

Armand's interest was clearly piqued. 'A while? Better still forever,' he said with a chilling smile.

'Forever – an interesting thought,' Guy agreed. 'First,

however, I need to speak to the Grand Master of the Templars, Robert de Sable.'

Edwina, a long dark cloak covering her silk gown, hurried towards the rear of the camp. Just ahead, close to a line of tethered horses, she saw a figure also swathed in a dark cloak, the hood drawn close to half conceal the wearer's face. 'Leila, you are here. I am sorry I am late.'

The young woman smiled and bowed her head respectfully. 'My lady, I feared that you might not come.'

'I promised I would, did I not?'

'Unfortunately, I have learnt that Frankish promises are sometimes broken.'

'I do not break my promises,' Edwina said very seriously, as she thrust a bag into Leila's hand. 'Money and a few necessities. Your escort, when he arrives, will have enough provisions for the journey.'

'Forgive my mistrust.' Leila smiled warmly at Edwina. 'You are a good person, I should not have let my thoughts waver even for a moment.'

Leila had looked after Edwina and expertly tended to her wounds for two days onboard the king's galley. Edwina had come to like the strangely enigmatic young woman and also come to pity her when she had learnt more about her past.

Leila was a Moslem and, unbeknown to Richard, the sister of an influential Saracen leader. She had been travelling in a caravan some years ago when it had been attacked. She had been captured and eventually sold as a slave to the brothel owner in Messina, where she had been forced to become a whore. Edwina had empathised even more with Leila's position because of her own brief brush with slavery. Also, because of her marriage to Hugh, she felt that she had a better understanding than most about being forced to prostitute oneself.

Leila had told her that she had been relieved when

Armand purchased her and sent her to serve such an important man as Richard. Hoping to eventually find a way to free herself from slavery, she had told the king that she had relatives in the Holy Land. To her delight, he had promised to free her once they reached the safety of Tyre. However, when their ships had been refused entrance to the city, she'd had no choice but to accompany the king to Acre.

Here in the camp, she had been quite alone, separated from Richard because of his illness and the arrival of his wife, and she had sought out Edwina. When the opportunity had arisen they had spent time together and Edwina had enjoyed Leila's company.

'I've found someone who will escort you through the Christian lines. No doubt you will be reasonably safe once you reach Saracen-held territory.'

Edwina had not wanted to involve Stephen in this plan because, despite the fact that Richard had promised to give Leila her freedom, he had not yet done so and at present she was still officially the king's slave. Instead she had asked Martin for his help and, much against his better judgement, he had agreed. He had found her a Turcopole – one of the many men of Arab and Frankish descent who served in the Christian army – who was willing to escort Leila to safety.

'You know that I will never be able to repay you for all your kindnesses to me, Edwina,' Leila said with feeling.

'I have enjoyed the times we have been able to spend together. You have helped me with my Arabic and taught me a little more about your people and their customs.' Edwina paused. 'I will not lie to you, Leila. I have other reasons for helping you as well.'

'Your friend, Berengaria,' Leila said with understanding. 'You told me that she has become far closer to her new husband since she has been nursing him. I am aware that my presence endangers that relationship. It would be better for her if I disappeared and she never has cause to even learn of my existence.'

'That is so.' Edwina saw the tall dark-skinned man she had spoken to yesterday with Martin walking towards them, leading two horses. 'It appears that understanding goes both ways.'

'It was fate that threw us together at such a propitious time,' Leila said very seriously. '*Qismat*, we call it. May God be with you, Edwina.'

'And you also,' Edwina said softly.

After watching Leila and her escort ride off, Edwina turned to walk back to Stephen's tent. Martin had wanted to accompany her here, as he did not like the idea of her walking around the camp alone. However, she had refused his offer because she did not want anyone else to be directly involved in Leila's disappearance, apart from the Turcopole, of course, who had been well paid for his silence.

She was sorry to lose a friend, because she considered Leila a friend even though their acquaintance had been brief. Now Leila would be free at last and would hopefully soon be reunited with her family.

Edwina's thoughts turned to Stephen. Berengaria had no need of her this evening and she was already envisaging the passion-filled hours she and her lover would spend together. She looked up at the sky. It would soon be dark and already the noisy pounding of the catapults had ceased, allowing an air of tranquillity to fall over the vast camp for a short while. It would be busy again as soon as fires were lit, meals cooked and soldiers spent time with their comrades sharing stories and drinking together. The peace did not bode well for her, however, as the camp was not a particularly safe place for women to walk around alone in daylight, let alone now when dusk was fast approaching.

Walking swiftly, she retraced her steps, past a smithy and a Hospitaller facility, which was fortunately currently bereft of new casualties. The ground had become even drier of late and the dust swirled around her feet, dirtying the hem of her cloak and gown. Stephen had told her that once there had been fields and verdant greenery surrounding the city but nothing was left of it now: it had become a barren wasteland fit only for warfare.

She skirted a large enclosure, which contained a large, very ornate blue tent, knowing that she had to hurry as the sun had just disappeared over the horizon and the light was becoming even dimmer. Night seemed to come almost in an instant in this part of the world and she feared she would find it more difficult to find her way in the darkness, so she increased her pace.

She was so intent on where she was going that she didn't notice anyone behind her and she jumped nervously as she heard someone say, 'My lady, you should not be walking around the camp alone.'

The knight, accompanied by a guard carrying a lantern, stepped in front of her. As the lantern was raised she saw to her consternation that it was Guy de Lusignan. 'Please.' She shielded her eyes from the sudden bright light.

The soldier moved the lantern away from her face as Guy said, 'Lady Edwina? What brings you here?'

'I was delayed on an errand for the queen,' she lied, 'and somehow lost my way.'

'Then you must allow me to escort you back to your quarters.'

She was tempted to refuse his offer, but she knew full well that it would be far more perilous to walk back alone than to be with him. 'That is kind, but I have no wish to trouble you, sire.'

'I would not have it any other way, it is my pleasure, my lady.' He took hold of her arm, gently but persuasively. 'As it happens I am heading in that direction as I have business with the king. First, if you would favour me with a moment, there is something I need to take with me.'

She had no choice but to accompany him across the compound and into his ornate tent. The queen's quarters were pleasant enough, but this was so much more luxurious. There were even carpets covering the ground. That had surprised her in the castle in Limassol, but she couldn't believe he would bring such precious objects to be used in here of all places. Surely the dust and grime would damage them irreparably.

Guy walked over to an ornately carved table. 'Could I offer you refreshment?' he asked. 'I have a rather ill-favoured wine or some sherbet, a taste most ladies seem to enjoy.'

Edwina wanted to keep this situation as formal as possible so she said, rather stiffly, 'I respectfully decline your offer, Majesty. I am not in need of any refreshment at present.'

'It is not necessary to stand on ceremony when we are alone, my lady. Perhaps you may require refreshments later,' he replied with a rather teasing smile tugging at his lips.

Edwina tensed. He had said 'later' as if he expected her to be here some time, yet he had told her that he would only be a moment. 'I cannot tarry, the queen is expecting me.'

'A pity.' Guy took hold of her arm and drew her over to a large table on which rested a parchment. It was stretched out flat and weighted down with a couple of small bronze statues. She could see that the parchment was covered by elegantly scripted lettering and parts of it were gilded. 'You cannot leave yet, Lady Edwina. I have something to show your first.'

'Show me?' His hand still held onto her arm quite firmly and she was filled with the sudden inexplicable urge to flee. Yet there was nothing out of place in his manner and there was no reason for her to feel like this.

'You may recall when we last spoke at the king's wedding, Queen Joanna mentioned that she had a gift for her brother – a family tree. She was kind enough to have a scribe copy it for me and it would please me if you would examine it.'

She was confused but also just a little curious. 'Why, sire?'

'Look here, my lady.' His finger pointed at a name near the top of the parchment. 'Fulk of Anjou, a name that might be familiar to you. Fulk married Eremburtge of Maine, and if you trace the line down you reach their great-grandson, Richard Plantagenet, also known as King Richard the Lionheart.'

He was presuming that she knew how to read, which she did fortunately, although she knew that there were those among the nobility who could not. Yet she couldn't make out the names for a moment as the letters swam before her eyes. 'Fulk,' she repeated. 'Yes, I see,' she added as her vision cleared.

'After Fulk's wife died, he married again, this time to Melisende of Jerusalem and they became the king and queen of the Latin Kingdom.'

Still she couldn't quite see why this should interest her but she smiled rather nervously at Guy and then returned her attention to the document. She watched his finger slide slowly down the other side of the parchment until it reached a name she recognised. 'Sibylla, your late wife,' she said rather awkwardly.

'Fulk's great-granddaughter,' he prompted.

She nodded, then because he appeared to be waiting for her to say something, she added, 'So Sibylla was distant kin to the king?'

'You ignore the obvious, Lady Edwina.' He stabbed his finger on another name and she feared in his zeal he might rip the parchment. 'Peter, the youngest son of Sibyl who was Fulk's daughter by his first wife.'

'So?' Edwina looked at Guy in confusion, not sure why this should mean anything to her. 'Sibyl, a similar name to your late wife's, but I do not see any other connection.'

'Do you not know your own heritage? Are you not aware of the names of your own grandparents?'

'No, my father would not speak of them. I know not why. My brother says that there was some kind of disagreement with him and his family.' She tensed anxiously as Guy pulled her round to face him. 'Does this document have something to do with me?' she asked haltingly.

'You, Edwina, are the great-granddaughter of Fulk of Anjou. Surely your father has at least mentioned that you are kin to your liege lord, the King of England?'

She had always wondered why Richard had been so kind to her, especially when she was very young, and now she knew why. 'I did not know,' she stuttered. 'I am obliged to you for telling me, but I do not understand why it should concern you.'

He smiled warmly at her as he placed his hands on her shoulders. 'Because you are also related to my late wife, Sibylla. Royal blood from both houses flows in your veins and now that you are free, my lady, I have decided to make you my bride.'

8

Edwina had run for what seemed like ages, darting around campfires, rows of horses and tents, ignoring the curious and sometimes concerned glances of the soldiers and knights she passed. Some had called out to her but she had ignored them and now, to her relief, she could see Stephen's tent.

Pausing, she took a deep breath, not wanting him to see how agitated she was as she tried vainly to forget all that had happened between her and Guy. Yet how could she, it still troubled her way too much. After he'd told her that she would be the perfect bride for him, she had pointed out quite politely that she had no wish to marry him. She had informed Guy that she was promised to Stephen and that they planned to be married as soon as her necessary term of mourning was at an end.

To her amazement Guy had appeared to be amused by her statement and had pointed out that in this life no one could be sure of anything. There was always the chance that the situation between her and Stephen might well change and circumstances might prevent her from marrying him. There had been something about Guy's manner that had made her fear for Stephen's safety, before she'd dismissed such a notion as totally foolish.

Feeling confused and troubled she had said that she could tarry no longer as she had to return to the queen, whereupon he had immediately pulled her into his arms and kissed her. To be honest, she had been rather surprised but she had not found it unpleasant and in a strange way she had been flattered by the fact that a king desired her so much. Soon the kiss became more passionate and his tongue began to sensually probe her mouth. She was sorry to admit it now but she had felt the first brief flutterings of sexual arousal and she had made no protest, letting him kiss her a while longer. However, his hand had suddenly and quite unexpectedly covered her breasts, massaging them through her gown, while his other hand reached beneath her skirts.

Sanity had returned and she'd slapped his face hard. Unfortunately the blow had not appeared to anger him; in fact it aroused him even more. He had pushed her roughly back against the table and held her pinioned there. He then lustfully kissed her again, while his hand inveigled itself between her thighs. Acting on instinct alone, she had kneed him hard in the balls. With a grunt of pain he had crumpled to the ground, then groaned noisily as he clutched desperately at his groin. Edwina had turned and fled.

Surely she could not be punished for protecting her own chastity, however much she might have harmed King Guy. She put a shaky hand to her hair. She had lost a number of precious bronze pins somewhere along the way and her careful coiffure was in disarray.

She could see a light in Stephen's tent, so he must be inside. Not until she was in his arms would she really feel safe. Taking a deep breath she stepped forwards, vowing not to tell him what had occurred. Knowing Stephen, he would immediately pick up his sword and stride off to challenge Guy de Lusignan and King Richard would not be happy about that. It would only complicate a difficult situation even more.

As she entered the tent, she saw Stephen immediately. Surprisingly he was naked, apart from a linen towel around his loins. He sat on a low stool while his squire attended to him. 'What is wrong?' she asked anxiously as she hurried forwards.

'Nothing of any consequence.' Stephen winced as Dickon, his squire, spread a thick greenish salve over the livid bruise she could see on her lover's left shoulder. It was massive and looked terrible, extending down his arm and across to his nipple.

'A sword blow, my lady,' Dickon explained as he stepped back and wiped the remains of the salve from his fingers. 'Fortunately my master's chainmail is of the best quality and protected him from even worse damage.'

'It looks painful,' she said as she examined it more closely. 'Are you sure there is no other damage, Stephen?'

He flexed his arm, wincing visibly once again. 'Just a brief encounter with some Saracens. I've survived far worse and the blow didn't even break the skin.'

'It looks bad enough to me.'

'And you look a little dishevelled, my love,' he said as Dickon picked up the jar of salve and left the tent. The squire was a thoughtful young man and wise enough to know that it was circumspect to leave them alone.

'Dishevelled?' She awkwardly touched her hair. 'I suppose I was just in a rush to see you.' He looked at her thoughtfully and she wasn't sure if she believed her or not. 'Stephen.' She stepped closer and put a tentative hand on his undamaged shoulder. 'I was hoping that tonight . . . but you are hurt and it might be wiser if I let you rest.'

'Nonsense, I am fine. Do not think that a Saracen sword blow is going to stop me.' He slid his right arm around her waist and eased her closer. 'It will ache and be stiff for a few days but it is not my sword arm and it will not prevent me enjoying the pleasures your presence offers me.' She dropped her cloak to the floor as he lifted up her skirts and caressed her thigh. 'Sit.' He pulled her closer until her legs touched his knees.

Parting her legs, she edged forwards and perched gingerly on his thighs. 'Are you sure this is wise?'

'What do you think?' His hand slid beneath the silk that was draped over his legs and his fingers touched her sex. Edwina gave a soft moan and jerked away the towel that covered his groin. His cock lay there curled up on the bed of his balls and she saw it twitch visibly as his fingers slid into the slit of her sex. 'Edwina,' he said softly.

She reached out and curved her fingers around his shaft, then stroked it tenderly until she felt it stiffen against her palm. 'Are you sure?' She caressed it more firmly, milking it until it hardened into a rigid rod, while she felt her body moisten under the pressure of his searching fingertips.

'So very sure,' he said. His hand cupped her buttocks and he slid her closer until her open sex was pressed against his swollen shaft.

She lifted herself, moving further forwards until he could guide his cock head into the entrance of her vagina. The warm pressure of his flesh seeking entrance felt delicious and she pushed herself downwards, savouring the feel of his hot hard shaft sliding deep inside her.

Stephen had always been fascinated by the desert. He found a strange wild beauty in the stark emptiness: the rolling dunes of golden sand that could shift so easily in the desert winds and the flat plains which appeared to stretch on forever, blending into the distant horizon so that it became difficult to see where the land ended and the sky began. When the sun was at its zenith and the heat grew overpowering it turned into an ethereal shimmering landscape which appeared as old and endless as time itself.

They had reached this oasis only a short time ago. The twenty Knights Templar who rode with him had chosen to camp in the shade of the trees, but he had erected his small tent close to the waterhole at its centre, which because of the lateness of the spring rains was at present more like a small lake.

Stephen sat cross-legged on the sandy ground admiring the magnificent beauty of his surroundings as the sun slowly set in the west. As it sank lower the dark outlines of the palm trees stood in stark silhouette against the blood-red sky.

He had forgotten how much he loved this land. Before the fall of Jerusalem there had been almost one hundred years of peace between Moslems and Christians. If Richard could achieve his aims and that peace returned, he would be happy to live here for a time but he was unsure if Edwina would feel the same.

As he thought of her, he recalled how upset she had been when he had told her that he had to leave for a while as the king had ordered him to lead this group of Templar knights to the castle of Sarak. It was the only fortress which still remained in Templar hands and by now most probably reinforcements were desperately needed.

Richard had recovered but while he was ill he had relied greatly on Stephen. So, not surprisingly, Stephen had been confused when the king had ordered him to go on such a relatively unimportant mission. However, when he had learnt that the grand master had specifically requested his involvement he knew that Guy had had a hand in this.

The Templars were extraordinarily loyal to the King of the Latin Kingdom, and it was clearly an attempt by

Guy to keep him out of the way for a while. Stephen was well aware of how much his behaviour must have infuriated Guy of late. He had refused to accept ill-conceived military advice from a man who had never managed to lead his forces to victory on even one occasion.

So be it, Stephen had thought. Frankly, if it hadn't been for Edwina, he would have been happy to leave Acre for a while. Even now, out here in the wilderness, he missed her, but he knew full well that she would be safe enough because she was under King Richard's protection.

As night fell, the darkness was accompanied by a peaceful silence, although now and then in the distance he could hear faint sounds coming from the Templar camp. No doubt by now the knights would be at prayer. Most of them had not served in the Holy Land before so he had let the few Turcopoles that had accompanied him stand guard tonight. They were more attuned to this land and he trusted their instincts, knowing that they would sense a Saracen patrol far earlier than he could. This part of the country was under Salah ad-Din's control but so far they had seen no signs of any Saracens and with luck they would reach Sarak without being spotted.

Stephen tensed, reaching for the dagger at his belt, as he heard a squeak and a faint scuffling sound. He had thought it safe enough to remove his chainmail but perhaps that had not been wise. A dark shape appeared not far away from him. He sprang to his feet and, by the silvery light of the moon, saw one of the Turcopoles striding towards him, dragging a slight figure which struggled in the soldier's firm grasp.

'My lord,' the man growled as he reached Stephen, 'I caught this boy trying to creep into the camp.' He threw the captive to the ground at Stephen's feet.

'You think he's a spy?' He couldn't see the captive clearly but he was quite slight and appeared to be dressed in Arab garments.

'Why else would he be here?' the soldier replied disparagingly, as he nudged the figure with his booted foot. But the boy, whose hands were tied in front of him, crouched there, head lowered, and did not utter a sound. 'Do you want me to question him?'

Stephen was about to say yes when the captive lifted his head and stared right at him. Moonlight caught the captive's eyes, making them appear an unearthly silvery blue. Stephen tensed. There was something troublingly familiar about the youth even though darkness disguised his features. Stephen's heart missed a beat. No, it couldn't possibly be, he told himself. 'No, I'll question him – you return to your post.'

'Yes, my lord.'

As the man hurried off, Stephen shoved the dagger back in his belt, grabbed hold of the captive and hauled him inside the small tent. It wasn't high enough for him to stand up straight in, so he had to crouch awkwardly as he closed the flap. He drew aside the shade that covered the flame of the lamp so that he could see the captive's face more clearly.

Angrily, Stephen ripped off the ragged turban and two fat golden plaits fell down over the captive's shoulders.' 'What are you doing here?' he exclaimed furiously. 'Are you mad?'

'Of course not.' Edwina's mouth was set in a stubborn line. He moved the lamp nearer to her and she blinked at the bright light. 'Why are you so angry with me?'

'Angry is not the half of it.' He sank to his knees in front of her. 'Do you realise how foolish this was? My men could have killed you by mistake. You could have been set upon by a Saracen patrol or lost in the desert and died of thirst. There are so many dangers here that you know nothing about.' Despite his furious words, part of him was pleased to see her. She looked beautiful, even dressed in her grubby tunic and loose trousers. 'It is a miracle you survived.'

'Did you know that you are even more handsome when you are angry?' She struggled into a sitting position and smiled coyly at him. 'Despite your concerns for my safety, are you not just the slightest bit pleased to see me?'

'No,' he said stubbornly, ignoring the love and desire he felt for this sweet, irritating creature. 'I am a knight, Edwina, and this is war. It is not a suitable place for a woman.'

'Yet the king brought Berengaria and I to Acre.' She tried to ease the rope from her wrists but it was tied too securely.

'A decision that I told him was foolish as it happens,' he said as he took the dagger from his belt again.

She smiled and held out her bound hands, but he did not move to cut her bonds, just glaring furiously at her. 'Well, are you going to release me?' she asked. 'Or would you prefer to leave me bound and just cut off my clothes instead?' She pursed her lips then smiled seductively. 'I confess I find the thought of you taking me while I am tied up quite stimulating.'

Stephen was exasperated: he wasn't getting anywhere. He exhaled very slowly. The seductive way she was looking at him and the images that her words had prompted in his head caused a surge of blood to fill his loins. 'Certainly not here and now but the thought does interest me.' Rather reluctantly, he cut the rope that bound her wrists together.

She rubbed her reddened wrists. 'The rope was digging into my skin. Your soldier did tie it incredibly tight but I didn't dare complain, let alone tell him who I really am.'

'You know that my anger was caused only by concern?'

'Of course.' She nodded and then contritely lowered her eyes until her thick lashes fanned her pink cheeks.

'And you admit that your actions were foolish?'

'Foolish maybe.' She looked up at him. 'But I had the uneasy feeling that something bad was going to happen to you.'

'And will your presence here prevent it happening?' he asked coolly as he tried to ignore the fiery lust that had ignited inside his body.

'I suppose not.' She flung herself at him quite unexpectedly and with so much enthusiasm that she pushed him over and they fell to the ground in a tangle of arms and legs. 'Do you forgive me?'

'I will have to be persuaded.' Rolling onto his back, Stephen grabbed hold of her and pulled her atop him. 'Will not the queen be concerned by your disappearance? She will fear that something terrible has happened to you.' He couldn't resist slipping his hand under her tunic to caress her bare back.

'She will not.' She sounded very confident. 'It was Berengaria who helped me arrange to follow you. It is amazing what a queen can do, especially when she is in possession of the king's royal seal.' Edwina wriggled down his body until her hips were pressed to his. 'She is to tell everyone that I am unwell and resting in my tent. So they will not even know that I am gone.'

'Richard will be furious if he finds out.'

'He will not. You should send one of your men to find my horse. I left it on the other side of the oasis.'

'Later.' Stephen was having great difficulty concentrating as Edwina seductively rubbed her pelvis against his groin. His cock was becoming harder by the moment.

She smiled, knowing quite well what her seductive

movements were doing to him. 'Stephen, I swear that I can feel –'

'I am well aware what is happening to my body,' he interjected in a strained voice.

Even from a distance, Sarak stood out in the barren landscape as a stark reminder of the power of the Knights Templar and it made Stephen think of the famous fortress of Kerak, which was built along similar lines and was said to be the finest military stronghold in all Christendom.

Although much smaller, Sarak was still a remarkable fortress and was designed to be easily defendable with only a limited force of men. Surrounded by high thick walls, it had four tall towers. Deep escarpments protected it on three sides, while the fourth had a wide, deep waterless moat which was only traversable by a drawbridge. Also Sarak was fortunately located on a promontory close to the Mediterranean, so it was relatively easy to ship in supplies. Stephen thought that this was no doubt why it had managed to hold out so long against the Saracens as he and his men rode towards it.

There were no Saracen forces surrounding the walls: they had left long ago, defeated by the determination of its defenders. Just a few birds circled its high battlements and their raucous cries penetrated the still air, sounding to Stephen like a warning of danger. The citadel had a menacing air about it and Stephen felt it closing in on him as his horse clattered across the drawbridge and into the bailey.

Telling himself not to be so foolish, he glanced back at Edwina. With her eyes lowered, her hair covered and dressed in a squire's uniform, which she had sensibly carried in her saddlebags, she looked every inch a squire, albeit a rather scrawny one.

He heard the ominous rattling of chains as the draw-bridge was raised and the heavy thud of the massive metal-studded gates being pulled shut. Stephen halted, his men lined up behind him, and looked around the large bailey. There was no sign of any civilian occupants at all, just a fair number of Knights of the Temple, in their white surcoats fronted by red crosses, and a few sergeants and squires of the order dressed in their usual black habits.

Stephen dismounted and walked towards the small group of knights who stood at the main entrance to the large inner keep. The commander of the garrison was Bernard le Motte. Stephen presumed that Bernard was the tall man in the centre of the group, who looked to be uncommonly thin. His grey hair was cropped very short and his skin was drawn so tightly over his sharp features that his face had an almost cadaverous air about it.

'Greetings.' The master, like all Templars, wore a thick beard because his order did not permit him to shave.

'The Comte de Chalais at your service,' Stephen said, feeling very conscious of all the inhabitants' eyes focused upon him alone. Usually he didn't find such evident curiosity troubling but he did so today. There was something eerily strange about this place and a slight shiver ran up his spine as he climbed the wide stone steps to the door of the keep.

'Comte.' A tense, almost unemotional smile crossed the man's tight features. 'I am the Master of Sarak, Bernard le Motte.'

Reaching inside his surplice, Stephen brought forth the letters he carried, which were wrapped in a leather wallet. 'Communications from His Majesty King Richard and the Grand Master of your order, Robert de Sable,' he said as he handed it to Bernard.

Judging by the brief moment of concerned confusion which ensued, the Templars did not know that a new Grand Master had been elected after his predecessor had perished at Acre. 'We were not aware,' Bernard said after he'd conducted a short conversation with his companions. 'We have lived in virtual isolation here for a long time.'

'I am sorry to be the bearer of bad news. Gerard de Ridefort died bravely in battle,' Stephen replied. Bernard was staring at him with eyes so dark they looked almost black in the bright sunlight. They had a strange flat quality about them which he found immensely unsettling.

Bernard nodded. 'Comte, you may not recall but we have met before, many years ago at court in Jerusalem.'

Stephen managed to hide his surprise, while thinking that he surely would have remembered such a strange-looking man. 'I regret I do not remember our meeting. However, I was very young and most probably not paying as much attention as I should have to the visitors at court.' He glanced back at his men, who had dismounted and were waiting patiently for orders beside their horses. 'I am sorry that I was unable to bring more reinforcements. Unfortunately, the Grand Master wished to keep as many men as possible with him for the final assault on Acre.'

'No doubt he explains it all in his letter.' Bernard turned the leather wallet in his hand but did not undo the ties that held it closed. 'We have managed to hold out against the Saracens for three years, and they no longer trouble us now.' He turned to whisper something to his companions that he clearly did not want Stephen to hear. 'Forgive me, you must be hungry and thirsty. Perhaps you would like to partake of refreshments in our rectory? I will have quarters prepared, but I must warn you that we live very simply here.'

'I am a soldier, I would not expect otherwise. Anything will suffice.' Stephen glanced back at Edwina who stood demurely behind him. 'My squire, Edward, can share my quarters. There is no need to trouble yourself by providing more than one room.'

Bernard le Motte frowned thoughtfully as he read the last of the three letters. The first two had been much as he had expected. There had been a greeting from King Richard, followed by a few encouraging words regarding the bravery of the knights defending Sarak and a couple of brief sentences about his plans to retake the Holy Land. The grand master's letter had recounted how Gerard de Rideford had died. Bernard was pleased that it had been a noble death. It was clearly the will of God that the former grand master had sacrificed himself for Christ. Apart from that there had been a brief explanation about the small number of reinforcements and the letter had finished with prayers for their continued success.

Bernard reread the letter from Guy de Lusignan. He had served the King of Jerusalem for many years and he felt concerned. Apparently the Comte de Chalais was close friends with Balian of Ibelin and they were, with other nobles of the Latin Kingdom, plotting to dethrone King Guy and make Princess Isabella queen. Bernard knew that he could not allow that to happen. 'Of course I will help you, my friend,' he said softly.

Bernard rose to his feet, filled with a determination to defend this noble cause. He had been chosen by God to help King Guy and King Richard destroy Salah ad-Din and drive the infidels from the Holy City forever. Nevertheless, he would have to be careful what he said to his knights: there were those among them who shared his zeal but might not agree with what he planned to do about King Guy's request, as it wasn't precisely legal according to the rules of the order. Other reasons must be found; perhaps heresy was the answer, he thought, as he rose to his feet.

Setting the first two letters on a nearby table, he placed the other in a secure secret pocket he'd had constructed inside his surplice. Usually it contained one of the three holy relics he owned, which were at present safely stored in his room. The Knights of the Temple were forbidden to own personal belongings. However, he felt that he was above such petty rules; the relics had helped him achieve success and had made him almost invincible.

'Master.' Brother Gerard hurried into the room. He acted as both chaplain and clerk in this small community and he was the only brother Bernard could trust with his deepest secrets. 'Is the news good?'

'You may peruse the letters.' Bernard pointed to the two missives. 'Then you can read them to the brothers when they eat their meal.' He paused, then added, 'I have other news from my friend, our noble king.'

'Long may he live,' Gerard said enthusiastically. 'He is well, I trust?' Gerard added with a tight smile. He did not say more but Bernard sensed that something was troubling him.

'He intends to marry soon a recently widowed noblewoman, Edwina de Montfort. Not only is she an heiress, she is kin to both King Richard and our dear departed Queen Sibylla.'

'Propitious news.' Gerard nodded. 'Very propitious. However –' he stepped closer to Bernard '– there is something important we must discuss right now. It is most unpleasant and concerns the Comte de Chalais.'

'Unpleasant?' Bernard enquired, hoping that whatever it was it might be something to aid his cause. 'In what way?

'As instructed, I had him watched,' Gerard replied. 'And it appears that the comte has an unnatural relationship with his squire.'

Bernard tensed. 'Are you certain about this?'

'Yes.' Bernard bobbed his head up and down nervously. 'I assigned Brother John the task of keeping a close eye on our guests. He was peering through the peephole into the comte's quarters when he saw them enter the room and bolt the door. To his consternation the comte and his squire then kissed each other passionately.'

'I must see this for myself.' Bernard's heart began to beat out of control and his palms felt sweaty as he strode from the room followed by Gerard.

It was only a few paces to the stone staircase and he climbed it quickly, hearing Gerard's laboured breathing as they reached the top. Turning left, he hurried forwards until he reached a small storeroom, which contained far more than mere supplies. Behind a concealed panel in the far wall was the entrance to the narrow tunnels that honeycombed the walls of this citadel. Few of the occupants knew of their existence, only Bernard, Gerard and a small number of select Templars whom he knew he could trust implicitly. Bernard had made use of the tunnels since he had become master, using them to spy on the few visitors they'd had, and on the acolytes in their first months of service, as well as members of the order he had come to suspect of misdeeds.

He, like all other masters, insisted that the members of the order slept in lighted rooms, always dressed in shirts, breeches and shoes. With many men confined in one place for long lengths of time, temptations existed. Therefore, brothers were forbidden to look upon each other when unclothed because it might encourage lewd sexual relationships between them.

Now it appeared that such a relationship was occurring in the comte's room. Bernard felt agitated as he opened the concealed door and stepped into the narrow passageway. Of course he had faced such uncomfortable situations before. However, in the past he had thought it his duty not to rely on hearsay and he had secretly witnessed what occurred first hand before deciding on a suitable punishment. The odd thing was that he couldn't seem to erase the perversities he had seen from his mind. When he lay down to sleep at night he saw them again and again in his head and even in his dreams, making his body burn with a strange fire that was difficult to extinguish.

As he walked along the dark passage he became more and more agitated. The hair shirt he had put on beneath his clothes only two days ago began to rub even more uncomfortably against the sweaty skin of his chest and back.

'Here,' Gerard whispered, pausing to silently draw back the wooden shutter that concealed the peepholes drilled in the stone.

Bernard leant forwards and put his eyes to the holes, his heart beating excitedly in his chest as he tried to ignore the strange sensations forming in his groin. The first thing he saw was the Comte de Chalais standing stark naked in the centre of the room. For some inexplicable reason the image burnt its way into his mind. He saw a wide muscular chest and powerful arms formed by hours of training and swordplay. The comte's skin was smooth with a faint golden tint, not white and pasty like his own. He couldn't help but admire the flat stomach and he tensed as he caught a brief glimpse of Stephen's sexual organs before he turned towards the bed. Now he was faced with a strong back, webbed with muscles, firm hard buttocks and powerful thighs, which were doing remarkably strange things to his equilibrium. He supposed it was because in his estimation nudity of any kind was sinful.

Forcing his eyes from Stephen, Bernard spotted the squire, fortunately not naked but dressed in shirt and breeches, standing by the bed. Just like his master, the boy must be steeped in iniquity because he cared too much for his appearance and had grown his blond hair long. It was drawn into a plait at the nape of his neck but Bernard could not gauge how wickedly long it actually was because the plait was tucked inside the neck of the boy's shirt. The squire was attractive with handsome, almost girlish looks. Perhaps that was why Stephen chose to use him in such an unnatural way.

Then Bernard glanced back at the muscular man. Stephen stepped towards the bed and Bernard shivered as he caught a glimpse of a cock that looked uncommonly large, although, of course, he was no expert on such matters. It hung against the sac of balls, slapping against powerful thighs as the comte moved closer to the squire. He said something that Bernard couldn't quite hear and the youth laughed and laid down on the bed on his stomach, his buttocks pointed towards his master.

With a muttered oath Stephen jerked down the squire's breeches to expose a creamy, perfectly formed naked bottom, which looked tempting even to Bernard. Hastily crossing himself, Bernard watched in lewd fascination. He found himself holding his breath in anticipation as Stephen curled his fingers round his cock and masturbated, rubbing his hand up and down the shaft until the organ grew thicker and larger, turning into a rigid rod of impressive size.

'Master,' Gerard whispered anxiously.

'Silence,' Bernard hissed, his excitement rising to fever pitch.

Bernard felt his own penis grow harder but studiously tried to ignore it, concentrating on his need to bear witness to this appalling incident. He saw Stephen ease the squire's legs apart then move, thrusting his cock deep inside the youth, who immediately gave a loud groan of pleasure. To be honest Bernard was unable to see this as clearly as he would have wished, because in the process of impaling the squire, the comte had moved and all he could see was the man's muscular buttocks thrusting lewdly back and forth. Even so he was captivated by the sight of the erotic movements, finding the vision so compelling that his own shaft grew even harder until it felt as if it might explode. There was almost an animalistic air about these two people enjoying such forbidden pleasures and Bernard was so very tempted to slide his hand under his surplice and press it against his aching cock.

Soon his breathing became as laboured as that of Stephen's, who was still energetically pumping into the willing squire. Bernard's heart missed a beat and his fingers curled, his ragged nails digging into the stone wall as Stephen withdrew and flipped the squire over. The boy's long shirt concealed his sex for a moment and then the comte ripped it off, revealing the surprising sight of two round firm breasts tipped by erect cherry-coloured nipples. Bernard's gaze slid down to the squire's groin, hardly able to believe it was a woman. What had possessed this knight to bring a woman, disguised as a boy, to this sacred place?

Yet he could not fail to be moved by her nakedness. In truth he might have envisaged it in his youth but he had never seen a woman unclothed before and it was a magnificently inspiring sight. He began to understand how such a sinful creature might have tempted Adam in the Garden of Eden. Her long golden hair confined in a fat plait flopped across one pert breast. As she lay there smiling seductively at the comte, she parted her thighs to reveal all of herself to the onlookers. Bernard swallowed and gave a soft sigh as he watched the line of wicked pink flesh opening up between her pale thighs. He so wanted to be there, naked on the bed with them, and he watched enthralled as Stephen eased his rigid cock back inside the woman again. As the thrusting started, she wrapped her legs around Stephen's lean hips and Bernard could not resist the temptation a moment longer. His hand surreptitiously reached beneath his surplice and he grabbed hold of his penis, rubbing it through the rough fabric of his breeches, while he watched the two of them rutting together.

Their pleasure appeared to rise as swiftly as his. He saw Stephen's muscles go rigid and he emitted a loud grunt as he climaxed. That noise was followed by a sharp scream from the woman as she too came. Confusion erupted inside Bernard's body as he felt a quite indescribable pleasure consume him. Then his own muscles tensed and his cock pulsed with a wild pumping pressure. The strange sensation was followed by a wonderful warmth and a powerful sense of release.

Unable to comprehend what had happened to him, he leant back against the far wall, shivering slightly as he became aware of a strange damp stickiness in his breeches and he realised in disgust that he had climaxed, something he had never allowed himself to do before, because self-gratification was a mortal sin in his eyes.

Yet none of this was truly his fault, he told himself: it had come about because of the Comte de Chalais's strange shameful behaviour. Bernard vowed that he would be punished for this as well as his other crimes. Turning, he leant towards Gerard. 'Go find the strongest sleeping potion we have, put it in a jug of our finest wine and send it to the comte.'

When she awoke Edwina was confused, very confused. She had opened her eyes to discover that she was lying on a hard narrow bed in a cell-like room with stone walls – a place she did not recognise at all. 'Stephen,' she gasped, although barely a sound escaped her lips as her tongue felt thick and swollen in her mouth.

'My lady, are you recovered?'

Edwina blinked to clear her vision and saw an elderly man with a white beard and wearing a black habit, leaning over her. 'Who are you?' she just managed to say, although her mouth felt as parched as the desert she had recently crossed.

'I am one of the brothers,' he said in a gentle voice. 'You have been unwell.'

'I need to see Steph– the Comte de Chalais.' She clutched nervously at the sheet that covered her, conscious that she was wearing a long-sleeved, high-necked linen shirt that did not belong to her. So someone must have dressed her in it, yet no one was supposed to know she was a woman. This man unfortunately clearly did. 'Please.'

'I will summon the comte, Lady de Moreville,' the man said soothingly. 'Or would you prefer that I call you Edwina?'

How did they know who she was? She remembered the letter of safe passage Berengaria had insisted on giving her, which had been concealed in her saddlebags. The queen thought it wise to carry it just in case she came upon a Saracen patrol. Salah ad-Din was known to be a noble leader and had always made a point of releasing ladies of rank when they had been captured by mistake. Yet that no longer mattered now. She had to ensure that

Stephen was not blamed for bringing her here. She knew how much the Templars disliked being forced to come into contact with women. For goodness' sake, they even refused to allow their knights to innocently kiss their own mothers once they had made their vows.

'Call me what you wish,' she mumbled thickly as she licked her dry lips, but there was little moisture in her mouth. 'Do you have any water?'

'I have a soothing drink that will quench your thirst,' the man replied. He gently lifted her head and held a goblet to her lips. Edwina drank greedily of the contents, which had a refreshing fruity flavour.

'Thank you,' she said as he lowered her head to the lumpy pillow again. 'Will you call the comte now – I must speak to him.'

'Soon,' the man said in a soothing voice.

Edwina strangely began to feel a little sleepy again for some inexplicable reason. 'What is wrong with me?' she asked, trying to force herself to stay awake.

'An ague brought upon by the desert heat,' he replied, moving away from the bed.

Edwina heard the sound of a door opening. Her head felt incredibly heavy as she turned to see who had entered, hoping that it was Stephen. Unfortunately it was not him, it was the master, Bernard le Motte. His presence made her feel uncomfortable as his cold dark gaze flickered over her for a moment. 'You have confirmed?' he asked the old man.

'As it said in the papers, it is she,' he said softly.

Edwina strained her ears to hear as Bernard said, 'One of the Turcopoles claims that she followed them and was spying on them as they made camp. What could cause such foolish behaviour? King Guy will be very concerned.'

What had Guy to do with her presence here, Edwina wondered in confusion. She wanted to sit up and ask for an explanation and then demand to see Stephen but she just didn't have the strength. Wearily she closed her eyes for a moment, and she was still trying to think of exactly what to say when sleep overwhelmed her senses again.

9

Clearly he had a hangover. This was Stephen's first thought as he struggled back to consciousness. There was a terrible pounding in his head and his lids felt as though they were glued together, while every muscle in his body screamed in pain. As clarity sliced through his muddled thoughts he realised that he was upright, or as upright as he was able to be. No wonder his arms and shoulders were protesting so much, the entire weight of his body was hanging on them.

He straightened his legs and that helped relieve the agony a little as he became aware, with a chilling blast of consternation, that he was chained hand and foot. What the hell had happened, he asked himself, as he looked at the rough stone walls of the small cell. There was a slight chill in the air so doubtless it was a dungeon somewhere below ground, and no wonder he felt rather cold as he was not wearing a stitch of clothing.

Was it possible that the Saracens had at last managed to break into the fortress and he was their prisoner? That did not seem likely but there was no other explanation for this perilous conundrum. Edwina, he thought with rising fear, what had happened to her?

Confusion mingled with his concern and magnified. Nothing made any sense as he could not figure out who had brought him here and confined him while he was unconscious. He'd no idea what time it was but judging by his aching muscles he had been hanging here for some time. Presumably he was still in Sarak, yet even so there were so many questions he could not answer.

Stephen tried to move his feet but his ankles were manacled and the chains attached to them were fixed to rings in the floor. He looked up. The chains attached to the manacles around his wrists were fastened to a pulley arrangement, so that they could be tightened or loosened at the will of his captors, whoever they happened to be.

He tensed as he heard the rattle of a key turning in a lock. Now he would have answers. He stiffened his resolve, fearing that whatever was to come would be far from easy. To his amazement, Bernard walked into his cell and whatever apprehension he had was replaced with white-hot fury. 'Master Bernard,' he shouted, 'why have I been confined in this humiliating fashion? You'll pay for this,' he added, pulling angrily at his chains.

The cold dark eyes looked him up and down with utter derision. 'We Templars abhor heretics.'

'Heretics!' Stephen exclaimed. 'I am no heretic, this is insane.'

Bernard glanced back at the Templar who hovered by the door. 'Leave us.'

The man disappeared and, as the door shut, Bernard smiled evilly and walked towards Stephen. 'You are confined here because the knights and brothers believe you to be a heretic.'

'And my accuser is?' Stephen challenged, trying to show no fear. Even to be suspected of heresy was troubling enough as it could lead to torture, perhaps even death,

'Your perfidy was revealed by our king, Guy de Lusignan.'

'So this is Guy's doing,' Stephen sneered. 'His words are generated by malice, nothing more. There is no truth in his insane accusations. Release me and I will prove it to you.' Bernard said not a word, so Stephen added, 'You know full well that his accusations are not true, don't you?'

'Truth is in the eye of the believer. I informed the members of my order that you were a heretic and they believe me.'

'I have no idea why Guy did this. We disagree over military matters but that is all,' Stephen argued in frustration.

'You deny then that you plotted with others to wrest the throne from my king.' Bernard circled Stephen like a predator might his helpless prey.

'Of course I deny it – that is as ridiculous an accusation as heresy.' Stephen was greatly troubled by his sheer helplessness. It wasn't a situation he was accustomed to and in this citadel he was surrounded by Templars who answered only to one man, Bernard le Motte. There was no one he could call on for aid apart from Edwina, and he had no idea what had happened to her. Unsure if Bernard yet knew the truth of her gender, he said, 'About my squire.'

'Yes, your squire, I was coming to that.' Bernard now stood so close they were almost touching, and the way he was looking at Stephen made him even more discomfited by his nudity. 'You bring a noblewoman here disguised as a squire and then you proceed to violate her in our guest quarters.'

'Violate!' Stephen exclaimed. 'I did not violate her.' His voice was trembling with indignation. 'She will tell you that herself.'

'Lady Edwina is not in a position to deny the accusations. And even if she were I would have no intention of questioning her about them. It would be far too upsetting for a noble lady to be made to recall such unpleasantness, especially one whom King Guy intends to marry. Her efforts to accompany you here were foolish and lacking in judgement but you had no need to conceal her identity from us so that you could force her to share your room.'

'I didn't force her to do anything,' Stephen shouted. 'And she is not marrying Guy, she is marrying me.'

'You live under great misapprehension, comte. The lady is to become our queen and you violated her.'

'If you believe that then why did she not cry out?' Stephen challenged. 'She had every opportunity to ask for your help.' He knew that he was getting more and more embroiled in Bernard's lies.

'For all I know you drugged her, or used some kind of witchcraft on her to make her accede to your vile lust. After all no woman would choose you above a king. I intend to send her back to King Guy as soon as possible,' Bernard said. 'While you, of course, will remain here as my prisoner.'

'No!' Stephen tried to lunge forwards but he was jerked back by his chains as the iron manacles dug into his ankles and wrists. However, he welcomed the pain, which didn't even come close to the agony in his heart. 'She will never marry Guy,' he said through gritted teeth.

'That is no longer your concern, there are other matters you now have to contend with.' Bernard stepped to the door of the cell and flung it open. 'Come,' he called.

A tall muscular knight entered the cell and in his hand was a whip with knotted leather strands. The man looked Stephen up and down quite impassively. 'He looks strong, he will probably be able to take a fair few lashes. Do I continue until he confesses?'

'No.' Bernard pursed his lips. 'Just a dozen strokes to soften him up a little. I want to take this investigation very, very slowly.'

Isabella was not happy, but then why should she be? Nothing was going to plan and it was all her husband's fault. She shivered at the mere thought of Conrad de Montferrat. She loathed him intensely and rued the day she had married him. Not that she'd had any choice in the matter; she had been coerced into it. Conrad was an old man in her eyes and a grizzled, remarkably unattractive warrior, with rough ways and little delicacy in his manners. He was no fit consort for a princess, let alone a queen. Why couldn't she still be married to her sweet charming Humphrey? Admittedly, he had no real interest in her physically as he was not attracted to women in that way, but he was charming, well read and very sweet natured. They had got on well together and she considered him her very best friend in the entire world.

She looked around her unhappily as she rode into the bailey of the castle of Sarak. It had an unpleasant, melancholy air about it. Although built on similar lines to Kerak it was a very different place. She knew Kerak well; she'd resided there from the age of eleven when she had been sent to the castle to live with the family of her future husband Humphrey de Toron.

Conrad should have taken her to Acre with him but he had stubbornly insisted she stay safely in Tyre. In truth he knew nothing about women because as soon as he had left she had made plans to join him. She was curious to meet the great Lionheart everyone was talking about. Amalric, the captain of her personal guard, had insisted that it would be safer to travel by sea and she had been quite happy when they set out because her journey would take less than a day. All was proceeding to plan until they'd spotted a large number of Saracen vessels. Knowing he would be unable to outrun them, the captain had insisted on taking refuge in the small natural harbour nearby, while she sought protection from the Templars of Sarak.

She jumped down from her horse and strode towards

the steps of the keep. Waiting for her at the door was a very sinister-looking Templar knight. Isabella frowned; she had never been at ease among the Templars, mainly because they were still loyal to her despicable brother-in-law, the infamous Guy de Lusignan.

'Princess.' The sinister-looking Templar bowed and then smiled politely at her. 'I am the Master, Bernard le Motte. We are honoured by your presence.'

She was convinced that he was lying. Most probably he greatly resented her unexpected arrival. 'I trust you will only have to endure it for a short time,' she replied very coolly.

'You may stay as long as you wish. I have arranged suitable quarters,' Bernard said. 'Nevertheless, we live very simply here so there will be none of the luxuries you are used to.'

Over the last few years she had lived a relatively nomadic existence, so she had brought most of what she needed with her. 'No doubt it will suffice,' she said, regally inclining her head.

'I will have food and drink brought to your room,' Bernard said, and she noticed how strange his eyes were – flat, dark and cold. He made her feel uneasy and she certainly didn't trust him. She would leave here as quickly as possible. 'I trust you will also provide suitable accommodation for my soldiers and Captain Amalric?'

'Of course.' Bernard looked towards a plump balding man in a plain black habit. 'Brother Gerard will take you to your room.'

Nodding, Isabella turned in a swirl of turquoise silk and strode into the keep. The interior was dark and surprisingly cool after the intense heat outside. It appeared that her chamber was on the second floor. She followed Brother Gerard up the wide stone staircase, conscious that he began breathing a little heavily before they even reached the top. He led her along a wide corridor and into a large, airy but rather sparsely furnished room.

'This will be perfect.' She smiled sweetly at Gerard who was now panting with exertion.

'If you have need of anything you have but to ask,' he said breathlessly then left, passing Isabella's maid Maria in the doorway.

'Mistress.' Maria looked curiously around the chamber, appearing a little uneasy. Isabella didn't find that surprising as Maria had not served her long and had never been away from Tyre before. Walking to the bed, Maria touched the plain, rather rough woollen blanket. 'The bed is soft enough but the linen will have to be replaced.'

'At least I'll be comfortable although I doubt anyone could rest easy in this place.' Isabella wandered over to the window. 'When the baggage arrives, find the blue silk coverlet and my soft blanket, and put some pillows on the bed as there is nowhere comfortable to sit.'

As Isabella looked down onto the large, remarkably empty bailey, she heard Maria say softly, 'This place has a most unpleasant air about it, don't you think?'

Isabella glanced back at her. 'It has, we will not be staying long. As you know the Templar knights make me feel uncomfortable.'

As she spoke two of her soldiers heaved a large wooden trunk into the room. Maria hurried to open it and began sorting through the contents as Isabella glanced out of the window again. She noticed a couple of men step out of what she thought were the stables. However, they were not Templars; they were dressed in the gaudy uniform of the Turcopoles. 'Did not Captain Amalric say that the only occupants of Sarak were Templars?'

'He did, no other troops at all,' Maria replied rather

distractedly as she pulled the blue silk coverlet from the trunk.

'Strange,' Isabella said thoughtfully as she leant out of the window a little further. Walking out of the entrance of the keep she spied two brothers in dark habits carrying a litter. Was the person they carried ill, she wondered curiously.

As a couple more Turcopoles left the stables, leading a string of horses, the brothers carried the litter past her window and she saw the wounded person more clearly. To her amazement she saw long blonde hair and it became obvious to her that this person was a woman. It appeared to her that they intended to fasten a horse to each end of the litter, presumably so that the woman could be taken from the citadel.

'Princess.' She heard Amalric's deep voice and she turned and smiled warmly at him. The handsome man had been the captain of her personal guard for a number of years.

'Amalric, I need you to do something for me.' She hurried over to him. 'There are some Turcopoles down in the bailey with a woman.'

'Woman? Who?' he exclaimed in surprise. 'Would not something have been said about her when we arrived?'

'I want you to go down there right now and question the Turcopoles, find out who she is. I have a feeling something strange is going on around her. If you have any problems making them answer questions send them to me and don't let the Templars stop you doing what I ask.'

Stephen was fast losing hope, which was unlike him, but he had never found himself in such a powerlessly perilous position before. It was not easy to remain positive when one was chained naked in a dungeon, a captive of the insane Templar Bernard le Motte. His muscles were cramping from the discomfort and there was no respite from his torment. After a time, to relieve the pain in his legs, he had been forced to relax and put most of his weight on his arms again until the agony became too much to bear, and then he'd stood for a time again.

The whipping had been bad but not quite as terrible as he had expected because Bernard had limited it to a few lashes, purely as a precursor for what was to come. Stephen knew that a torturer played on his victim's fears – the anticipation of pain was almost as bad as the torture itself. Fortunately during his punishment he had managed not to cry out, which was good as, judging by Bernard's expression, he enjoyed watching his victims endure pain. He was a zealot of the very worst kind and used the excuse of his religion to carry out his own perverse plans.

Stephen had been in dangerous situations before and always found a way to escape but he could see no way out of this. There was no point on relying on Richard to rescue him, no doubt he was too busy at Acre, and if he did not return it would be presumed that he'd been killed by a Saracen patrol. Salah ad-Din was known to be a very noble man and Stephen thought that at present he would rather be in his hands than in those of the Templar Master.

Once again he let his knees relax, gritting his teeth as his arms and shoulders screamed complaint, while the tension made the skin on his back pull against the lash wounds. His only comfort in all this was that Edwina was at least safe while Bernard believed that Guy wished to marry her. With his fanatical loyalty to his king, he would do her no harm and would ensure that she was safely returned to Acre.

Yet there was no way he would let her marry Guy under any circumstances, so he had to find a way to escape. She was a determined woman so she wouldn't marry the man willingly but she would be forced to if her liege lord, Richard, ordered it. It was possible that if he did not return, Guy might find some way to persuade the Lionheart to let him make Edwina his wife.

Stephen had no idea how long he had been here or even whether it was day or night. There was a dim lantern in his cell, fuelled by a candle. One of the Templars had come in a short time ago to replace the candle and give him a couple of sips of water – not enough to quench his raging thirst, but enough to keep him alive. He brought with him a leather bucket so that Stephen could relieve himself but the man had not unchained him so the experience had been humiliating to say the least.

A while ago he had briefly thought that his torture might be coming to an end. There had been noises outside, a banging on his cell door and raised voices. He'd shouted out in a cracked voice but to his disappointment the mayhem had eventually subsided.

He had tried to question the Templar who tended him about what had happened, but the man had refused to say anything.

The tearing pain in his upper body was getting worse and, to relieve the pressure, Stephen took his weight on his legs again. He let his head fall forwards until his chin rested on his chest and then closed his eyes. It was unlikely he would sleep, but he hoped he might eventually pass out and the agony would subside for a while.

He heard the cell door open but he didn't bother to raise his head or open his eyes; either it would be one of the Templars or Bernard come to gloat, he thought with weary resignation. Then he heard a gasp of horror that could only have come from a woman. 'Edwina,' he croaked through cracked lips, opening his eyes and forcing his head upright.

'No. Not Edwina,' said a soft melodious voice.

He saw an immensely beautiful young woman walking towards him. She looked like an angel but she couldn't be because she had long dark hair and angels were always blonde, weren't they?

'Stephen, is that you?' she said in a troubled voice. He heard her turquoise silk skirts swish softly as she walked towards him. 'Can you hear me?'

A soft hand stroked his cheek.' Yes, I hear you,' he managed to gasp as she held a cup to his lips. It contained only cold water but it tasted better than the finest wine to him.

'Not too fast, drink slowly.' She drew the cup away before he'd finished all the water. Stephen was confused; there was a familiarity about her that he couldn't explain. Brow wrinkling, he stared at her as she glanced at the rather agitated-looking Templar hovering in the doorway. 'Release the prisoner from his chains.'

'I cannot.' The man anxiously wrung his hands.

'You dare refuse me,' she said imperiously, her dark eyes blazing. 'Captain Amalric,' she called out.

That name was familiar also. Stephen tried to remember but pain had muddled his thoughts, holding half-recalled memories trapped beneath the surface somewhere.

'Princess,' the Templar said fearfully, 'there is no need for this. The master says this man is a heretic.'

'There is every need,' she insisted in a tone that allowed no dissent. 'He is no heretic and if King Richard gets to hear of how you have treated one of his most loyal knights he will have you executed.'

'Isabella?' Stephen remembered the pretty dark-haired girl he had once known so well. 'Is it you?'

'Yes.' She smiled affectionately at him. 'I was very taken with you when I was young. Don't you recall that I told you that I would marry you one day?' Memories came rushing back to him while at the same moment she caught sight of the wounds on his back. 'That swine whipped you as well?'

As she spoke, a tall good-looking, brown-haired man pushed the Templar aside and strode into the cell. 'Amalric!' Stephen exclaimed.

'Yes, it has been a long time.' His expression was full of concern. 'Before they departed, your Turcopoles told me that you were here. Yet the Templars denied this and refused to reveal your exact whereabouts so I knew something was wrong. I searched the citadel and came to the conclusion that you might be in this cell. But they would not let me enter until the princess ordered them to do so.' He stepped over to the hook that held Stephen's chains in place. 'I'll lower them slowly.' He glanced over at Isabella. 'We need one of the men to support him; I doubt he'll be able to stand alone.'

'I'll manage,' she said determinedly.

'No, Princess. You cannot hold him up alone,' the Templar said, reluctantly moving to aid them. Bending, he removed the pins that held the manacles in place around Stephen's ankles. 'You hold him captain, and I will loosen the chains. Once the pressure is off his arms, I will release the manacles around his wrists.'

'I will help,' Isabella stubbornly insisted. 'You cannot take his weight alone.'

Amalric positioned himself on the other side of Stephen and placed a supportive arm around his waist. As he felt the chains loosen a shade, Stephen could not stop an anguished groan escaping from his lips. Stepping forwards, the Templar reached up and undid the manacles around Stephen's wrists. His arms dropped limply down and, as the blood flowed into his tortured limbs, the pain returned, different but just as excruciating. He tried to remain upright but his knees sagged, yet Amalric and Isabella held onto him, just managing to bear his weight.

'Princess, you should not be doing this,' he gasped.

'Nonsense,' she said as she helped Amalric lower Stephen onto a straw-stuffed mattress that one of her soldiers had, just at that moment, dragged into the cell.

For a minute or two, Stephen almost lost consciousness as they positioned him carefully until he was lying prone on his stomach. Vaguely, he heard Amalric curse under his breath as he examined the lash marks on Stephen's back. 'Princess, we will have to get someone from the infirmary to attend his wounds.'

'No. They'll not lay a hand on him. I'll tend him myself,' Isabella said. 'Send one of the men for the necessary supplies.' She sank to her knees beside Stephen. 'And you, Amalric, inform Master Bernard that I wish to speak with him urgently.'

Once her men had departed, Isabella glared at the Templar who still lingered in the doorway watching her. 'Get out of my sight if you don't want to endure the wrath I intend to bring down on your master's head.'

Now that his limbs were not being tortured, a measure of clarity was returning to Stephen's mind. Previously the pain had driven all thoughts of modesty from his mind but now it returned in abundance. 'I'm sorry,' he mumbled in embarrassment.

'For what?' She crouched close to his face as she reached for the remains of the cup of water she had left on the floor.

'For being naked.'

'And a most stimulating sight it would have been,' she whispered seductively. 'If I had not been more concerned with your well-being at the time.'

'Isabella –' he strained his neck to look up at her '– are you flirting with me?'

'What, here, in this cell? I might do so if we were in more comfortable surroundings.' She trailed a gentle finger down his back, carefully avoiding the lash marks, until she reached his unmarked buttocks. 'Even like this your body is beautiful, Stephen. You have grown into a remarkably handsome man.' She moved even closer so that he could feel her warm breath on his cheeks. Her hand rested on his buttocks. 'You were way too skinny and rather gangly-looking when I first met you.'

'And you were but an irritating child if I recall correctly,' he said as she kissed his cheek. 'Now you have grown into an extraordinarily beautiful woman.'

Edwina's dreams were more like nightmares because her bed swayed from side to side and jolted now and then, while she felt incredibly hot as if something was burning her face. Yet when she awoke, silence and darkness surrounded her. Then she saw campfires and dark figures moving about before she was taken aback by a strange face looming over her. 'Bashir, she is awake.'

'What's happening?' She sat up. Her head felt fuzzy, her stomach decidedly queasy and the skin on her face was hot and tight as if it had been burnt by the sun. Fortunately she was clad quite demurely in a long shirt and loose-fitting breeches. Yet no one could think she was a boy now as her hair had come loose from its plait and fell around her shoulders and down her back.

'Don't you remember?' The man called Bashir squatted beside her and she recognised him as the Turcopole who had captured her in the oasis only a few days ago – or was it days? She couldn't quite recall. She put a hand to her head. 'The last thing I remember is being in Sarak.'

'The commander of the fortress ordered us to escort you back to Acre. You've been ill and you slept all the way so far.' He grinned and his teeth looked very white in his suntanned face. 'You make quite a convincing boy, my lady.'

'And the comte?' she asked.

'He remains at Sarak to help plan the defence, so the commander Bernard le Motte said.' He frowned. 'Somehow I did not quite believe him and I never laid eyes on the comte before we departed, which I found troubling. There was another man who questioned me about him and you. He wore a uniform I did not recognise. Do you think something might be amiss?'

'I don't know.' She was confused, her brain was not working properly and she was finding it quite difficult to think logically. 'What should we do?'

'If he does not follow us to Acre in a couple of days, I will find his friend Martin. He can speak to King Richard and have more men sent back to Sarak to discover the comte's whereabouts. In the meantime my only concern must be you.' He handed her a goblet which one of the other men had just given him. 'The brother who tended you said that this would help clear your mind when you awoke.'

Edwina took the cup and cautiously sipped the contents, which had a remarkably pleasant flavour. 'Thank you.' She was still smiling at Bashir when she heard a faint, rather high-pitched scream followed by anguished shouts.

'Saracens!' Bashir sprang to his feet. 'Stay here,' he said to her then glanced at his companion. 'Guard her well.'

As he ran off, Edwina tossed aside the goblet. Even the word 'Saracen' caused a shudder of fear to rip through her body, suppressing all the questions about Stephen that still filled her mind. She peered into the darkness, just able to see dim figures fighting each other as she heard angry shouts and swords clashing against swords. Occasionally, she saw a brief flash of light as moonlight caught the slashing blades. Soon, the sounds of battle were intruded upon by the anguished screams of the wounded.

As chaos continued around her, she looked at the Turcopole left to guard her. 'Give me a weapon,' she begged.

Wordlessly, he tossed her a small sharp dagger. It was not what she had expected, a sword would have been better. Perhaps he was right – she knew how to use one but she was a far from proficient swordfighter. Grasping the dagger firmly, she rose a little unsteadily to her feet just as she saw two dark menacing figures running towards her.

'Run,' the Turcopole hissed as more figures followed them. He stepped protectively in front of her. 'It's your only chance. Find somewhere to hide.'

He sounded determined but the tension in his voice told her he feared that all was lost. Judging by the many dark shapes she could see, the Turcopoles were greatly outnumbered and had little or no chance of survival.

Edwina turned and ran, stumbling over the uneven ground, slipping now and then on the sandy soil. If only she could try escaping with shoes on instead of always in bare feet, she thought, her terror tinged by insane amusement. She was forced to slide to a halt as two men unexpectedly stepped in front of her. Realising she was virtually surrounded, she anxiously tried to dart around them. But one managed to grab hold of her and jerked her roughly towards him. Lashing out wildly, her blade sliced into his forearm. He gave a grunt of pain but didn't let go, just wrestled the dagger from her grasp and clamped his fingers around her throat. Gasping for breath, she struggled as his grip slowly tightened.

'Wait!' she heard his companion say in Arabic and to her relief the grip lessened enough for her to take a few strangled breaths. 'Bring a torch,' he shouted to one of his men, who was busy with some of the others examining the dead and wounded.

Fortunately it was too dark for Edwina to see what was happening properly but she heard a man moaning in pain, then there was an unpleasant gurgling sound followed by silence. Clearly they wanted no prisoners and no one left alive. Filled with terror, she tried to close her ears to the terrible sounds of slaughter. Suddenly, her captor threw her to the ground and she crouched there unsure whether it would be better to die or survive.

Edwina blinked nervously as a torch was produced and the flickering flame was held close to her face. 'By the will of Allah,' she heard one man say, 'a woman, with hair like spun gold.' He touched her face and she felt blood from the wound she had inflicted drip onto her cheek. 'We will take her back to Nasir al-Din.'

10

Isabella waited anxiously in her room. It should be time by now. Vespers was long gone, darkness had fallen and the brothers had recently celebrated compline – the last mass of the day. Now the citadel was eerily silent and no one was walking the empty corridors, although there were still guards on the outer walls. She hoped that she was right about all the Templars being asleep as she opened the door and peered out into the dark corridor.

She had been tending to Stephen for three days now. He was strong and was recovering swiftly. The lash marks had crusted over and were starting to heal. Even so the zealous Templar Bernard had refused to free him and they'd had a number of heated discussions during which she had drawn on her rank and regally demanded that he free Stephen. Still he had refused, claiming that he only owed allegiance to the pope, the grand master and to a lesser extent to his king Guy de Lusignan. Stephen was safe enough for now but she doubted he would be when she left Sarak. Then Bernard would start abusing him again. She had contemplated using force to get her way but she didn't have enough soldiers with her to defeat the entire Templar garrison.

Instead she had decided to provide the tools to let Stephen help himself. Recalling the uncanny ability he'd had with locks when she had known him years ago, she'd had Amalric fashion a pair of lock picks which Stephen now had in his possession. If he managed to get out of his cell, as she hoped, he should be reaching her room soon. Here he would be safe at least until she and Amalric figured out a way to smuggle Stephen out of the fortress. Bernard would not dare demand to search a royal lady's room and Amalric knew that he and his men were watched constantly so they could not be implicated. Once Stephen was found to be missing, during the ensuing chaos, Amalric intended to creep out of the fortress and plant evidence which would lead them to believe that Stephen had escaped via the small postern gate, which was used to bring in supplies.

At last she heard a faint noise and she turned to see Stephen, clad in a tattered pair of breeches and a shirt, running towards her. 'Quick,' she whispered, filled with relief. She pulled him inside her room, shut the door quietly and slid the heavy bolt in place.

'The lock was an easy one once I had the tools to pick it.' He grinned as he placed the two metal picks on a low chest.

'No one saw you escape?'

'As luck would have it, the Templar on guard was asleep.'

'There was no luck in that, Stephen.'

He inclined his head. 'I am amazed by your talents, my lady.' Stephen glanced around the room, smiling when he saw the silk throws, pillows and other fripperies. 'I see that you do not travel light.'

'Does any princess?' Isabella had deliberately worn her most provocative gown. It was very low cut and the silk clung to the curves of her body like a second skin. It had been a gift from Humphrey who liked lovely things. Even if he had not been interested in bedding her, dressing her beautifully had been of paramount importance to him. She was certain that Conrad wouldn't notice if she dressed in sackcloth, yet she could feel Stephen's eyes casually perusing her body and she hoped he liked what he saw. He was a remarkably attractive man and, as he looked her up and down, she felt her nipples tighten and a pleasant warmth fill her stomach. Was this the instantaneous sexual attraction that sometimes turned into love? It was something she had never felt before.

'To be truthful I am not acquainted with many princesses,' he said with a teasing smile.

She knew that if she closed her eyes right now she would be able to see him naked as she had a couple of days ago. Even while witnessing his pain and distress, she had been moved by the sight of his muscular body and generously sized sex. She had to admit that she had also been highly aroused even if she had also been a little ashamed of her feelings at the time.

'I thought you would wish to wash.' She pointed to a basin of water. 'It should still be reasonably hot.'

'I suppose a bath is impossible?' he asked with a smile so wicked it took her breath away and turned her legs to water.

'Have you ever met a Templar who confessed to enjoying bathing?' She laughed. 'Most likely they consider it sinful as they appear to do most other things. They are far more devout than the nuns in the convent where my stepsister, Sibylla, was raised. Master Bernard would most likely have a fit if I demanded enough hot water to bathe in. He only endures my presence here and is most eager to be rid of me.'

'And no doubt your concern for my welfare infuriates him.' Stephen walked over to the basin. 'Yet your arrival here proved to be my salvation. Would you mind if I removed my shirt to wash?'

'Mind!' She looked at him in disbelief. 'You were naked when I first laid eyes on you again, so a bare chest will not upset my feminine sensibilities.' She could not tear her eyes from him as he ripped off the filthy tattered shirt, which she would not have expected even a peasant to wear. Isabella watched entranced as he wiped his face, then his chest and under his armpits. Her imagination ran riot, creating sensual visions that made her body ache with desire for him.

He had such firm muscles and taut golden flesh, while his stomach was flat and most probably near as hard as iron. Just recalling the sight of his manly parts made her feel extraordinarily light headed. 'Do not put that back on,' she said as she looked in disgust at his filthy shirt. 'Amalric has left you some of his clean garments. They may be a little tight but they will suffice. However . . .'

'However, what?' he enquired, running his fingers ruefully over the heavy stubble on his chin.

She didn't answer for a moment; she was too focused on the droplets of water glittering like gems on his muscular chest and the tempting arrow of fine dark hair that tracked down towards his groin. 'You need to wash the rest of yourself, do you not?'

'Despite the fact that you have already seen me naked in such untoward circumstances, I cannot willingly stand unclothed in front of you – a royal lady.'

'You are way too honourable.' She picked up a towel and handed it to him. 'If my modesty concerns you, Stephen, then I will turn my back.'

She took a few steps towards the bed and turned away from him. Her ears were attuned to even the slightest sound and she heard what she thought was a faint rustling as he removed his tattered breeches. This was followed by a splash as he wrung out the cloth in the water. Isabella waited until she thought he would be fully engrossed in washing, then glanced furtively over her shoulder just in time to see him carefully wiping his nether regions.

Scared that he might see her looking, she averted her eyes again, unable to control her emotions. Stephen was magnificent and lust consumed her every thought. She'd had two husbands already although she was not yet twenty. Humphrey had bedded her very infrequently, because he felt it his duty, but she had never found it arousing, just awkward and rather embarrassing. More often than not his desire had waned before they'd even reached the point of copulation. Now there was Conrad, who was at least thirty years older than her. She found him repulsive as he was crude, quite ill mannered and only interested in warfare, with no understanding of a young woman like her. Thank goodness he had only bothered to bed her a few times because when he had she'd loathed the uncomfortable experience. Was it so wrong to desperately desire a man and have him desire her as well?

Her thoughts were interrupted by Stephen appearing at her side, a towel wrapped securely around his lean hips. 'The clothes, where are they?'

Gathering her courage together, she turned and put a tentative hand on his shoulder. 'You realise that we will be together in this room for some time. At least until Amalric figures out a way to smuggle you out of the fortress.'

'So it appears.' His expression told her nothing, his stance unresponsive.

Rather nervously, she trailed her hand down over the hard planes of his chest, allowing her fingertips to brush teasingly against one flat nipple. 'Stephen, my life has not pleased me so far. I have been obliged to marry men I did not want or desire.'

'I know that.' His green eyes were focused on her face. 'It could not have been easy for you.'

She swallowed awkwardly, still keeping her hand on his chest, conscious that she could feel the steady beat of his heart. 'I would ask a boon of you.' Isabella suspected that he knew what she wanted, yet he made no attempt to come to her aid and she was forced to continue. 'I am well aware that your heart lies with another and that you are concerned for her safety. I would not wish her to be forced to marry Guy. He is pompous, selfish and untrustworthy, yet even I would find him more agreeable that Conrad.'

'You dislike your husband that much?' he asked gently.

'Yes.' She felt tears fill her eyes and tried to force them back, determined not to weep. 'Princesses have little or no say in their choice of husbands.'

'Yet I believe you cared for Humphrey?' He didn't appear to expect an answer from her. 'You were only twelve when you married him, better half a man such as him than an elderly warrior like Conrad who might not have been concerned about your youthful innocence.'

'I give thanks for that. Humphrey was like a brother to me,' she replied. 'Nevertheless I fear that I will never know what sexual desire is let alone spend a night of passion with a man who desires me. You could change that, could you not?'

Stephen was silent for a moment and she feared that he intended to reject her out of hand. 'So you ask this of me, Isabella, in return for saving my life?'

'I ask nothing that you are not prepared to give.' She turned away from him but tensed as she felt a strong hand clasp her shoulder. Stephen pulled her back and twisted her around. He slid his arms around her waist and eased her closer until her full breasts were crushed against his chest, with nothing between their bare flesh but a sliver of pink silk.

'God forgive me,' he murmured before his lips covered hers, his tongue sliding sensuously into her mouth. She shivered in surprise and reached out to cling onto him as the kiss deepened and became more passionate. Her body seemed to melt as a wild heat coursed through her veins, the warmth of a desire she had never felt before.

Then he was edging her towards the bed, but when he let go of her she had to hold back her cry of dismay, fearing that he had changed his mind. 'Take off your dress,' he said huskily as he discarded his towel.

Isabella's hands trembled as she struggled with the lacings. Stephen gave a soft chuckle and slipped it from her body himself. Men had seen her naked before but never like this in the heat of passion. She blushed shyly as Stephen's lustful gaze raked her naked body. He placed a hand on her breast, then massaged it gently and pulled at the sensitive teat until she gave a pleading moan.

'Tell me again that you want me,' he growled as he eased her down onto the soft mattress, tossing aside the pillows that got in his way.

'I want you,' she whispered rather demurely, although she felt far from demure as his gaze raked her body once more and she shuddered with suppressed excitement. Then he touched her again, his hands tenderly following her soft feminine curves as a wild need invaded every fibre of her being. 'So much,' she murmured as he possessively caressed her breasts, pulling at both nipples until they stiffened and began to ache. Then he fastened his lips around one teat and began to suck on it hard. Isabella's body melted into the mattress as the pulling sensation travelled down her body to her groin.

While his mouth lingered on her breasts, his hands slid downwards to stroke her flat belly, then eased their way between her thighs, sliding into the narrow slit of her sex. As he caressed her secret flesh, she felt the moisture gather there, giving extra fluidity to every smooth movement of his fingertips. Slowly those fingers slid inside her and stroked the soft interior with such sweetly arousing movements that she thought she would go insane with delight. She savoured a pleasure the like of which she had never known before.

So this was lovemaking, she thought distractedly. How wonderful it would be to share pleasure like this night after night. Now that she had tasted the honeyed sweetness of this illicit passion she wanted more.

All of a sudden Stephen removed his fingers, spread her legs wide and, with one smooth movement, replaced his fingers with his mouth. Isabella was utterly taken aback, not knowing something like this was even possible. It felt so wicked and yet so good. Stephen's searching tongue was moist and slippery, the seductive movements playing a magical melody on a tiny nub of flesh she had never know existed before. It felt so blissful. Then, to her amazement, she felt that snake of a tongue wriggle inside her and the pleasure became so perfect she found herself threading her fingers through Stephen's dark hair and pressing his face hard against her sex.

She was climbing towards something wonderful but, before she could reach it, he pulled her back from the brink. He slid his body atop hers, his groin pressing demandingly against hers. Supporting his weight on his strong arms he kissed her again and she tasted the musky flavour of her own secretions on his lips.

'I'll not hurt you,' he whispered, lifting his hips so that he could reach down and guide his engorged cock into the opening of her sex.

Even the tip felt huge and she recalled how large he was even unaroused, far bigger than anything she'd known before and, for a moment, the thought made her body stiffen nervously against his.

'Relax,' he purred as he moved his hips just a shade, gently easing his solid shaft inside her. He proceeded slowly, a finger's breadth at a time, until her body stretched to accommodate his and he was buried to the hilt, his groin pressed close to hers.

Stephen smiled and his green eyes locked with her brown ones as he began to thrust, gently at first then a little harder. Her eyes widened in amazement as she felt the intense sensations, which gradually magnified and grew inside her, layer upon layer, until she thought nothing could get any better.

Yet it did, as she wrapped her arms around him, her palms pressing against his buttocks to encourage him onwards, urging him to pump harder and even more vigorously. Soon she felt it, a powerful sensation, blossoming and expanding like a ripple did when a pebble hit the water until it grew into a powerful wave of wild unimaginable delight. It swept over her, carrying her up into a world of sweet bliss she had never dreamt of let alone experienced before.

In the past Edwina had listened in fascination to Stephen's tales of the harems but she was finding the reality of it all very different. Life here was far more luxurious than she had expected it to be and, to her amazement, the women did not appear used and abused by their master; in fact they seemed extraordinarily happy to be living here.

After a long trek across the desert in the company of grim-faced Saracen soldiers, knowing full well that they had brutally slaughtered the Turcopoles, she had been pleased to arrive at this place, which she learnt the Franks called Ibram. It had once belonged to the most important nobleman in the Latin Kingdom, and now it was ruled by Nasir al-Din, a distant relative of the great Salah ad-Din himself.

She had told her captors that she was a lady of King Richard's court before they had left her here, knowing that she would have to be patient and wait until she was ransomed. It would take a while to send a message to Acre and sort the matter out, so she had accepted that she would have to endure living here for a short while.

When she had first stepped into the harem, beautiful women in outrageously scanty garments had taken charge of her. They had not expected her to speak any Arabic so she had stayed silent and listened to their idle chatter as they led her to a separate bathing facility and stripped off her clothes. The large pool of warm scented water felt like heaven after the grittiness and heat of the desert.

After a long luxurious soak and a hair wash, she had been handed over to a hugely overweight man who had pummelled and massaged her skin with sweet-scented oils. She had been embarrassed by her nudity, of course, but he did not display any desire for her and she'd known instinctively that he was a eunuch. Stephen had told her of the young male slaves who were emasculated at an early age so that they could safely guard the women in the harems.

Her hair had been combed and dried, kohl applied to her eyes and then she had been dressed in a silk skirt and an embroidered bolero that barely covered her breasts. She had been led to a cool shady room, given food and then told in hesitant Frankish to rest. Having no choice, she had done as they asked and surprisingly had slept long and deeply.

Her days henceforth had passed in idleness; the women here seemed to do nothing but eat, sleep and chatter near constantly. Some played music on strange Arab instruments while others danced, but none of them did anything one could consider remotely useful and there were servants to cater to their every whim. No wonder some of them were plump, because they spent their days in happy indolent luxury.

Yet by now Edwina was becoming very bored and she knew every inch of this place because she had walked around it numerous times. The rooms were all exotically decorated, some even with pictures on the walls, and the floors and high-arched ceilings were covered in elaborate mosaics. The harem was constructed around a central courtyard filled with plants and flowers and at its centre was an ornamental pool filled with strange-looking fish.

Today Edwina had been watching the fish for some time as they darted to the surface, gobbling up the tiny insects that landed on the surface of the water. It was getting a little too hot, so she wandered back into the cool interior of the harem. At this time of the day, most of the women slept for a while. She passed plump scantily dressed women snoozing on low couches and upon piles of cushions on the floor. Soon she thought she would go insane with boredom, and her patience began to wane a little. If only someone would tell her how things were progressing – how long did it take for a ransom to be paid, for goodness' sake?

She heard a noise and looked towards the source of the sound, just in time to see a group of people enter the harem through a door which was usually kept locked and was always heavily guarded. It was the same door through which the concubines came and went when they were summoned by their master. All of them appeared quite happy to go and they often returned with generous gifts and elaborate jewellery.

Edwina stared curiously at the woman in the centre of the group, who wore cobalt-blue silk and was far more demurely clad than the concubines. A veil covered her dark hair and the lower part of her face so that only her kohl-ringed eyes were visible. Judging by the amount of gold she wore she was a woman of some importance. She was accompanied by two maidservants and a tall attractive man with skin as dark as pitch, who looked too fit and muscular to be a eunuch.

When the woman spotted Edwina watching them, she walked purposefully towards her. 'Frank, here come,' she said in atrocious French.

There was little point in ignoring her command so Edwina approached the woman and, unsure of the lady's position in the household, curtsied. The woman delicately pulled the veil from her face and rewarded Edwina with a regal smile.

Reaching out she touched Edwina's long blonde hair. 'Like gold, most unusual,' she said in Arabic to the women accompanying her. 'Her skin is unusually pale. Her cheeks have been coloured by the sun but that will soon fade. My lord will like her, I am sure.'

Presumably she was referring to Nasir al-Din, Edwina thought, as she stared at the woman rather curiously. In the West she would be classed as attractive rather than pretty, as she had rather strong features and full lips, while her skin was an appealing dusky-brown colour.

'I do not like the way the Frank is looking at me,' the woman complained.

'My name is Edwina, Lady de Moreville,' Edwina said politely in Arabic.

'You speak our language?' The woman was surprised.

'Not very well,' Edwina admitted. 'To become fluent takes time.'

'Time you now have,' came a reply, which Edwina did not like overmuch.

'I think not. I expect to be ransomed very soon.'

'Ransom?' The woman smiled. 'I came here looking for you, Ed Winna, my lord wishes to see you.'

'Your lord?' Edwina queried. 'You mean your master Nasir al-Din?'

The woman was clearly taken aback by her reply and

the guard interjected coldly, 'You disrespect the Lady Jamilah, she is Nasir al-Din's first wife.'

'My apologies,' Edwina said quickly, recalling that Saracens could take up to three wives if they so chose. 'Would the meeting have anything to do with what is to happen to me? I know that negotiating a ransom can take a long time.'

'You misunderstand, Ed Winna. He now considers you one of his concubines and he wishes you to share his bed tonight.'

Bernard looked irritably at the knight standing in front of him, who had a rather insolent smile on his face. 'So you say that King Guy has changed his mind and now wants the man he calls a traitor freed and you come here to escort him back to Acre?'

Armand nodded. 'I showed you his seal to confirm that I act only for him, did I not?'

'And are you at liberty to tell me why?' Bernard had no wish to admit yet that the comte had somehow escaped. He knew that the princess had helped him but he could not prove it and he was not foolish enough to confront the royal lady when he had no evidence to back up his claim. His men had searched every inch of Sarak and found no trace of Stephen, and Captain Amalric informed him that one of the horses they'd brought from the galley was missing and clothing had also been stolen. He had sent knights out to search the surrounding countryside but all they had found was a pile of discarded clothing; the garments that Stephen had been given to wear in his cell.

'Before I give you my reasons, could you confirm that you have destroyed King Guy's original letter?'

'Of course,' Bernard lied.

Armand nodded. 'Very well. You told me that, when you discovered who she was, you sent the Lady Edwina back to Acre. Well, when she arrived she appeared rather concerned for the comte's safety and King Guy thought it likely that King Richard would send a large contingent of knights here to find his friend. So he wants the comte moved away from here.' Armand looked thoughtfully at Bernard. 'Sometimes it is wiser not to write things down, just in case. Many things can happen between here and Acre,' he added obliquely.

Bernard nodded: so Guy didn't really intend for Stephen to return to Acre, but he was not prepared to put that in writing, which was a wise move in the circumstances. The fewer people who knew of such matters the better. Bernard wondered how he was going to tell this insolent young pup that Stephen had escaped.

Armand de Mirabel strode through the corridors of Sarak filled with fury at the ineptitude of Bernard le Motte. How could a Templar of such standing be stupid enough to let a prisoner escape from his dungeons and then ride out of a heavily guarded citadel unchallenged? Taking a deep breath in order to control his anger, Armand stopped to take stock of the situation, knowing that a change of plan was in order here.

He tapped his finger against the letter he carried. Guy had obtained it from his friend the grand master. It was an order to the Templars to give whatever aid Armand required of them. To be honest he did not think even Guy realised how much power this gave him.

It was logical to assume that the meddling princess had helped Stephen escape. Armand had made a point of learning all he could about Stephen and he was aware that he and Isabella had known each other in the past. Most likely the princess had managed to smuggle Stephen onboard her galley, which was still at anchor close by. However, there was another alterative. Would she have been indiscreet enough to conceal him in her bedchamber, knowing full well that Bernard would never dare to insist on searching there for fear of offending her?

Armand pursed his lips thoughtfully – it was a distinct possibility. Women were not logical creatures and did the most foolish things at times. Isabella was now an extraordinarily beautiful woman, so he'd heard, and she had been forced into marrying Conrad, a grizzled middle-aged warrior who probably displayed little interest in her. On the other hand, Stephen was a very attractive man and very well endowed, he recalled from the visit to the brothel in Messina. Amazingly attractive, Armand thought, allowing his own desires to surface for a moment before he determinedly suppressed them again.

First he had to discover if his presumptions were correct and he knew exactly how to do that. He frowned. Who would Bernard have placed his trust in? Knowing the way the Templar hierarchy worked, it would probably be the chaplain, Brother Gerard. Striding swiftly along the corridor, he tried to remember where the chaplain's quarters were located.

Armand had not been entirely truthful with Bernard. The Templar believed that Armand was working for Guy but he had used the King of the Latin Kingdom just like he used everyone else, in order to follow his own personal agenda. He had come here to get Stephen out of Sarak but he had his own reason for doing so. This war was just as much about politics in Armand's estimation as it was about religion.

As luck would have it, before he had walked very far he spotted his prey in the corridor, waddling towards him. 'Brother Gerard,' he called out, 'I have been looking for you.'

'My lord.' Gerard stopped in front of him, appearing very nervous. 'How can I help you?'

Armand smiled charmingly in an effort to put the man at his ease but his sexual allure didn't appear to work on this fat little man, who continued to stare at him as if he were the spawn of Satan. 'I would like to know the whereabouts of the Princess Isabella's chambers. I feel in the circumstances that I should pay my respects to her before I leave.'

'You leave so soon?' Gerard sounded relieved.

'Now that my quest appears so fruitless, I have no choice but to do so,' Armand replied. 'There is no way I can search an entire desert for one man. The princess . . . ?'

'She is resting. She has spent all her time in her chamber the last few days.' He cleared his throat. 'One can only presume she is unwell. We have orders not to disturb her under any circumstances and she even insisted that her maid be given a separate room.'

'And you did not question this request?'

Gerard shrugged his shoulders. 'Who dares question royalty? They are a law unto themselves. Master Bernard is obliged to treat the princess with great delicacy. Fortunately the captain of her guards tells me she intends to depart for Acre tomorrow.'

'No doubt your master will be relieved?' The polite part of this conversation was at an end. Armand took hold of Gerard's arm, feeling him flinch nervously as he drew the brother towards a window embrasure. 'Do you know what this is?' He placed the grand master's letter of authority under Gerard's nose.

'I do,' he confirmed, looking in anguish at Armand. 'What do you want me to do? Nothing untoward, I hope. I am loyal to Master Bernard.'

'Nothing untoward, to be sure,' Armand assured him. 'Now tell me where the princess is housed.'

'She is in the chamber usually reserved for the grand master when he visits.'

'So you are unable to spy on her then?'

'Spy, my lord?' Gerard said hesitantly. 'I do not know what you mean.'

'It is not just you and Master Bernard who are aware of the tunnels honeycombing this citadel. The grand master knows of them also – so I require you to tell me.'

'That is the reason why that room was selected for our grand master, because there are no hidden tunnels in that part of the main keep.'

Armand smiled and patted his arm. 'How difficult was that? Now if you will but direct me to the princess's room.'

Armand walked along the corridor following Gerard's instructions to the princess's rooms. He paused at the top of the stairs; her room was along that corridor and the plans, which he had memorised just in case, said the entrance was just around here. He stepped into the small chamber, which contained freshly laundered garments for the garrison, then closed and bolted the door so that he would not be disturbed. Only those who built Sarak knew of this particular tunnel; that knowledge had not been passed on to the Templars, and he had no idea why. It was fortunate that he had the necessary resources to discover such well-kept secrets.

He moved aside a pile of clean shirts. According to the plan, the entrance was on this wall – he just had to find it. Armand examined the plain dark-wood panelling, unable to see any sign of a concealed door. Gently he tapped the wood until the tone sounded a little hollow and he thought he might have found the right spot. He applied a little pressure but nothing moved. Clearly this had not been opened for years. He examined the panelling more closely until he saw a fine line, which might be mistaken for a flaw in the wood. It was clogged with dirt. Wincing with disgust, he ran one carefully tended fingernail down the narrow gap until he had removed a thin serpentine line of grime from the crack. Pushing harder this time, he heard a slight squeak as the panel moved, gradually displaying the tunnel he had been seeking behind it.

Armand had nothing to light the tunnel, so he knew that he would have to find his way as best he could using the daylight from the small room. Opening the panel as wide as possible, he stepped cautiously into the tunnel, which smelt rank and stale. As he walked, his feet disturbed the dust of many ages, sending motes into the air, which clogged his nostrils and made him want to sneeze. He could hear a strange rustling sound, which he suspected were piles of dead insects that he was crushing beneath his boots as he walked.

Armand moved deeper into the tunnel until he found a small panel of wood on the wall, which made a slight grating sound as he pulled it aside. He put his eyes to the holes but disappointingly all he saw was a pretty maidservant sitting in the window intent on her sewing. Sliding the panel shut, he moved on but the light didn't reach this far and now he was stepping into total blackness, which was quite disorientating. It meant he had to run his hands along the stones at eye level until he found the next set of spyholes. The wood of the panel appeared to be crumbling slightly and he slid it aside with great delicacy.

His presumptions had been correct. Bernard had been foolish to believe that the princess would never think to conceal Stephen in her bedchamber. There he was, standing close to the window. Armand swallowed hard and pressed his hands against the stones in front of him – Stephen was not wearing one stitch of clothing and he looked magnificent.

Armand had never been one to differentiate, he was drawn equally to both men and women and he had been attracted to Stephen the moment he had laid eyes on him. He would never have admitted that to anyone; knowledge like that made one vulnerable. The princess might have acted foolishly but she had good taste in men and he recalled how she had looked when he'd last seen her – a rather plain-looking, tiny scrap of a child. My, how she had changed, he thought, as she rose naked from the bed and walked towards Stephen. She looked like some exotic goddess of old. She was indeed remarkably beautiful, with pale skin, long black hair and a stunningly voluptuous figure. He couldn't blame Stephen for being tempted by her: what man wouldn't be?

When Stephen turned towards her, Armand saw the lash marks on his back and he frowned. Bernard had far exceeded what Guy had asked of him and Armand was not altogether happy about that. Guy had hoped that with Stephen out of the way Edwina would eventually succumb to his charms and agree to become his queen, but he was stupid enough not to have thought beyond that and make further plans for the future disposal of his rival. Armand had known from the start that Guy was lacking in many skills including those of planning and leadership. To be honest he did not even like Guy very much but he had been extraordinarily easy to manipulate so far.

Armand had always enjoyed voyeurism; it was a titillation of the senses. He watched entranced as Isabella passionately kissed Stephen. Then she sank to her knees in front of him, tenderly caressing the sac of his balls, while she curved her hand around his generous shaft and pumped it gently. It grew and hardened almost instantaneously. She smiled, and then slid her full pink lips over the bulging tip, gradually drawing it deeper into her mouth.

Gripping the stones hard, Armand shivered with desire, so wanting to be there with them, tasting the delights of both their bodies. He could feel his arousal growing as Isabella slid her lips up and down the rigid shaft, while Stephen groaned and threaded his hands through her jet-black hair. Armand was tempted to stay and watch and masturbate himself to a climax but he had other matters to attend to before he could indulge in such pleasurable pastimes. He was frustrated, there was no denying that, as it had been so long since he'd tasted another's flesh. There had been little or no opportunity for sexual encounters since reaching Acre and he was fastidious enough to avoid visiting the rough and ready creatures who served the common soldiers of the camp.

Forcing himself to pull away, he began to edge back along the tunnel. It was a relief when he stepped back into the sunlight-filled room and he was able to breathe fresh air again. Brushing the dust from his surplice, he picked up a clean towel and wiped the grime from his face and hands. Tossing the soiled towel in the tunnel, he pushed the door shut and concealed it with a large pile of linen.

It didn't take long for him to make his way to Isabella's room. He knew he would be intruding on their lovemaking but they'd been alone long enough the last few days to satisfy all their rabid sexual appetites. He rapped on the princess's door, hoping no Templars were lingering surreptitiously close by to hear him. A door opened further along the corridor and the maidservant walked anxiously towards him.

'My lord, the princess does not want to be disturbed.'

'I have been sent here by King Richard. I need to speak to her urgently,' he said in a loud voice as he knocked harder.

Eventually, he heard the sound of a bolt being drawn back and the door opened a crack. Armand could just see the princess, her face flushed with sexual desire, her hair in disarray. 'What is amiss?' she asked imperiously.

'I need to speak to you in private.'

'Not now.' She went to push the door shut but he acted too quickly, putting his shoulder to it and forcing it open.

She stepped back, eyes wide in fearful surprise as he barged into her bedchamber. The maid moved to follow him but he pushed her back and slammed the door in her face, then slid the bolt in place. Immediately, he turned to look for Stephen but the comte was better prepared than he had expected. Armand tensed as he felt the tip of a sword blade pressed to his throat.

'Armand! What are you doing here?' Stephen, clad only in a pair of breeches, said in surprise, as he continued to keep his sword pointed as Armand.

'Forgive me, Princess. I am Armand de Mirabel. Unfortunately the blade at my neck prevents me from bowing.' Armand glanced at Isabella, who didn't appear overly embarrassed that she was dressed just in a loose robe. 'I am pleased to see, Stephen, that you've not perished somewhere in the desert as Master Bernard led me to believe.'

'You haven't answered my question,' Stephen pressed.

'It appears I interrupted you both at a rather inopportune moment,' Armand said coolly, certain that Stephen had no intention of harming him. 'I apologise for that also. But my intrusion is necessary, Princess, if you want your ... er ... friend, Stephen, to get safely away from Sarak.'

'Why would you want me safely away from here?' Stephen clearly did not believe him. 'I've suspected for a while that you are working with Guy, so don't deny it. And it was Guy who got me into this perilous situation. I'm not a fool, Armand.'

'I never thought you were.' Armand swallowed; if he moved even a fraction the blade would pierce his flesh.

The broadsword was heavy but so far Stephen's muscular arm hadn't wavered at all. 'Would you mind if I made myself more comfortable?' He looked towards a nearby chair. 'You can tie me down if it would make you feel safer.'

'I'm faster than you, Armand. You'd be dead before you'd even have drawn your sword.' Stephen lowered the blade. 'Sit.'

Armand moved forwards and sat down, lacing his hands in his lap. 'As you say, I've been working with Guy – it was he who sent me to Sicily because he wanted one of his men close to Richard. However, as I got to know the Lionheart I began to respect him immensely; he is a remarkable man and a great warrior. Guy foolishly lost his kingdom to the Saracens but I truly believe that Richard is capable of defeating Salah ad-Din and recapturing Jerusalem and I intend to do all I can to help him.'

'Go on,' Stephen prompted, appearing quite unmoved, which irritated Armand as for once he had more or less spoken the truth.

'As far as your imprisonment in Sarak goes, you know that Guy planned all this to keep you out of the way for a while?'

Stephen nodded and glanced back at Isabella before he said, 'Because he has set his sights on Edwina.'

'Just so.' Armand nodded. 'However, he puts his throne in peril by doing so. King Richard is your friend and if he discovers Guy planned all this –'

'Presupposing I survive,' Stephen interjected.

'That is why I am here. I have made a decision. I no longer own any allegiance to Guy: he is a fool and not worth serving. Now I pledge my sword only to King Richard the Lionheart and his loyal knights, which of course includes you.'

11

'This is ridiculous, I am not one of his concubines,' Edwina insisted anxiously as the two maidservants stripped off her clothing, while the Lady Jamilah watched calmly, displaying no emotion. Edwina supposed she could have put up a fight, but no doubt then the guard would have intervened and that would have been even more humiliating. 'Please stop them, my lady.' Edwina looked pleadingly at Jamilah as she tried unsuccessfully to cover her nakedness with her hands.

'You are a concubine, because my husband deems it so,' Jamilah said firmly, displaying not one iota of jealousy. 'You exist now purely to give him pleasure.'

Edwina straightened, and no longer tried to cover herself because it was a fruitless exercise. 'I am a noble-woman. A lady of King Richard's court, and I am betrothed to one of his most trusted lieutenants.' Desperation, unfortunately, made her voice waver a little. 'The Lionheart will pay a generous ransom for me.'

'Nasir al-Din is wealthy enough already. He has no need of Frankish gold,' Jamilah replied as the guard picked Edwina up and plonked her down on the large bed.

He held her there firmly, taking hold of one of her flailing arms so that the maidservants could lash it to one of the posts of the bed with silken cords. Soon her other arm was tied as well and she looked helplessly at Jamilah. 'Does this not trouble you?'

'Why should it?' Jamilah asked, her expression betraying none of her thoughts. 'Ed Winna, usually my husband takes his time. He likes his women to be fully instructed in all ways of pleasing a man.' She sighed. 'For some reason he has decided that he cannot wait for that and he has decided to take possession of you this very night.'

Jamilah looked at the guard, who immediately forced Edwina's legs apart so that the maids could also fasten her ankles to the end posts of the bed. This was even more humiliating than she feared it might be as everyone in this room could see the most private parts of her body. Jamilah stepped forwards and looked thoughtfully at her sex.

'Your body hair should have been removed by now, but it is even paler than the hair on your head so it is not wholly unattractive. Perhaps this new diversion might give my husband an extra facet to his pleasure. Come,' she said to the servants and they and the guard followed her from the room.

Edwina had not given in to her fate quite yet. She pulled at her bonds, jerking them as hard as she could in an effort to free herself, but her struggles were to no avail. She heard the door open and, unable to face her humiliation, closed her eyes. It could only be Nasir al-Din who entered, and she feared to see what he looked like. For all she knew he could be an ugly-looking fearsome Saracen warrior or a disgusting old man.

She heard someone moving towards the bed but she still kept her eyes firmly shut, embarrassed by the obscene way her body was displayed. For a moment there was nothing but silence and she tried to remain in control of her shattered emotions. Yet she still jumped nervously when she felt a hand trail across her stomach and down the curve of her hip.

'There is no need to be afraid,' he said in a deep voice that sounded as smooth as silk. For a second she had not realised that he had spoken to her in fluent French tinged with just the faintest of accents. Part of her was curious to see this man – after all she was expected to couple with him – yet a voice was nothing to judge someone by and she feared she might find him repulsive. 'Will you not look at me?' he asked as a firm hand took hold of her chin and turned her face towards him.

Very reluctantly, she opened her eyes and found herself staring at a young, surprisingly attractive man, probably about the same age as Stephen. Of course, he looked like a Saracen, with dark olive skin, black hair and dark eyes, and like all Moslem men he wore a beard, but it was small and neatly trimmed. Edwina had not expected him to be this good-looking and, although his face was square jawed and his features inherently masculine, there was a gentleness in his expression that made her feel just a little less terrified. Nevertheless she knew that, like voices, looks could be deceiving.

'Do you want to converse in your language or Arabic?' he asked her.

'I didn't think it was conversation you had in mind.' Judging by his response to her words he wasn't used to women being this brutally frank with him.

'Edwina.' He smiled. 'There is far more to lovemaking than mere sex. Communication is also a part of it. Now answer my question.'

'How could anyone conduct a conversation in such a humiliating position?' When he didn't answer but continued to stare at her expectantly, she added, 'I do not speak Arabic that fluently.'

'Then today it will be French, which pleases me.' He sat down on the side of the bed. 'My father held a noble Frankish lord hostage for a couple of years. It was from him I learnt to speak your tongue. He was a clever man, a knight of some standing, and I liked and respected him.'

He did not have to tell her this and she had no idea

why he was doing so. If he wished to put her more at ease all he had to do was untie her. 'I too am a hostage, am I not?'

'Yet you are no knight,' he said with a teasing smile, as he ran his fingers through her pale silken locks.

'Yet you could still ransom me. I've heard that Salah ad-Din never keeps noblewomen captives: he always frees them with or without payment of a ransom.'

'I may choose to follow Salah ad-Din but he is not my liege lord. I am my own man and I do what I like. And I have chosen to keep you for myself.'

'Will you not at least untie me?' she pleaded. Now that he was close to her she could smell an exotic spicy odour on his skin that was quite tantalising to her senses.

'Untie you?' He chuckled. 'The man who captured you told me you were a wildcat. I hear that you wounded him – cutting him quite deeply.'

'I was only defending myself,' she argued. 'I have no weapon now. What harm can I do to a great warrior such as you?'

'A wildcat with a silver tongue.' He ran his fingers down her cheek. 'I prefer to keep you tied and that is an end to it. My women do as I command; I allow no dissent.'

He stood up and slipped off his elaborate robe. Beneath it, to her consternation, he was naked. Foolish woman, what else did you expect? Yet he was, she noticed, a fine figure of a man with the muscular build of a warrior. Unbidden, her eyes slid downwards; his generously sized cock and balls were surrounded by a black ruff of pubic hair. She was tempted to look closer because his penis appeared a little different from Stephen's, but she wasn't sure why and she didn't want to keep staring at him.

'Do I disappoint you?' He seemed amused by her curious examination.

'That is a question for me to ask you, is it not, my lord?' There was no point in fighting the inevitable, she knew that now. She was aware that men responded to honeyed words better than resistance, but she had no wish to become like his other servile, obedient concubines. 'Tell me – do I disappoint you?'

'Jamilah would never have had you brought here if she suspected you might not please me. I have never had a Frankish concubine before. I will be interested to discover how passionate Western women are.' He ran his hands caressingly over her breasts, then played with her nipples, rolling them between his finger and thumb until they stiffened. He did not repulse her: she found him quite attractive, but she did not want him and that was an end to it, so she felt no desire, just a mute kind of acceptance as he toyed with her breasts. Perhaps if she remained unmoved he would decide he did not want her after all.

Nasir replaced his fingers with his lips and, as he lashed her nipples with his tongue and then sucked on them tenderly, she at last felt just the faintest flicker of response from her body. Yet she did not want it so she fought to remain unmoved.

'Fear does not nurture desire, does it, Edwina?' he said softly. 'Yet I do promise that you have no need to fear me. Your life can be pleasant here and far more comfortable than the battlefield of Acre.'

Perhaps he sensed that she did not wish to reply. She modestly tried to pull her legs together, until the silken ropes dug deep into the skin of her ankles. Desperation and the fear that this man could eventually make her desire him, forced her to pull even harder against her bonds, as he pressed the palm of his hand against her pubic mound and ran his fingers through the blonde hair that guarded the entrance to her most private parts.

'Please no,' she couldn't help saying.

'Don't fight the inevitable,' he purred as his fingers gently explored the slit of her sex. 'Your body is made for pleasure.'

She could have argued against this and told him that it was hers alone to control and did not belong to him. Nevertheless she sensed that he wouldn't listen to her. Women were lesser mortals in his eyes. Also she had to admit that she didn't find his intimate caresses that unpleasant, even if she had no wish for her body to react to them. In an effort to keep her thoughts away from sex, she stared up at the ceiling, focusing on the elaborate carvings and trying to pretend that he wasn't touching her.

So far she had succeeded and she knew that she was still dry and not ready for intercourse. However, it appeared that Nasir was equally determined to make her respond to him. He moved to crouch between her legs, leaning so close to her sex that she felt his warm breath brush the sensitive skin of her inner thighs. He spread the lips wide with his fingertips so that every part of her secret pink flesh was open and exposed to him.

Trying to ignore what he was doing to her, she concentrated hard and attempted to count the lacy patterns on the ceiling, yet she still jumped in surprise when she felt something as light as thistledown brush against her most intimate parts. It tantalisingly caressed her clitoris, the most acutely sensitive part of her body. The touch was insubstantial yet highly erotic and whispering fragments of pleasure set her nerves alight.

'Do you like that?' she heard him say and curiosity made her glance down at him.

She saw Nasir drawing the tip of a brightly coloured

feather over the interior of her sex lips and once again teasingly across her clitoris. Tiny tendrils of desire wriggled their way inside her, and she shivered at the strangely different sensations. 'Not at all,' she lied.

He smiled. 'Your body betrays you, Edwina,' he said using the feather again and, as the fronds brushed her sex, she felt the sensations grow and expand like the roots of a strange exotic plant worming its way into every part of her body.

'If you untie me, you can see how passionate I can become,' she challenged invitingly.

'I do not need to untie you; I have all I need right here.' He dropped the feather and dipped his fingers into a small pot which had been left beside the bed. Tenderly, he anointed her sex with the slightly sticky ointment and, as it touched her sensitive inner flesh, she felt an odd tingling sensation, followed by a surge of something far stronger.

'What have you done to me?'

'You Franks are so strange. You think that sex is somehow sinful, yet it is one of mankind's greatest delights. My only aim is to help you see that it can bring you nothing but bliss.'

'We only equate sex with love.' She tried to ignore the sudden aching desire to be touched down there again and for his fingertips to continue on their sweet sensual exploration of her body.

'Yet you marry for power and wealth, not love,' he challenged, seeming only entertained by her reluctance to submit to him.

By now the strange fire the ointment generated was working its way deep into her sex and up into her groin. She now wanted him desperately; well, her body did, even though her mind resisted such wildly outrageous demands. She struggled to ignore the lust he was arousing in her as he moved astride her hips until his cock and balls were resting warm and heavy on her upper stomach.

'I would like to put my shaft into your mouth, so that your lips can make love to me,' he said huskily as he leant towards her. The tantalising smell of his spicy-scented skin filled her nostrils.

'Then why not do so?'

'Because you have sharp teeth.' He kissed her gently on the lips and she was tempted to open her mouth and let this kiss become more passionate, yet she had a stubbornness inside her that made her continue to resist. Still she could not totally ignore the fact that the ointments he had used were stimulating her senses in a most peculiar way. 'And I have not enough trust in you as yet.'

He curved his fingers around the root of his cock and rubbed it briskly. She watched it grow into a rigid rod. Now she knew why it looked so different; there was no ring of extra flesh to protect the tip and the head was already fully exposed.

Nasir must have suddenly realised what was confusing her because he gently touched the tightly stretched skin on the domed head of his cock with his index finger. 'It is part of our beliefs. They cut away the excess skin when we are young boys. It increases sensitivity and makes intercourse even more enjoyable for a man.'

'But not a woman,' she responded as her heart beat faster and she tried to pretend that his warm flesh wasn't pressed intimately close to her.

'Let us see.'

He moved, positioning himself between her thighs, and Edwina had never felt more powerless or exposed. Yet the silken bonds were almost invigorating in a perverse way because she had no choice but to submit to his sensual demands and she knew now that he had no intention of harming her. Despite all her determined thoughts to the contrary, this man was fully capable of arousing her senses and making her desire him.

She had often fantasised about Stephen tying her hands before he made love to her but unfortunately she had never been bold enough to suggest it – apart from that night in the oasis – and now it was too late. Too late for everything she cared about, it seemed. She couldn't be that many leagues from him but she was in a different world where nothing was the same as it had been before and most likely would never be again.

Maybe if she hadn't been so helpless, Nasir wouldn't have been so aroused, but judging by the size of his cock now, he clearly was. She felt it press demandingly against the mouth of her sex, then with one smooth thrust the shaft was buried deep inside her and his hips bore down on hers. The burning lust the ointment had caused, coupled with the sensation of fullness, made her draw in her breath in surprise. She couldn't contain her soft sigh as he started to move, thrusting into her hard and fast like a man possessed. The sensations grew more powerful, rising swiftly and strongly inside her. Yet she didn't want to climax as she was convinced it would be a betrayal of the love she felt for Stephen.

All of a sudden, Nasir lifted his body a little, taking the pressure off her hips. Yet he thrust even harder, while his hand reached down between them and his finger pressed demandingly against her engorged clit. That, coupled with the stimulation of the ointment, set her senses alight, sending a burning flame through her body, which ignited into an orgasm that swept through her like an all-consuming fire.

Stephen was not at all sure he was doing the right thing, but what other choice did he have if he wanted to get out of Sarak in one piece? Isabella had originally planned to smuggle him out of the fortress dressed as one of her soldiers. But their helmets left their faces bare and, with his features uncovered, it was likely he would be recognised, and no doubt Bernard would have no compunctions in imprisoning him again. On the other hand, Armand had the parchment from the grand master, assuring him of the Templars' aid, so even if they did recognise him Armand had the power to prevent them taking him captive again.

Nevertheless, Stephen did not trust Armand. He was one of those men who oozed charm and sincerity but one could never be sure if he was telling the truth or not. Stephen tightened his hold on his reins, pleased to be at last seated on his warhorse and dressed in his own armour once again. At least his helm concealed most of his features and, like Armand, he wore the deep-blue, gold-crested tabard of the knights of Jerusalem. Now he looked no different from the knight who had accompanied Armand into Sarak. He had been left behind and it had been arranged that he would leave the fortress with Isabella's forces on the morrow.

Still he felt uneasy, forced to rely on the one man he neither liked nor trusted. Yet no one challenged them as they rode through the gate and across the drawbridge. Urging their mounts into a faster canter, they rode away from the place Stephen had no wish to ever return to again.

'See, was that not easy?' Armand looked back at Stephen and smiled. 'You should have had more confidence in me.'

Stephen nodded. 'Remarkably easy.' He was aware that he had to keep his wits about him from now on.

'The men who escorted me here are camped over the next ridge.' Armand pointed in the direction as he slowed his mount to a trot.

'I give thanks for your help,' Stephen said, manoeuvring his horse so that he was riding beside

Armand for a moment. 'However,' he said ruefully, 'Princess Isabella changed her mind at the last moment and begged me to accompany her instead of travelling overland. After all that she has done for me I could not in good conscience refuse her request.' As he wheeled his horse around, he shouted, 'I'm sorry. I'll see you back in Acre. May God be with you, Armand.'

According to Amalric, the narrow track that led down to the small natural harbour lay in a valley to the south west of Sarak. At the end of the valley, close to the shore, some of Isabella's men would be waiting to take him and his warhorse on board. As he galloped towards it, Stephen thought that Armand would not be altogether surprised by his actions. He had made it very clear to Armand that he found it difficult to trust him. Despite all Armand's assurances Stephen couldn't quite believe that he had come all this way just to rescue him. He suspected that Armand had his own secret agenda, which might or might not involve Guy.

He slowed his mount a little as he reached an area of stone-strewn terrain, not even bothering to glance back to see if Armand was following him. In truth he did not know if he was friend or enemy but if it came to a fight, Stephen knew he was the better and more experienced warrior. Nevertheless he hoped it would not come to that.

His horse's hooves raised a swirling cloud of dust as he descended the track into the valley. It was very narrow in places so he slowed his pace to a steady trot. However, when he rounded a sharp bend in the track, he caught sight of a large group of horsemen some distance ahead of him.

'Saracens!' Stephen pulled his horse to an abrupt halt and turned swiftly, in a skitter of stones and dust, hoping they hadn't yet spotted him. He was greatly outnumbered and he had only two choices – run or fight. Stephen drew his sword, urging his mount back along the path he had just traversed, knowing he would have to chance going back to Sarak to warn Amalric, otherwise Isabella and her men might walk into a trap.

He saw Armand approaching him but he was some distance away as yet. 'Run,' he yelled, hoping he was in earshot. 'Saracens close behind me.'

Armand drew his sword but stupidly continued riding towards Stephen, not away to safety. It was then that Stephen saw another group of Saracens chasing after Armand and he realised why he hadn't turned back. He glanced anxiously to his right, aware that here the sides of the narrow valley were so steep it would impossible for a mountain goat, let alone a horse, to climb. They had no choice but to stand their ground and fight. He looked back to see the other Saracens coming up behind him quite fast.

As Armand drew almost abreast of him, now also brandishing a sword, Stephen shouted, 'We have to fight, there's no retreat.'

Armand gave a loud unintelligible yell and astonishingly rode straight at him, slashing his blade downwards, and just missing Stephen's mailed fist. There was a loud scraping sound as blade skittered down blade. 'Damn you, fool! The Saracens, not me!' Stephen yelled angrily.

Armand just wheeled his horse around and attacked Stephen again. 'Put down your weapon,' he screamed as he slashed wildly at Stephen.

Stephen was the stronger man and easily parried the blow. Enraged by Armand's stupidity, he slammed the heavy hilt of his sword down hard on the young man's hand, forcing him to loosen his hold on his weapon. As it fell to the ground, Stephen shouted in fury, 'God's blood, Armand. What are you playing at?'

In response, Armand turned and galloped straight

towards the advancing Saracens, who had now slowed their mounts to a steady walk. Stephen was surrounded, totally outnumbered. There was no way to escape a fight and he thought Armand had lost his mind completely until he saw the Saracens part to allow him through. Then, to his consternation, Armand turned and joined the enemy.

Stephen felt adrenaline-fuelled battle lust fill his veins as he swore under his breath, vowing to kill as many of them as possible, starting with the traitor Armand. He tightened his hold on his broadsword, holding his horse in check, waiting for just the right moment to launch his suicide attack.

Armand raised his hand. 'Surrender, Stephen,' he yelled, his voice echoing eerily around the valley. 'I have no wish to harm you.'

'Harm me,' Stephen snorted in disgust, furious that he'd trusted this Saracen spy. 'I'll fight and die rather than surrender.'

'You will not.' Armand nodded to his companions and a number of them raised their bows and pointed their arrows at Stephen. 'I do not lie. They have orders to take you alive, so my men will just shoot your horse from under you. I assure you there is no way you will escape.'

Still swearing angrily under his breath and heaping a multitude of curses down on Armand's head, Stephen reluctantly threw down his sword.

Edwina, now dressed a little more demurely in a long pink silk undergown and a short elaborately embroidered tunic, walked into Nasir's chambers. These rooms had become very familiar to her over the last few days as he never seemed to tire of her company.

To those around her she appeared to have accepted her fate, although deep inside she still railed against it. Nasir had released her from her bonds as soon as he had taken her for the first time and surprisingly she had not been bundled back to the harem, but had remained with him all night. As he had slumbered beside her, she had reluctantly been forced to admit to herself that she had not disliked having sex with Nasir, and when he had taken her again in the morning she had relaxed and enjoyed the experience. Although sex it was; she could never consider it lovemaking, because she didn't care for him as she did Stephen.

It was strange, she considered, as she sat down on the bed and looked at Nasir, who was sitting a table reading some official parchments: she had never realised how stimulating and satisfying sex could be for a woman even when her heart wasn't involved.

Oddly enough she had come to like Nasir, who was an extremely intelligent and cultured man – not at all what she had expected a Saracen nobleman to be. He thought very differently from her but he was an interesting and charming companion and their relationship was not based purely on sex: he appeared to enjoy spending time with her as well. When she had told him how bored she was in the harem, he had arranged for a teacher so she could improve her spoken Arabic and learn to read and write it as well.

Yet, despite this, she missed not having friends, as even in a harem full of women she had not been able to become close to any of them. There were undercurrents she had never noticed when she first arrived: small groups of women banded together against each other and disagreements were caused by petty jealousies and arguments over who had the nicest clothes or most expensive jewellery. Now that she was installed as a favourite and had a far more important position in the harem, they either treated her with disdainful resentment or tried to become her new best friend because she had influence with their lord and master. She was relieved, therefore, that Nasir had now arranged for her to have her own suite of rooms so that she could shut herself away from them, although the rooms were already overflowing with the many gifts of clothing and jewellery he had given her.

'Did you enjoy your lessons today?' Nasir set aside the parchment he was reading and turned to look at her.

'Very much.' She smiled and relaxed back among the cushions, thinking that he looked very handsome today; his dark-green burnous suited his colouring.

'Your teachers tell me that you learn remarkably quickly for a woman.'

She laughed. 'I doubt that is true. Not all women are bereft of brains, my lord.'

'The women I know are not interested in matters that concern men,' he said pensively. 'You are unlike other women, Edwina. You have the mind of a man in a woman's body. I find it a tantalising combination.'

'You've not met many Frankish women but I assure you that there are others like me. King Richard's mother, for instance. She is a great diplomat and one of the most respected women in Christendom. And his sister, Joanna, is far cleverer than I.'

'Come here.' Nasir beckoned to her.

All her instincts told her to refuse, but she stood up and walked towards him. Edwina saw no point in disobeying Nasir on such an inconsequential matter. She didn't know him well enough just yet to gauge how he might react if she did disobey him. There was always the possibility that he might withdraw her lessons as punishment.

'I was thinking,' she said cautiously as he pulled her onto his lap.

'That's all you ever do.' He smiled indulgently at her.

'Once I have learnt Arabic, I should like to try to learn more about your people and your culture.'

'And you could study our holy book?' He kissed her cheek and stroked her golden hair, which he insisted she always wear loose around her shoulders. 'That would please me greatly.'

'Your wish is my command,' she said with a teasing smile. 'In return you could perhaps allow me to visit the market with some of the other concubines. Even perhaps ride with you sometimes?'

'One step at a time, my dove.' He eased up her skirt so that he could caress her thighs, then slipped his hand between them. Edwina shivered with pleasure as his cool fingers invaded the warm valley of her sex, gently stimulating her until she gave a moan of delight. 'The first time I touched you here, you were dry and unresponsive. Now your body becomes moist immediately.' He sounded pleased. 'It appears that Western women are passionate after all.'

'Yes it does,' she managed to gasp as his searching fingers slid inside her and began to move in a most tantalisingly seductive way.

'Do you want me?' he whispered against her cheek.

'You know I do,' she murmured as he somehow managed to stand up, while continuing to hold her in his arms.

He must be extraordinarily strong, she thought, as he carried her to the bed and laid her down upon it. She watched him with rising anticipation as he stripped off his burnous and joined her.

'If you want me, you can have me.' He began to undo the tiny buttons that ran down the front of her tunic, ripping them in his haste to remove her clothing.

* * *

It seemed to Stephen that they had been travelling for days, barely resting at all, and he was feeling exhausted. He didn't find the searing heat as easy to cope with as the Saracens did, especially while carrying many pounds of chainmail on his body. Most of the Saracen cavalry who accompanied him wore only lightly padded garments designed for this climate, as they relied more on their speed and manoeuvrability than strength. His mail was chafing his skin in places, as he had had no chance to remove it, let alone undress and wash since they set out. He was chained hand and foot when they did stop to rest and, even while riding, Stephen's wrists were kept permanently manacled together.

They had crossed the desert and the fertile plains of Sephora, riding through almost endless green fields, orchards of olive trees and acres of sugar cane; it was a verdant part of the country with good supplies of water. Now, only a couple of hours later, they were climbing out of a barren valley. The hills of Nazareth were just to the south of them and, as they reached the top of the ridge, Stephen saw the desolate place known as the Horns of Hattin. Well over three years had passed since the battle but all around him were the sad remnants of the defeated Christian army. Just by the side of the track was a skeleton of a horse, and in every direction were piles of human bones, picked clean by the vultures, which still circled high in the sky. Just ahead he saw another skeleton, this one still clad in its rusting chainmail, with a decapitated head lying alongside it, still wearing its battered helmet.

'It is a sad sight, is it not?' he heard Armand say, and he looked to up to see the man he now loathed urging his mount forwards to ride beside him. This was the very first time Armand had spoken directly to him since he had been captured.

'Why should it trouble you?' Stephen asked derisively.

'Because I fought here.' Armand looked at the remnants of the carnage, an unreadable expression on his face. 'On the side of the Christians as it happens.'

'Then when all was lost you became a turncoat and sided with the Moslem victors, I presume?' Stephen said in utter disgust.

'You make too many presumptions on matters you know nothing about.' Armand dug his spurs into the sides of his horse and cantered away from him.

To Stephen the pitiful remains seemed to go on forever. It wasn't surprising because the Christians had fought with at least twenty thousand men, and the Moslems even more. The heat had become so intense that even the Saracens seemed troubled by it as they stopped to share out the last of the water before setting off again.

Only a short time later, Stephen was urging his exhausted mount down into a valley and, in the distance, he could see the cool blue waters of the Sea of Galilee sparkling invitingly in the sunlight. He had never felt so hot in his life before; he was soaked in sweat and his sopping shirt and sodden gambeson seemed to be welded uncomfortably to his body. No doubt he stank appallingly. He lifted his bound hands and pushed back his mail coif so that the faint breeze coming off the sea could blow through his perspiration-sodden hair.

Ahead was a place he knew well, the town of Tiberius. The walled town had once been the home of his godfather Raymond and Stephen had resided there for a fair proportion of the time he had spent in the Holy Land. At the centre of the town was the citadel, which now sadly flew only Saracen flags from its high battlements.

Peasants, who were working in the fields, stopped as

they approached and stared curiously at him. Most probably they had not laid eyes on a Frankish knight for some time. More people stopped to stare as they rode through the gate and into the town itself, which was crowded with people and looked to be a prosperous community. As well as Moslems, he saw a few Armenian Christians and a number of Jews, who had chosen to remain here under Saracen rule. There were others, with pinched pale faces and ragged clothing. They were most likely Christian slaves and Stephen couldn't help wondering if he would soon share their fate, presupposing he survived, of course. Yet logic told him that Armand would not have brought him all this way just to kill him: he had something else in mind for him.

Stephen's horse clattered across the drawbridge and entered the citadel itself. Here it did look different, because in the middle of the large central courtyard was a massive yellow silk tent, which had a banner fluttering from one of its tall centre posts. Stephen stiffened in surprise, recognising the insignia of the Sunni leader the Saracens called Salah ad-Din. He wasn't happy about being Armand's prisoner but at last he was going to lay eyes on the great man himself – the charismatic leader who had united the Arab world.

As one of the soldiers grabbed hold of the reins of Stephen's horse, Armand approached him looking irritatingly at ease in his ornately decorated Saracen hauberk, with burnished silver panels on its front.

'Get off your horse,' he ordered.

Stephen dismounted and two of the soldiers took hold of his arms while Armand strode over to the yellow pavilion and spoke briefly to a dark-clad mullah at the entrance. Beckoning them forwards, Armand walked inside, followed by Stephen and his guards.

Stephen was a little disappointed when he caught sight of Salah ad-Din for the first time, sitting cross-legged on a low couch. Somewhere in his mind he had equated him with his own handsome young king. But then Richard was only in his early thirties, while Salah ad-Din was 54, well into middle age, and time had not been kind to him. He was very slim with dark weather-beaten skin and a large slightly beakish nose, and his long dark hair and beard were streaked with grey.

'My lord.' Armand stepped forwards and bowed low before the great general. 'It is my honour to bring you a very special prisoner.' Salah ad-Din nodded his head and looked thoughtfully at Stephen, his eyes resting on the grubby blue tabard on which the crest of Jerusalem was still visible through the grime.

'Special prisoner?' he spoke in a weary, rather resigned tone.

Stephen was manhandled forwards until he stood directly in front of Salah ad-Din. When their eyes made contact he realised with a jolt of surprise that he sensed something unique and powerful in this man.

'May I present Stephen, Comte de Chalais – King Richard's friend and most trusted lieutenant. He works closely with the Lionheart and is well acquainted with all his future plans. Under expert questioning he will be forced to reveal all he knows. Now that we have lost Acre, the correct intelligence is of paramount import-ance, is it not?'

So Acre had fallen. Stephen was unable to hide his start of surprise, and Salah ad-Din had been sharp-eyed enough to notice his reaction. 'So you did not know, comte.' He turned questioningly to Armand to act as interpreter.

'There is no need, I speak your language,' Stephen interjected. 'And you are right, I did not know that Acre had fallen.'

'It may hearten you to know that I did not like the terms of surrender.' Salah ad-Din smiled wryly. 'The commanders of the city did not bother to acquaint me of the details until the deed was done.'

Stephen was surprised that he was admitting to a weakness within his ranks. 'Sometimes, my lord, our men do what we do not expect them to do.' He stared pointedly at Armand.

Salah ad-Din nodded sagely, then added, 'And are you indeed conversant with all King Richard's plans?'

'I am. I helped him formulate them. However, I regret that is all I am prepared to say on the matter,' Stephen replied.

'Despite the fact that my eager young commander would wish to use every painful means at his disposal to force the answers from you?'

The thought of being tortured would horrify even the strongest man but Stephen could not in good conscience tell the Saracens anything that might result in the loss of Christian lives. 'I have no doubt that this man, who I know as Armand, will be overzealous in his efforts to force the information he wants out of me. I pray that I can be just as zealous in preventing him from doing so.'

'I would have expected no other answer from one of the Lionheart's knights.' Salah ad-Din rose to his feet and stepped over to Stephen. 'Release your hold on him,' he ordered the soldiers as two servants hurried forwards. One offered Salah ad-Din a goblet of liquid, while the other held a medium-sized metal box. As Salah ad-Din flipped open the lid, Stephen saw that it was lined with wood and packed full of ice – a very precious commodity in heat such as this. Salah ad-Din put two generous scoops of the ice into the silver goblet and handed it to Stephen. 'Rose water cooled with the snows of Hemon,' he said. 'Now drink.'

'I am honoured.' As Stephen lifted the goblet to his lips, he heard Armand's indrawn hiss of breath and he knew full well why he was angry. Arab custom said that if one offered a prisoner food and drink his life was safe and no harm would be done to him. He was doubly thankful to Salah ad-Din as he drank deeply, feeling the liquid cool his burning throat. 'I give thanks for your generosity,' Stephen added as he solemnly handed Salah ad-Din the empty goblet.

'You are most welcome.' Stephen could have sworn that he saw Salah ad-Din's lip twitch as if he were amused by Armand's horror at the gesture. Stephen began to think that he could well come to like this man.

'Now tell me.' Salah ad-Din stared deep into Stephen's eyes. 'If I unchain you, will you give me your parole – your solemn vow as a knight that you will not try to escape?'

Stephen nodded, knowing that in time a ransom would be negotiated to free him. In the meantime he hoped he might be given the opportunity to get to know Salah ad-Din much better. 'You have my word as a knight.'

12

Edwina sat on a low divan while elaborate henna patterns were painted on her feet and the back of her hands in preparation for the ceremony. It was something that she didn't like to think about even though she knew she had to. Nasir had decided to make her his second wife, which meant that she now had no chance of ever getting away from him. When he told her of his decision she had not dared to say she didn't want to marry him as she had already learnt from the other woman that one did not say no to Nasir. First Guy, now Nasir, she thought sadly – why did the wrong men always want to marry her?

'This is the material.' Jamilah showed her a scrap of peacock-blue silk embroidered with gold thread. 'It will suit your colouring.'

Edwina did her best to look enthusiastic even though she was feeling very morose and wanted only to wring the neck of the brightly coloured singing bird that Jamilah had just brought to her as a gift. It was singing in a high-pitched tone almost constantly and the noise was getting on her nerves. 'It is very pretty. If you think it suitable then I will have it.'

'Why don't you show more interest in the clothes you will be wearing for the ceremony?' Jamilah asked.

'I will be covered from head to foot in a veil, so no one will see me anyway.'

Fortunately, Jamilah missed the cynicism in her words. 'But Nasir will see you. Don't you want to look beautiful for him?'

'Of course I want to please him,' Edwina replied. 'I'm just a little tired, that's all.'

'Are you with child?' Jamilah had been married to Nasir for four years but had not yet fallen pregnant. Edwina had been told that Jamilah feared Nasir might divorce her because of her barrenness. However, if she as his second wife was able to give him the sons he craved, most likely Jamilah's position was safe. 'It would be wonderful if you were, would it not?' she said, her expression softening.

'I am not, Jamilah.'

'A pity.' Jamilah stroked her cheek. 'When my lord told me that he planned to marry you, at first I was concerned. It seemed strange for him to take a Frankish woman for a wife. Now I think it might be a wise choice as it will help him understand your people more.'

'I hope it will.' Edwina forced herself to smile at Jamilah even though she felt like curling up in a ball and weeping; however she didn't even have the privacy to do that at present.

The henna patterns were finished and the maids held out Edwina's hands for inspection. Jamilah smiled and then waved the maids away. 'Now we should prepare as our guests will be arriving soon.'

'Guests?' Edwina knew that a number of Saracen noblemen had been invited to the wedding but only men held any positions of importance in this culture and they would not be allowed in the harem.

'Yes. Guests.' Taking hold of her wrist, Jamilah pulled Edwina to her feet. 'The wives of some of our most influential emirs and the sister of Taki el-Din, who is Salah ad-Din's nephew.'

'I did not know that they would bring female relatives with them.'

Jamilah patted her cheek affectionately. 'You still have much to learn.'

Her presence sometimes irritated Edwina but she was glad of the friendship, even if it was prompted by selfish motives on Jamilah's part. The two women walked into the main chambers of the harem and the concubines immediately moved aside for them. Edwina was treated with great respect now that it was known she was to marry Nasir.

Suddenly, the impressive beaten copper doors at the main entrance swung open and a crowd of veiled females, all chattering excitedly, entered the harem. They clearly knew Jamilah well because when they spotted her their veils were tossed aside and they hurried towards her. Soon Edwina found herself being examined intently on all sides before she was embraced by numerous soft-skinned, heavily perfumed women. She was reasonably fluent in Arabic now but they were all talking at once in high-pitched voices and she became confused, unable to fully understand what was being said. It didn't appear to matter, however, as she didn't seem to be required to say anything.

Yet one woman kept apart from the others and had not removed her veil. When Edwina found the opportunity she stared at her curiously, wondering who she was. She was dressed in black silk, heavily embroidered in gold, and her dark kohl-ringed eyes kept staring thoughtfully at Edwina, making her feel a little uneasy. 'That is the sister of the great Taki el-Din,' Jamilah whispered in her ear. 'I've not met her before. She keeps herself apart from others, so I'm told.'

Edwina, for some inexplicable reason, began to feel a little strange. Perhaps it was all the fuss that was being made of her. Then the lady in question suddenly stepped towards her. Her large number of gold bracelets made a pleasant tinkling sound as her cool fingers took hold of Edwina's hand. 'Come,' she said in a husky voice.

She guided Edwina out of the room into the bright

sunlight of the garden and, perhaps because of her important position, no one moved to follow them. They walked in silence to a stone seat, which had been placed in the shade of the trees. She sat, beckoning Edwina to join her.

Edwina sat down, so wanting to stare at her and try to discern her features through her veil. Then, at last, it was pulled aside and she saw the woman's face. 'Leila!' Edwina exclaimed in disbelief.

'Thanks to you I reached my family safely.' Smiling warmly, Leila leant forwards and kissed Edwina's cheek. 'When I heard that Nasir was to marry a blonde Frankish captive, it never entered my head it might be you.'

'It is a long story.' Edwina sighed. 'It will take some time to recount.'

'Time we have,' Leila said reassuringly. 'The ceremony is not for three days.'

'It is so good to see you again,' Edwina said with feeling, determined not to let herself cry. It had been so long since she'd had a friend to confide in and she was still hardly able to believe this fortuitous coincidence was possible. 'You never told me how influential your brother actually was.'

'Antecedence does not matter when one is a slave. It seemed unimportant at the time. Nevertheless, when I returned to him, he welcomed me with gladness in his heart, caring for me enough to allow me to put all my sad memories behind me. He knows what terrible things happened to me but no one else must ever learn of them, Edwina.'

'They never will,' Edwina replied sincerely.

Leila looked pensively at her for a long moment. 'Now you have to tell me, do you really want to marry Nasir al-Din?'

The tears came, unbidden, but Edwina made no

238

attempt to hold them back now. 'No, of course not. I still love Stephen. But what choice do I have?'

'One always has choices,' Leila said, taking hold of Edwina's hand. 'And now I am here, we can figure out what they are.'

Stephen gave a loud groan of pleasure, his eyes focused on the exotic supple-bodied houri who sat astride his hips, his cock buried deep inside her. She leant back, increasing the pressure on his swollen shaft, and began to rhythmically contract her internal muscles. Stephen groaned again as she milked his cock expertly, the delicious sensations setting his nerves afire. She was the only woman he had ever had sex with who was capable of this and the sensation was utterly amazing.

Unable to just lie there and be pleasured by her a moment longer, he levered himself into a sitting position and grabbed hold of her. She twined her arms around his neck as he pulled her towards him, crushing her breasts against his muscular chest.

She gave a soft laugh and pressed her soft lips to his. Stephen kissed her long and deeply, savouring the taste of her cinnamon-flavoured mouth as her tongue twined erotically around his. Yet all the time she was keeping up the relentless milking motion on his shaft and he feared he might climax too swiftly.

'Not so strongly,' he growled as he grabbed hold of her buttocks.

Ever obedient, she complied, easing the contractions down a little, slowing their pace, but the sensations were still wildly stimulating and he could almost feel his balls rising and tightening, ready to climax. Salah ad-Din had treated him more like an honoured guest and sent him lovely young slave girls to share his bed at night. This one had come to him a number of times before and tonight Stephen was determined to make her climax before him. He knew her clitoris was extra sensitive but so was another part of her body. Slowly he slid his fingers into her buttock crack and she gave a loud sigh of pleasurable anticipation.

'Please, master,' she begged as he gently pressed his finger against the taut brown ring of her anus.

'Move your hips,' he instructed.

She lifted her body and slammed it down against his groin, hard, increasing the pressure on his cock as she somehow managed to continue contracting the muscles of her vagina at the same time. As she worked them harder, Stephen slid his finger deep inside her, hearing her submissive moan of delight. Her body reacted immediately, going rigid for a moment as she climaxed. Her internal rhythmic contractions went out of control, growing stronger and stronger until they were too much for him to bear. At last he let go, and was consumed by a violent orgasm that seemed to go on forever as if her body were trying to drain him dry.

Wearily, Stephen rolled onto his side, pulling her with him, his cock still buried inside her. They lay there, limbs entangled as their sensual excitement slowly waned. For a long extended moment Stephen felt content – well, as content as he would ever be far away from the woman he loved. Tenderly, he clasped the dark-haired slave girl in his arms, wishing she were Edwina.

As his breathing slowed he began to relax, hoping he could rest for a short while before this sensual creature tried to arouse him again. However, the tranquillity of the moment was disturbed by a loud rapping on the door. Without even waiting for him to answer, a soldier opened the door and stepped into the room.

'I'm sorry, my lord,' the man said, lifting the oil lamp

he held so that Stephen could see him more clearly. 'Salah ad-Din wishes to speak to you.'

Rather awkwardly, Stephen disentangled himself from the girl and sprang to his feet. 'Right now?' he asked in surprise. It was late, probably well past midnight.

'Yes.' The man nodded. 'I have orders to escort you to him immediately.'

Stephen saw the man's eyes stray towards the voluptuous young woman sprawled naked on his divan. Most probably he was wondering why a Frankish prisoner was being treated like an honoured guest. Stephen knew full well how unusual his situation was here and he had Salah ad-Din to thank for that.

'One moment.' Stephen strode over to a bowl of cold water and splashed his face. After wringing out a cloth he swiftly washed himself; it was such a warm night that the water on his skin dried almost immediately.

As he turned, he discovered the girl had risen from his bed and was holding out a long pale-blue robe. Slipping it on over his head, he shoved his feet into soft leather slippers. 'I'll return soon,' he told her. 'Wait for me in bed.' By the time he left she was happily ensconced on his divan again.

At this time of night the citadel seemed deserted as he followed the guard, not to the wing where Salah ad-Din had his rooms, but down the wide staircase and out of the main door of the keep. Stephen had free run of the castle and spending so much time here had brought back many happy memories. With nothing productive to do, he spent much of his time in the library, which was even more extensive now than when his godfather had owned it.

Salah ad-Din had told Stephen that he preferred sleeping in a tent because he had been a warrior on the move from place to place for so long. However, to ensure his safety, his guards insisted that he spend his nights in his room in the citadel. It was easier to protect him there as there had already been a number of attempts on his life.

It appeared that he had remained in his pavilion tonight, and it felt pleasantly cool as Stephen stepped inside the large tent. As usual, when it was dark, Salah ad-Din was surrounded by a number of lamps as at his age his eyesight was failing a little.

'I am sorry to wake you,' Salah ad-Din said.

'You did not. I was otherwise occupied,' Stephen replied.

Salah ad-Din smiled knowingly. 'I asked you to come because I would like your advice.'

'Of course.' Stephen was surprised by the request. In the four weeks he had been here he had got to know Salah ad-Din quite well and if they had not been ostensibly enemies he now would consider him a good friend. They often ate their evening meal together and talked of many things, but never about Richard's plans; Salah ad-Din appeared to have made a point of avoiding that subject entirely.

Stephen knew much about the great man's past now and equally his captor knew just as much about him. He had even found himself telling him about Edwina and his deep abiding love for her and they had talked of Salah ad-Din's family as well. Stephen had also met Salah ad-Din's brother al-Adil, a respected Saracen general, a number of times. Not surprisingly, Salah ad-Din had also been eager to know more about Richard, who he appeared to admire greatly because of his renowned skill as a warrior.

'Sit.' Salah ad-Din pointed to a low couch set at right angles to his.

As Stephen sat down, Salah ad-Din leant forwards and poured red liquid from a jug into a silver goblet.

'Wine?' Stephen queried in surprise, as Moslems abhorred and avoided alcohol.

'The best Burgundy, so I am told.' Salah ad-Din smiled. 'I have to offer you something, do I not, in return for your advice?'

'I give it willingly,' Stephen said as he tasted the wine and found it very pleasant. However, it was odd how quickly one lost the taste for it; he'd not missed it overmuch.

Salah ad-Din picked up a parchment and handed it to Stephen who looked at it thoughtfully, recognising a number of the names. 'A list of Frankish prisoners, I presume?'

'Yes.' Salah ad-Din nodded. 'When Acre surrendered it was agreed that certain named Christian captives would be released.'

'So why should you want my opinion on this?'

'I don't.' Salah ad-Din sighed. 'The problem is finding them all. Many great Moslems fought with me and they all took prisoners but no adequate records were kept.'

'So there are prisoners on this list that you cannot, as yet, locate?' Stephen concluded, handing the parchment back to Salah ad-Din.

'Exactly,' he confirmed. 'It has been agreed that we can pay in instalments. A portion of the two hundred thousand bezants has already been sent to Acre.' He tapped his fingers on a cushion at his side. 'And I have arranged for the True Cross of your faith, which we captured at Hattin, to be brought from Damascus as soon as possible, but because of the problems with the prisoners I fear that all the terms will not be fulfilled in time.'

'Can you not negotiate for more time?'

'The Lionheart, not surprisingly, grows weary of the delays. My spies tell me that he believes I do this on purpose to anger him. Now I am told that he threatens to execute all two thousand seven hundred Moslem prisoners he has in his possession if I delay the matter further.' Salah ad-Din leant forwards worriedly. 'I cannot have that on my conscience. Do you believe, Stephen, that he would actually commit such a terrible act?'

Edwina had lost all sense of distance and time since she had been travelling with the Saracen caravan. The hot, near stifling days seemed endless and the nights just as long. Also she found it incredibly uncomfortable wearing the all-encompassing dark clothing as well as a veil over her face all the time. Yet she had to dress like the other women and at least no one in the caravan had the slightest idea what she looked like, let alone who she was. Then there was the camel she was riding; it wasn't the most comfortable transport and the odd swaying motion made her feel quite queasy at times. However, it was better than being forced to walk or ride one of those small pathetic-looking donkeys.

Her escort on this journey, Hadid, had once served as a Turcopole but he had been taken prisoner at Hattin and sold into slavery. However, he would not be a slave much longer as Leila had promised him his freedom if he escorted Edwina to safety.

All the time they had been travelling, Edwina had been worried about Leila, fearing that Nasir might have discovered by now that her friend had helped her escape. Leila had dressed Edwina as her maid and smuggled her out of the harem and then arranged to have her travel to Acre in this caravan. Hopefully, Nasir would not have discovered that she was missing for some time as, just before she left, she had pretended to feel unwell and had taken to her bed with orders that she was not to be disturbed.

Leila's brother was a very important man, so Edwina hoped that no one would dare to even suggest that Leila had aided her escape. Nevertheless, she had made Leila promise that she would send word to Acre in a week or so to confirm that she had returned safely home with her brother and that all was well with her. Despite the assurances, all the time she had been travelling Edwina had been waiting apprehensively for Nasir's soldiers to suddenly appear and drag her back to him.

Unexpectedly, the long line of people, donkeys, camels and horses stopped and Edwina saw Hadid hurry forwards to find out what was happening. He returned a few moments later and pulled at her camel's reins, ordering it to kneel. She hung onto the wooden front of the saddle as it pitched violently, before the creature came to rest on its knees. 'What's wrong?' she asked Hadid as she dismounted rather inelegantly, hampered as she was by her voluminous clothing.

'Apparently there is a large group of Templar knights some distance ahead and the caravan master fears they might attack. He is considering turning back and taking a different route.'

'Templars? Then we must be quite near Acre,' she said, suddenly realising that if they did attack she could be slaughtered along with everyone else. She had heard stories of Templars attacking innocent travellers in the past.

The leader of the caravan approached, agitatedly waving his hands to seek Hadid's advice on the situation. However, Edwina was in no mood to wait for this matter to be settled: she wanted to reach the Christian lines as soon as possible and the Templars could help her to do just that. Ripping off her veil, she said to Hadid, 'I'll sort this out, they will have to listen to me.'

Picking up her skirts she strode to the front of the caravan; judging by their expressions of amazement, her behaviour clearly horrified most of the other male passengers. Nevertheless, she wasn't concerned about that; all her concentration was focused on the large group of Templars waiting menacingly some distance ahead. One of the knights detached himself from the group and galloped forwards to bar her way. 'Halt – go no further,' he called loudly in badly pronounced Arabic.

'Let me pass,' she said haughtily as she threw off her headdress to reveal her blonde hair. 'I want to speak to your captain or whoever is in charge.' When he did not move and continued to stare down at her, she added, 'I am Edwina, Lady de Moreville, one of the queen's ladies-in-waiting.'

Perhaps he didn't believe her, because he did not even respond, but then she saw the entire body of knights moving towards her. One knight rode faster than the others and reached her first. After dismounting, he hurried towards her and she felt just a shade apprehensive. 'Edwina,' he said haltingly as he pulled off his helmet, 'is that really you?'

'Guy!' In the normal course of events she would not have been altogether pleased to see him, but she was so relieved to see someone she knew that she did not protest when he pulled her into his arms and kissed her. 'Please, my lord,' she said as he looked down at her, an expression of relief on his face. 'The people in the caravan – let them pass. It was they that brought me to safety.'

Guy looked back at the Templars. 'Stand back. Let them all pass unhindered.'

Clearly he was in charge, because the knights immediately withdrew from the narrow track, while two of the Templars rode to the head of the caravan, presumably to let them know they could carry safely on their way. It was then that Edwina saw Hadid hurrying anxiously towards her. 'My lady,' he called out. 'I was concerned.'

'He is my servant,' she told Guy as he hugged her rather too overenthusiastically again.

'I thought you were dead. We all did. The queen has been inconsolable.'

'I am here and I am very much alive.' She smiled awkwardly at Guy. 'Stephen – is he here at Acre?'

'Stephen?' Guy paled visibly. 'Of course, you do not know.'

'Know what?' She feared that she did not want to hear the answer.

'He is dead. We received word that he was killed by Saracens just outside Sarak.'

Edwina remembered nothing else as a cloud of blackness enveloped her.

Stephen stirred on the hard divan, realising that he was still in Salah ad-Din's tent. They had talked for ages and tiredness, coupled with the fair amount of wine he'd drunk, had made him eventually drift off to sleep. It couldn't be long until morning, but the sky hadn't lightened as yet. Most of the lamps had gone out but there was one flickering in the corner which gave off just enough light for him to see a dark form asleep on the other divan. Stephen smiled as he heard Salah ad-Din give a loud snore, then the tent grew quiet again.

He was just about to close his eyes and try to sleep a while longer when he heard a noise, which was so faint he thought he might have imagined it until he saw a figure miraculously step through the walls of the tent. He tensed anxiously, realising that the fabric must have been cut as the dark figure disappeared for a moment in the shadows. Then he saw it again, moving menacingly towards Salah ad-Din; judging by the outline, the man appeared to be carrying a curved dagger in his raised hand.

Stephen sprang from the divan, his long tunic flapping awkwardly around his bare legs, as he threw himself at the assailant, wishing he had a weapon to hand. Obviously not expecting anyone else to be in the tent, the attacker was caught by surprise, and the full weight of Stephen's body bore him to the ground with a jolting thud. Stephen immediately tried to gain the upper hand and they grappled together, rolling around as he fought for possession of the dagger. There was a metallic thud as they collided with a small table and its contents fell onto the carpet. The attacker was strong but eventually Stephen managed to gain control, jerking the man's hand back, twisting his wrist cruelly so that he was forced to release his hold on the dagger. It fell to the ground and Stephen went to grab it but it was so dark he couldn't see where it had fallen.

By now he hoped that the noise would have alerted the guards outside that something was wrong. Clearly the attacker thought so as well and, elbowing Stephen in the side, he struggled to his feet. As he went to flee, Stephen grabbed hold of his ankle and pulled him back, stoically ignoring the kick in the gut he gained for his trouble. Throwing himself atop the man, Stephen locked his fingers around the assailant's throat. He gave a strangled groan, his arms flailing, then he must have somehow found the dagger because Stephen felt a sudden searing pain in his arm. Gritting his teeth against the agony, he clung onto the assailant, reaching out frantically to try to keep the man from stabbing him again.

At that moment turmoil erupted around him. Many hands grabbed hold of Stephen and he was hauled away from the attacker and forced to his knees. His arms were pulled behind him and forced so high up his back they felt as if they might pop from their sockets at any moment. The flame of a torch spluttered near his face and he blinked in the sudden bright light.

'Stephen?' he heard al-Adil say.

'The other man,' Stephen gasped breathlessly, twisting his head to see the masked assailant kneeling close by him, similarly held down.

'Let the comte go,' Salah ad-Din's voice rang out authoritatively. 'Can't you see he is wounded?'

They let go of him and Stephen slumped forwards, crouching on his knees as he felt warm blood seeping from his stab wound, staining his sleeve and blossoming out like a scarlet flower. He was lifted up and placed on a divan while a soldier tied a cord tightly around his upper arm to stem the bleeding.

Meanwhile al-Adil had picked up the bloodstained dagger and was examining it closely. He handed it to Salah ad-Din and uttered one word. 'Hashshashin.'

Salah ad-Din had told Stephen that this strange sect had tried to assassinate him before. Stephen knew of them – they were feared by both Moslems and Christians alike as they carried out assassinations for money and political motives. They were Moslems, yet their leader owed allegiance to no one and they were a law unto themselves.

'So the Old Man of the Mountain has yet to give up on me,' Salah ad-Din said with a twisted smile as he looked at the assassin. 'I would like to know why he wants me dead so desperately.'

The man did not answer and al-Adil bent and ripped off his mask to reveal none other than Armand. 'Eventually one of us will succeed,' he said to Salah ad-Din with an expression of utter derision on his handsome face.

So why was he doing this, Stephen wondered in

amazement; first Frankish knight, then Saracen and now assassin? 'Why in God's name, Armand?' he muttered.

'You will never understand,' Armand said coldly. 'Just know this, most of what I told you was true. You were just a pawn, Stephen, a convenient way to get close to Salah ad-Din.'

'Do you think we can make him talk?' al-Adil asked his brother.

In response, Salah ad-Din beckoned forwards one of the guards and held out his hand for his scimitar. 'No.'

Stephen was no stranger to bloodshed but he couldn't bear to look at this. He turned his head away, closing his ears to the sickening sound as Armand's head was cut from his body with one fell swoop of the sword.

'I can go no further.' Al-Adil turned to look at Stephen. In the distance the sea glittered a pale greeny-blue, behind the city of Acre. 'You will tell the Lionheart that the next instalment will be with him in two days?'

Stephen nodded. 'And I will do my best to explain about your difficulties in locating all the listed prisoners.' He frowned. 'Unfortunately Richard has his faults – he is not a patient man.'

'At least he might listen to you.' Al-Adil smiled sadly. 'It has been good to know you, Stephen. And I am grateful because my brother owes you his life.'

'He owes me nothing,' Stephen said as a soldier moved forwards to hand him the lead rein of his packhorse, which carried his old chainmail and gifts Salah ad-Din had given him for Edwina and the king.

Stephen now wore a magnificent hauberk made out of thousands of tiny engraved metal discs, interleaved like the scales of a fish. It was light yet amazingly strong and looked magnificent, a deep burnished gold glittering like burning embers of fire in the bright sunlight. No doubt Richard would envy it greatly.

'One more thing,' al-Adil said, appearing rather concerned. 'About the message I received this morning.' The Saracens used trained birds to carry messages and Stephen had seen one of the white doves flutter down to the oasis where they were camped early this morning. 'It came from Acre and concerned your Edwina.'

'What about her?'

'She is to be married this very day to Guy de Lusignan.'

'Guy!' The bright future Stephen had envisaged disintegrated in an instant.

'Edwina believes you dead, it appears, and she is to be married the second hour after noon.' He looked up at the sky. 'You still have time to stop it, my friend. And may God go with you.'

'And you also,' Stephen yelled back to him as he spurred his horse forwards, down the Hill of Carobs towards Acre.

The gates of the city were open and thronged with people. There were still soldiers camped outside the walls and Stephen could see men deconstructing catapults and loading them on wagons, while more men were hard at work repairing the damage to the walls that had been done by their very own war machines. As Stephen galloped full tilt towards the entrance, people moved out of his way, but he was forced to slow down to almost walking pace as the crowds became thicker.

He calculated that it wouldn't take him long to reach the royal palace, where no doubt Richard was housed, and then he would put a stop to this union between Edwina and Guy. He knew that she would never go ahead with the ceremony once she learnt that he was still alive. But, as he steered his mount through the mass of people at the gate, soldiers stepped forwards to bar his way.

'Where do you think you are going, Saracen?' one challenged as he pointed his long-handled pike at Stephen.

'Saracen! I'm no Saracen, you fool,' Stephen said angrily, suddenly realising that in this armour and with his dark hair and beard he might well resemble one. 'Look closer,' he said, assuming an air of noble arrogance. 'I'm the Comte de Chalais, King Richard's right-hand man.'

The soldier glanced questioningly at his companions, clearly not believing him as Stephen's magnificent Arab stallion, another gift from Salah ad-Din, pawed the ground restlessly.

'The Comte de Chalais is dead,' one of the soldiers announced. 'Killed by one of your Saracen comrades.'

'Dam you, I'm not dead. Get out of my way.' He didn't have time for this unnecessary delay: every moment counted. Stephen's hand automatically reached for his sword as more soldiers surrounded him.

'Try that and you'll regret it, Saracen!' The soldier waved his pike in Stephen's face. 'Now keep your hands away from your weapon and dismount.'

Anxiously, Stephen scanned the crowd but there was no one here he knew who could vouch for him; he was on his own. Yet he had to act fast as even the slightest delay could take Edwina away from him again. His stallion was well trained and, at the flick of his reins, it began to turn restlessly, distracting the soldiers just enough to allow Stephen to draw his sword and at the same time urge his horse forwards. His stallion leapt past the soldiers and, as they uselessly tried to bar his way, he slashed out, his sword blade cleaving the pike shaft in two.

He galloped along the paved street, forcing people to scatter in all directions. He might well have got away if a number of mounted Templars hadn't moved to prevent his escape. Stephen had no wish to fight them as well so he pulled his mount to an abrupt, slithering halt, jumped from his horse and ran into the throng of people, hoping to somehow lose himself in the crowds as the soldiers and Templars bore down on him from both directions.

A number of French soldiers spotted him and, as they drew their weapons, he had no choice but to turn and face his attackers. Swinging round, sword in hand, he muttered a prayer to the Almighty under his breath, knowing that he would have to surrender and fearing that by the time his identity was confirmed it would be too late to stop the wedding ceremony.

'Stephen – is that you?' He heard a voice calling from some distance away. A dark-clad man shoved past the soldiers and ran towards him.

'Martin, thank God.' His prayers having been answered, he lowered his sword.

Berengaria looked anxiously at Edwina as they entered the church. 'Are you quite sure about this?'

'I am not sure of anything any more,' Edwina replied. Truthfully, she felt totally numb. Her life had stopped the moment she had learnt Stephen was dead and without him nothing had any meaning to her now.

'Broken hearts do not mend easily.' Berengaria squeezed her hand reassuringly. 'Why marry Guy now? Wait, give yourself time, Edwina.'

'Time for what?' she asked, confused by the fact that she was unable even to cry. 'He has been so persistent of late. Eventually, it was easier just to say yes to his proposal. Why should I care what happens to me now?'

'I do not think you are doing the right thing,' Berengaria whispered as they walked up the aisle towards

King Richard, who was waiting to escort Edwina to the altar. 'I begged Richard to stop you but he says that it is your right to marry if you so wish.'

Edwina focused her eyes on the tall, magnificently dressed monarch who was to give her away. She couldn't even bear to look at Guy standing expectantly at the altar beside the archbishop, who was to conduct the ceremony.

'Lady de Moreville.' Richard gallantly held out his arm as Berengaria let go of her hand. 'Are you ready?'

Edwina's throat felt so tight now that she couldn't even force a yes from her lips, so she nodded mutely. Placing her hand lightly on Richard's arm, she walked with him towards the man she was going to marry, barely conscious of the many nobles who'd gathered in the church to witness this momentous union.

They had almost reached the altar when she heard a loud noise as if the heavy oak doors of the church were being hammered open. This was followed amazingly by the clatter of horse's hooves coming towards her and for a moment even she was aroused from her unhappy lethargy as she wondered what was happening.

'What!' Richard exclaimed as he swung round in amazement.

He pulled Edwina with him, and she tensed anxiously as she caught sight of the menacing-looking Saracen bearing down on them. Drawing their swords, a number of nobles ran forwards to protect the king, but before they could apprehend the Saracen his horse came to a slithering halt and he sprang lithely from his horse. 'Forgive the untimely intrusion, Your Majesty, but it was necessary,' he said in a loud achingly familiar voice as he bowed to the king.

'Stephen?' Richard gasped in disbelief.

There was a murmur of surprise from the assembled congregation, while Edwina stood there totally dumbstruck as the icy coldness that had surrounded her heart began to melt in the warmth of her lover's presence. Stephen was alive!

'I appear to be a little late for the ceremony,' Stephen said as one of the noblemen silently took control of the situation and proceeded to take hold of the horse's reins and lead it out of the church.

Edwina, meanwhile, stared at Stephen, hardly able to believe this was happening, and knowing that, if she hadn't been holding onto Richard's arm, her legs might well have given way.

'Your arrival is unexpected and rather untoward,' Richard said gruffly, and then he grinned. 'But it is forgiven. Put aside your weapons, gentlemen.' Pushing aside the sword-wielding nobles surrounding him, he stepped over to Stephen and clapped a hand on his shoulder. 'My friend, I am so glad you are alive.'

'Majesty,' Stephen acknowledged, and then as he looked at her his expression filled with so much love that she was overwhelmed. 'Edwina.'

She wanted to say so much, but her mind and her heart were so full of emotion she could not speak for a moment and it was Berengaria who came to her rescue.

'Husband.' She stepped forwards and touched Richard's arm. 'It appears that King Guy has decided to beat a hasty retreat before the ceremony has even started.' Richard did not appear overly surprised as he glanced back at the altar where the archbishop now stood alone. Somewhere in the distance a door banged loudly as Guy left the church, knowing full well that Edwina would not marry him now.

'It seems a pity to deny the archbishop a ceremony, does it not? So if there were two people here who wished to be married would it not be circumspect to do so?' Richard said with a wide smile as he looked expectantly at Stephen.

'Will you?' Edwina heard Stephen say.

She stared at the man she had thought she'd lost and her heart was filled with so much joy she felt it might explode. 'Yes,' she said, reaching for his hand.

Visit the Black Lace website at
www.black-lace-books.com

FIND OUT THE LATEST INFORMATION AND TAKE ADVANTAGE OF OUR FANTASTIC FREE BOOK OFFER! ALSO VISIT THE SITE FOR . . .

- All Black Lace titles currently available and how to order online
- Great new offers
- Writers' guidelines
- Author interviews
- An erotica newsletter
- Features
- Cool links

BLACK LACE — THE LEADING IMPRINT OF WOMEN'S SEXY FICTION

TAKING YOUR EROTIC READING PLEASURE TO NEW HORIZONS

LOOK OUT FOR THE ALL-NEW BLACK LACE BOOKS – AVAILABLE NOW!

All books priced £7.99 in the UK. Please note publication dates apply to the UK only. For other territories, please contact your retailer.

HOTBED
Portia Da Costa
ISBN 978 0 352 33614 9

Pride comes before a fall . . . but what if that descent becomes the wildest ride of your life? Two sisters – Natalie and Patti – become rivals when they challenge each other's daring on a dark, downward spiral where nobody is quite who or what they seem, and where transgressing sexual boundaries is the norm.

Coming in October 2007

THE SILVER COLLAR
Mathilde Madden
ISBN 978 0 352 34141 9

Eleven years ago a powerful ancient werewolf ripped Iris's life apart. One full moon night it attacked the two people she loved most in the world, killing her twin brother Matthew and leaving her boyfriend Alfie changed forever. Iris and Alfie vowed revenge on the Beast, but when Alfie began to show a twisted loyalty to the creature who had made him, Iris lost him too.

    Now, Alfie is back in Oxford where Iris – still haunted by her dead brother – is heading up the Vix, a shadowy organisation dedicated to killing his kind. But Alfie needs Iris's help or what the Beast did to him that night may yet prove fatal. His body is fragmenting – the rules that govern his transformations into a wolf are changing. His only hope of keeping his deadly beast under control is the Silver Collar – an ancient artifact currently owned by the Vix. But Iris isn't prepared to help Alfie secure it until he agrees to defy the rules of his kind and help her avenge Matthew's death.

    Alfie and Iris both think that what happened between them eleven years ago has destroyed the love and trust they had for each other forever. The Silver Collar shows them that they're both wrong.

THE CAPTIVATION
Natasha Rostova
ISBN 978 0 352 33234 9

In 1917, war-torn Russia is teetering on the brink of revolution. A Russian princess, Katya Leskova, and her family are forced to leave their estate when a mob threatens their lives. Katya ends up in the encampment of a rebel Cossack army; the men have not seen a woman for months and their libidos are out of control.

When the Cossack captain discovers Katya's privileged background he has no intention of letting her leave the camp. Against the turbulent background of a country in turmoil, Katya and the captain become involved in an erotic struggle to prove their power over each other.

Coming in November 2007

SPLIT
Kristina Lloyd
ISBN 978 0 352 34154 9

A visit to Heddlestone, a remote village in the Yorkshire moors, changes librarian, Kate Carter's life. The place has an eerie yet erotic charge and when Kate is later offered a job in its puppet museum, she flees London and her boyfriend in order to take it.

Jake, the strange and beautiful curator and puppeteer, draws her into his secluded sensual world, and before long she's sharing his bed, going deeper into new and at times frightening explorations of love and lust. But Kate is also seduced by Eddie, Jake's brother, and his wild Ukrainian wife, and she becomes tangled in a second dark relationship. Split between the two men, Kate moves closer to uncovering the truth behind the secrets of Heddlestone, ever sensing danger but not knowing whether the greatest threat comes from ghosts or reality.

WILD KINGDOM
Deanna Ashford
ISBN 978 0 352 33549 4

Salacious cruelties abound as war rages in the mythical kingdom of
Kabra. Prince Tarn is struggling to drive out the invading army while his
bethrothed – the beautiful Rianna – has fled the fighting with the
mysterious Baroness Crissana.

But the baroness is a fearsome and depraved woman, and once
they're out of the danger zone she takes Rianna prisoner. He plan is to
present her as a plaything to her warlord half-brother, Ragnor. In order
to rescue his sweetheart, Prince Tarn needs to join forces with his old
enemy, Sarin, whose capacity for perverse delights knows no civilised
bounds.

Black Lace Booklist

Information is correct at time of printing. To avoid disappointment, check availability before ordering. Go to www.black-lace-books.com. All books are priced £7.99 unless another price is given.

BLACK LACE BOOKS WITH A CONTEMPORARY SETTING

☐ ALWAYS THE BRIDEGROOM Tesni Morgan   ISBN 978 0 352 33855 6   £6.99
☐ THE ANGELS' SHARE Maya Hess   ISBN 978 0 352 34043 6
☐ ARIA APPASSIONATA Julie Hastings   ISBN 978 0 352 33056 7   £6.99
☐ ASKING FOR TROUBLE Kristina Lloyd   ISBN 978 0 352 33362 9
☐ BLACK LIPSTICK KISSES Monica Belle   ISBN 978 0 352 33885 3   £6.99
☐ THE BLUE GUIDE Carrie Williams   ISBN 978 0 352 34131 0
☐ BONDED Fleur Reynolds   ISBN 978 0 352 33192 2   £6.99
☐ THE BOSS Monica Belle   ISBN 978 0 352 34088 7
☐ BOUND IN BLUE Monica Belle   ISBN 978 0 352 34012 2
☐ CAMPAIGN HEAT Gabrielle Marcola   ISBN 978 0 352 33941 6
☐ CAT SCRATCH FEVER Sophie Mouette   ISBN 978 0 352 34021 4
☐ CIRCUS EXCITE Nikki Magennis   ISBN 978 0 352 34033 7
☐ CLUB CRÈME Primula Bond   ISBN 978 0 352 33907 2   £6.99
☐ COMING ROUND THE MOUNTAIN   ISBN 978 0 352 33873 0   £6.99
     Tabitha Flyte
☐ CONFESSIONAL Judith Roycroft   ISBN 978 0 352 33421 3
☐ CONTINUUM Portia Da Costa   ISBN 978 0 352 33120 5
☐ COOKING UP A STORM Emma Holly   ISBN 978 0 352 34114 3
☐ DANGEROUS CONSEQUENCES   ISBN 978 0 352 33185 4
     Pamela Rochford
☐ DARK DESIGNS Madelynne Ellis   ISBN 978 0 352 34075 7
☐ THE DEVIL INSIDE Portia Da Costa   ISBN 978 0 352 32993 6
☐ EDEN'S FLESH Robyn Russell   ISBN 978 0 352 33923 2   £6.99
☐ ENTERTAINING MR STONE Portia Da Costa   ISBN 978 0 352 34029 0
☐ EQUAL OPPORTUNITIES Mathilde Madden   ISBN 978 0 352 34070 2
☐ FEMININE WILES Karina Moore   ISBN 978 0 352 33874 7
☐ FIRE AND ICE Laura Hamilton   ISBN 978 0 352 33486 2

☐ WILD CARD Madeline Moore   ISBN 978 0 352 34038 2
☐ WING OF MADNESS Mae Nixon   ISBN 978 0 352 34099 3

BLACK LACE BOOKS WITH AN HISTORICAL SETTING

☐ THE AMULET Lisette Allen   ISBN 978 0 352 33019 2 £6.99
☐ THE BARBARIAN GEISHA Charlotte Royal   ISBN 978 0 352 33267 7
☐ BARBARIAN PRIZE Deanna Ashford   ISBN 978 0 352 34017 7
☐ DANCE OF OBSESSION Olivia Christie   ISBN 978 0 352 33101 4
☐ DARKER THAN LOVE Kristina Lloyd   ISBN 978 0 352 33279 0
☐ ELENA'S DESTINY Lisette Allen   ISBN 978 0 352 33218 9
☐ FRENCH MANNERS Olivia Christie   ISBN 978 0 352 33214 1
☐ LORD WRAXALL'S FANCY Anna Lieff Saxby   ISBN 978 0 352 33080 2
☐ NICOLE'S REVENGE Lisette Allen   ISBN 978 0 352 32984 4
☐ THE SENSES BEJEWELLED Cleo Cordell   ISBN 978 0 352 32904 2 £6.99
☐ THE SOCIETY OF SIN Sian Lacey Taylder   ISBN 978 0 352 34080 1
☐ UNDRESSING THE DEVIL Angel Strand   ISBN 978 0 352 33938 6
☐ WHITE ROSE ENSNARED Juliet Hastings   ISBN 978 0 352 33052 9 £6.99

BLACK LACE BOOKS WITH A PARANORMAL THEME

☐ BRIGHT FIRE Maya Hess   ISBN 978 0 352 34104 4
☐ BURNING BRIGHT Janine Ashbless   ISBN 978 0 352 34085 6
☐ CRUEL ENCHANTMENT Janine Ashbless   ISBN 978 0 352 33483 1
☐ DIVINE TORMENT Janine Ashbless   ISBN 978 0 352 33719 1
☐ FLOOD Anna Clare   ISBN 978 0 352 34094 8
☐ GOTHIC BLUE Portia Da Costa   ISBN 978 0 352 33075 8
☐ THE PRIDE Edie Bingham   ISBN 978 0 352 33997 3
☐ THE TEN VISIONS Olivia Knight   ISBN 978 0 352 34119 8

BLACK LACE ANTHOLOGIES

☐ BLACK LACE QUICKIES 1 Various   ISBN 978 0 352 34126 6 £2.99
☐ BLACK LACE QUICKIES 2 Various   ISBN 978 0 352 34127 3 £2.99
☐ BLACK LACE QUICKIES 3 Various   ISBN 978 0 352 34128 0 £2.99
☐ BLACK LACE QUICKIES 4 Various   ISBN 978 0 352 34129 7 £2.99
☐ BLACK LACE QUICKIES 5 Various   ISBN 978 0 352 34130 3 £2.99
☐ BLACK LACE QUICKIES 6 Various   ISBN 978 0 352 34133 4 £2.99
☐ MORE WICKED WORDS Various   ISBN 978 0 352 33487 9 £6.99

❏ WICKED WORDS 3 Various   ISBN 978 0 352 33522 7   £6.99

❏ WICKED WORDS 4 Various   ISBN 978 0 352 36603 3   £6.99

❏ WICKED WORDS 5 Various   ISBN 978 0 352 33642 2   £6.99

❏ WICKED WORDS 6 Various   ISBN 978 0 352 33690 3   £6.99

❏ WICKED WORDS 7 Various   ISBN 978 0 352 33743 6   £6.99

❏ WICKED WORDS 8 Various   ISBN 978 0 352 33787 0   £6.99

❏ WICKED WORDS 9 Various   ISBN 978 0 352 33860 0

❏ WICKED WORDS 10 Various   ISBN 978 0 352 33893 8

❏ THE BEST OF BLACK LACE 2 Various   ISBN 978 0 352 33718 4

❏ WICKED WORDS: SEX IN THE OFFICE Various   ISBN 978 0 352 33944 7

❏ WICKED WORDS: SEX AT THE SPORTS CLUB   ISBN 978 0 352 33991 1
     Various

❏ WICKED WORDS: SEX ON HOLIDAY Various   ISBN 978 0 352 33961 4

❏ WICKED WORDS: SEX IN UNIFORM Various   ISBN 978 0 352 34002 3

❏ WICKED WORDS: SEX IN THE KITCHEN Various   ISBN 978 0 352 34018 4

❏ WICKED WORDS: SEX ON THE MOVE Various   ISBN 978 0 352 34034 4

❏ WICKED WORDS: SEX AND MUSIC Various   ISBN 978 0 352 34061 0

❏ WICKED WORDS: SEX AND SHOPPING Various   ISBN 978 0 352 34076 4

❏ SEX IN PUBLIC Various   ISBN 978 0 352 34089 4

❏ SEX WITH STRANGERS Various   ISBN 978 0 352 34105 1

❏ PARANORMAL EROTICA Various   ISBN 978 0 352 34132 7

BLACK LACE NON-FICTION

❏ THE BLACK LACE BOOK OF WOMEN'S SEXUAL   ISBN 978 0 352 33793 1   £6.99
     FANTASIES Edited by Kerri Sharp

To find out the latest information about Black Lace titles, check out the website: www.black-lace-books.com or send for a booklist with complete synopses by writing to:

Black Lace Booklist, Virgin Books Ltd
Thames Wharf Studios
Rainville Road
London W6 9HA

Please include an SAE of decent size. Please note only British stamps are valid.

Our privacy policy
We will not disclose information you supply us to any other parties. We will not disclose any information which identifies you personally to any person without your express consent.

From time to time we may send out information about Black Lace books and special offers. Please tick here if you do <u>not</u> wish to receive Black Lace information. ❏